THE HAND OF WAR

AN OMEGA THRILLER

BLAKE BANNER

RIGHTHOUSE

ISBN-13: 978-1-63696-336-5

ISBN-10: 1-63696-336-6

Cover design by: Damonza

Printed in the United States of America

www.righthouse.com

www.instagram.com/righthousebooks

www.facebook.com/righthousebooks

twitter.com/righthousebooks

THE OMEGA SERIES
Dawn of the Hunter (Book 1)
Double Edged Blade (Book 2)
The Storm (Book 3)
The Hand of War (Book 4)
A Harvest of Blood (Book 5)
To Rule in Hell (Book 6)
Kill: One (Book 7)
Powder Burn (Book 8)
Kill: Two (Book 9)
Unleashed (Book 10)
The Omicron Kill (Book 11)
9mm Justice (Book 12)
Kill: Four (Book 13)
Death In Freedom (Book 14)
Endgame (Book 15)

The mind is its own place, and in it self
Can make a Heav'n of Hell, a Hell of Heav'n.
What matter where, if I be still the same,
And what I should be, all but less then he
Whom Thunder hath made greater? Here at least
We shall be free; th' Almighty hath not built
Here for his envy, will not drive us hence:
Here we may reign secure, and in my choyce
To reign is worth ambition though in Hell:
Better to reign in Hell, then serve in Heav'n.

John Milton, Paradise Lost

ONE

His face was deceptively flabby. You'd be forgiven for thinking he was a weak man. But there was steel in his eyes. He watched me without emotion, observing me from his large, black leather chair. Through the plate glass window behind him I could see the morning sun, molten copper on the East River, and the Four Freedoms Park on Roosevelt Island. I had told him my story—my edited version of the story, minus the murder and the conspiracies —about how Marni was like a sister to me, we had lost touch over the last few years, and now I was trying to get in contact with her again.

He raised an unruly eyebrow and heaved a big sigh.

"Mr. Walker, I don't really see how I can help you. I am not at liberty to release Dr. Gilbert's contact details."

"I don't expect you to, Mr. Staines. But if Marni's address to the conference is on Friday 18th, she will be here for at least a week. What I was hoping was that you could get a message to her for me, and then perhaps she could contact me."

He spread his hands and made an unhappy face. "Mr. Walker, this is the United Nations, not a hotel switchboard. I have an international conference to organize..."

I interrupted, fighting down the pellet of anger in my belly. "Mr. Staines, I hear you. You are not interested in the personal problems of the speakers at your conference. That's fine. But it so happens that her father was killed and my father stepped in as her surrogate dad. We grew up together like brother and sister. All I am asking is, will you see her before the conference?"

He sighed again, noisily. "Yes."

"Would it interfere an awful lot with your busy schedule to hand her a piece of paper with my name and telephone number on it, and say, 'Please call him'?"

He was good at sighing. I guess he got a lot of practice because he sighed at every opportunity. That's how you get good at things in life. Now he sighed again and held out his hand. I put my card in it and stood up. "Thanks."

When I got to the door, he said, "Mr. Walker."

I turned.

"I'll tell her you were persistent and would very much like to hear from her."

Something like a smile moved his jowls and just for a moment he looked like a kindly St. Bernard.

I nodded once. "Thanks again."

I stepped out of his office and into what looked like a vast set for a *Star Trek* movie. The words 'sterile environment' seemed to be encoded into the architecture and the décor, along with an obscure, subliminal message about the destiny of mankind. It appeared to promise a future in which everybody would smile and all behavior would be 'appropriate', all genders and all races would be not so much equal as the same, though displayed in an appropriate rainbow of aesthetically pleasing variations on a theme. And that theme was to be inoffensive. Inoffensive to whom was not clear—a great abstract United Nations ideal, where nobody would ever disagree because nobody ever asked difficult questions. Because difficult questions could be offensive. And therefore inappropriate.

Especially if they were questions about the United Nations Ideal.

I stepped out into the early May sunshine and as I walked through the ugly, iron gates onto First Avenue, I hesitated and looked both ways, as though I were not sure where I wanted to go. It gave me a chance to spot the Omega men who were waiting for me. They were in the garden at the bottom of the steps that lead up to 43rd Street. I acted like I hadn't seen them, crossed over the road to make it easier for them to follow me, and started walking toward the parking garage on West 40th, where I'd left my car.

I knew they'd parked up the road at a meter, where they could keep watch and follow me when I came out. So I stepped into the entrance to the garage and stood with my back against the near wall, where they wouldn't see me, staring at the screen of my cell phone. A minute later they walked past. There were two of them. They had that unmistakable look of men who were clones of each other, who spent too many hours in the gym, having fantasies about living the 3D shooter dream, and not enough time looking into the eyes of dying men, or men who wanted to kill them.

THE HAND OF WAR | 5

I moved after them and matched my stride to theirs. They were dressed in off the peg Armani, because that was the uniform, and they drove a dark blue Audi, because that was what you drove if you were a black ops bad boy. They were the living embodiment of the UN promise. As they came up to their car I called out in my most pleasant voice, "Oh, excuse me!" and ran two steps to catch up.

They both turned. The nearest one was six-two and built like a brick shithouse. He looked at me with expressionless eyes in a pale, unfeeling face. That changed when I broke his knee with a short, sharp kick to the side of the joint. I didn't waste time following up. I'd heard it snap and I knew he was out.

His pal was a bit taller and more athletic. He was gaping at his fallen comrade and at me. It is estimated that a person takes a full four seconds to react to an unexpected attack. It may be three in the case of a highly trained operative. If you count out three seconds, it isn't hard to imagine how much damage you can do in that time.

I stepped in close and rammed the heel of my right hand up into his jaw. He said, "Oh..." like he'd suddenly gone dizzy, and his legs went wobbly. As he exhaled, I rammed my fist hard into his solar plexus and, as he doubled up, I took hold of his collar and the seat of his pants and rammed his head against the side of his dark blue Audi bad boy car. In all it took about as long as he would have needed to react to my breaking his friend's leg.

I knelt down beside that broken friend now and looked deep into his pale eyes. His skin was the color and texture of butter. He was sweating and trembling. I reached inside his jacket and pulled out his Glock. I released the magazine and put it in my pocket. I checked to see if he had any other weapons. He'd started to whimper, clutching at his knee. A couple of people passed and frowned at us, but when they saw the Glock they kept moving.

He was clean so I pulled his cell from his jacket and handed it to him. He took hold of it but I didn't let go. I forced him to look into my face.

"Tell Ben to back off. The next pair of primates he sends to follow me I'll kill. Get a job you're qualified for, will you?"

I left him sobbing and dialing and went up to my car.

Ben was Omega's mouthpiece. My father had been a big shot in the organization before he'd died; before Marni had killed him. And Ben had been his right hand man. When I'd buried my father at the family graveyard in Weston, outside Boston, Ben had tried to persuade me to join Omega, to step into my father's shoes. But I knew by then that my father had grown to hate Omega and everything it stood for. Since that time I had been searching for Marni, not to exact revenge, but because on his deathbed, my father had made me promise to take care of her and keep her safe. She had not made it easy[1].

Marni was important to them because her research, and most of all her father's research, if exposed, could bring Omega down. So Omega wanted Marni either on side or dead. Ben and I had finally reached an uneasy truce at their office in the Pentagon. At least I had allowed them to think we had. I would find Marni, they would give me any help I

---

1. See *Dawn of the Hunter*

asked for, and in exchange I would try to persuade Marni to talk to them[2].

But Marni had stopped communicating with me. She had vanished without a trace—until a week ago, when I had seen in the *New York Times* that she and Professor Philip Gibbons of Green College, Oxford, would be speaking at the United Nations International Conference on Climate Change and Overpopulation. I had been in Houston at the time, but I had dropped what I was doing, climbed in my Zombie 222, and headed east. I knew that this might be my last chance to talk to her. Omega would be weighing up the situation, figuring that if they had Marni at the UN, they didn't need me. With both of us dead, they'd be in the clear.

So I had to get to Marni before they got to her, and before they got to me.

The Zombie 222 is an electric car produced by a couple of crazy geniuses in Texas. It has the body of a 1968 Mustang Fastback, but its twin engines deliver eight hundred bhp, one thousand eight hundred foot-pounds of torque, straight to the back wheels. She'll go 0-60 in just over one and a half seconds, and she is totally silent.

As I slipped out of the parking garage, I saw the Tragic Two still on the sidewalk. The guy with the broken leg seemed to have passed out. The other one was on his knees, holding his head. I didn't feel bad for them. They were lucky to be alive.

Among the things I had inherited from my father, apart from a manor house in Weston and a butler to go with it, there was a penthouse apartment on Riverside Drive, in

---

2. See *Double Edged Blade*

Bloomingdale. That wasn't my style, and I kept telling myself that when this was all over I would return to my small house in Wyoming, where I had briefly been happy, fixing cars.

But that had been in another life. And besides, who said this would ever be over?

I took First Avenue as far as 79th Street and then crossed the park to the Upper West Side. I rode the elevator to the tenth floor and let myself in. It was a family-sized apartment. My father had bought it when I was a young kid—when my brother and I had been young kids. My mother, accustomed to the high life in London, had complained that Weston was going to drive her crazy. The bohemian, arty set had suited her better, but in the end it turned out it was not Weston that was driving her crazy, it was my father. My father was driving us all crazy.

Now that the apartment was empty, it seemed to swell to three times its size, and to be three times as empty. A family home without a family is like a body without a soul. It's unsettling to look at. Physically it has not changed, yet it becomes pitiable, and uncomfortable to be with.

I went to the kitchen, cracked a beer, and stepped onto the terrace. Across the canopy of trees, the Hudson lay heavy and massive, almost black in the late morning sun. It seemed to foreshadow something, like a black tide spreading imperceptibly over the city.

I took a pull of the cold beer and told myself that's what happens when you start thinking; you start getting ideas. My cell rang. I forced myself to let it ring three times before I answered.

"Yeah, Lacklan Walker."

The line was silent so long I was about to repeat it. Then I heard an intake of breath, and Marni's voice. It had been a year since I'd heard it, but it was as fresh as though it had been that morning.

"Lacklan, it's me, Marni."

"Hi, you're a hard woman to get hold of since you hang out with university professors."

"Lacklan, let's not make this any harder than it is. You need to stop pursuing me..."

"*Pursuing* you?"

"Lacklan, listen to me..."

"No. I'm not going to listen to that shit. Do you know how many times I risked my life for you in Turret? *You* asked me to follow you! You *asked* me to follow you to Tucson! You were mad at me that I *didn't* follow you to Washington! And now you tell me to stop *pursuing* you?"

"Lacklan, I know this is hard to understand..."

"It's not hard. It's impossible!"

"Do you want me to hang up?"

"No!"

"Then stop storming at me every time I open my mouth."

I drew a deep breath and let it out slow. "I'm sorry."

"This is not your fight anymore, Lacklan. You need to give it up."

"Can I answer without you hanging up?"

A small sigh. "... Yes, of course."

"First of all, what makes you say that? And second, what makes you think you get to decide whose fight this is?"

"Lacklan, I can't get into this discussion with you. But you need to understand... You *have* to back off!"

"Why?"

"What you did in Arizona. It was insane. You are so violent, *so* destructive!"

"Do you know what they were doing at Biosphere 3?"

"... Not exactly, no. But..."

"I do. Do you know who was investing money in that research?"

"Lacklan, listen to me!"

"Do you?"

"No!"

"I do! And among others it was the Sinaloa drugs cartel. And every one of the programs they were funding involved some form of mind control. Those insane, violent things I did drew media attention to them, and the programs were shut down."

"You were not meant to do that."

"Meant? Meant by who?"

"You were supposed to follow to Washington."

"Supposed by who, Marni?"

"You are not dependable. You are not reliable, Lacklan. You go off half cock and start killing people."

"Now you listen to me, Marni. If you'd talked to me, instead of trying to use me like a pawn, maybe I would have followed to Washington. And maybe you, and whoever is doing all this 'meaning' and 'supposing', would have seen the need to put an end to the Biosphere 3 project. But let's be clear about one thing, anytime you try to use me as a pawn, it is not going to work, because I am nobody's pawn, Marni!"

She sighed loudly. "You see? This is exactly why..."

"You think? Maybe it's you who hasn't understood.

Because from where I am standing, this whole damned business is about not letting people become drones. Let me ask you something, Marni."

"What?"

"When was the last time that you, or one of your pals who do so much 'meaning' and 'supposing'..."

"Please, stop saying that."

"When was the last time you shut down an Omega program?" I waited. There was no reply. "When was the last time you were inside their office in the Pentagon?"

This time she said, "You were at their office?"

"Yeah. From where I am standing, the one thing you *have* managed to do, aside from getting Professor Engels tortured and killed in Tucson, is to kill my father, the one high-ranking ally we had inside Omega."

"*What?*"

"Oh, now you want me to talk?"

"He killed *my* father, Lacklan!"

"I know. Are you forgetting that I hated that man all my life? He lived several hours after you shot him, Marni, and he told me everything. He made me promise, before he died, that I would look after you and keep you safe."

"I can't believe it."

"Well you'd better believe it. You and your pals may know a lot about climate and social geography, but you don't know shit about warfare. And so far you are screwing up at every step of the way. You need me, Marni. You don't understand your enemy. We *need* to talk."

"Lacklan, I called you to tell you to back off and desist."

I shook my head, even though she couldn't see me. "That's not what you want."

"Philip doesn't trust you."

"Who the hell is Philip?"

"Professor Gibbons."

"What the hell would he know?"

"Will you *please* stop being so aggressive!"

I breathed and counted five, backwards. "You know me, you turned to me when you left Weston, I was there for you. I destroyed the sun beetle farm, I destroyed the Biosphere 3 Project. What more do you need, Marni?"

"He thinks…"

"*Fuck* what he thinks!"

"No! Lacklan! Can't you see? It is precisely this bullying, aggressive attitude that makes it *impossible* to work with you! If there was one thing your father was right about, it was this!"

"OK, OK, OK! With the greatest respect for Professor Gibbons, you are better qualified to know whether I can be trusted or not than he is." A long silence. "And you know I can be."

"Yes, I do."

It was my turn to sigh. "Let's talk, in person. Then take me to meet Gibbons. There is a lot I can tell you about Omega." I hesitated, then said with heavy meaning, "We need each other, Marni. You know we do."

She was silent for a long moment. Then, "It's a shame you didn't realize that five years ago in London."

"Yes. I made a mistake. But this is not the time to discuss that."

"OK, Lacklan. I'll talk to Philip."

"You leaving the decision up to him?"

"No. We'll meet, but I need to discuss it with him. I'll get back to you."

"When?"

"Soon, Lacklan! Stop pushing so hard. In the next day or so."

I thought for a second. "They are hunting for you, you know that. The longer we delay, the greater the danger to you. Don't spend a week agonizing over this, Marni. You made a decision—the right decision—now we need to act."

"I know. *Stop pushing!* I'll get back to you."

And then the line was dead.

I finished my beer, went inside, dropped my phone on the bookcase, and threw myself on the sofa. After a while, to numb the ache of the silence, I switched on the TV. I scrolled through the channels, not seeing the images or listening to the voices, just searching for something I didn't know and couldn't find. Finally I got up and went to the kitchen to make some early lunch. I'd left the TV on a news channel, and as I cracked eggs into a bowl and started beating them, the litany droned in the background. I put the toast in the toaster, and went to lean on the doorjamb.

"...in a surprise development, former President Dick Hennessy is to address the United Nations Conference on Climate Change and Overpopulation next week, replacing former Vice President Al Gore. Alia Fadel interviewed him for the Right Now Program this morning..."

The screen was filled suddenly with the image of Alia Fadel sitting in a comfortable chair, gazing at Dick Hennessy. He was starting to look old, but he still had the eyes and the smile of a letch. She was nodding while he was talking.

"I'm real glad, Alia, that the United Nations has organized this conference, especially in view of the fact that we have pulled out of the Paris Accord. World leaders really need to get around the table and talk these issues through. As you know, Al has had a deep interest in climate change for a long time, and I know he was real excited about addressing the delegates, so when he asked me to stand in for him, I was real honored to accept..."

The shot cut back to the studio and the anchorman. "And you can catch the whole interview later this evening at a quarter after six..."

I went back to the kitchen and poured the beaten eggs into hot butter. As I watched it congeal I wondered to myself if there had ever been a time in human history when mankind had not been divided into parasites and hosts; the few, spreading fear—terror—and the many, pliantly believing what they were told, and offering up their lifeblood in exchange for... For what? The promise of guidance and leadership toward a promised land that was always just beyond the horizon, but never reached.

Because once you reach the promised land, the one thing you no longer need, is a leader.

TWO

THE CALL CAME AT SEVEN AM THE NEXT DAY, AS I was stepping out of the shower after my morning run. I dried my hands and my hair and wrapped the towel around me before answering. The screen displayed a cell number I didn't recognize.

"Yeah, Walker."

The voice that answered was English and cultured, and had that unmistakable Oxford resonance to it. "Good morning, Mr. Walker. This is Professor Gibbons. Forgive me for calling so early, Marni said you would be up."

I knew what he was going to say, but I asked anyway. "What can I do for you, Professor Gibbons?"

"I wonder if we could meet and talk."

"I'm sorry. I have to keep my schedule free."

There was a barely perceptible sigh. "May I ask what for, Mr. Walker?"

I could feel the anger building in my belly and tried to control it. "I am expecting to meet Marni."

"That is what I want to talk to you about..."

"No. That is what I am going to talk to Marni about, because, Professor Gibbons, my meeting with her is none of your business."

"That is where you are mistaken, Mr. Walker. It is very much my business."

"How's that?"

"I can't discuss it with you on the telephone. Please, meet me at the Bethesda Fountain at nine o'clock this morning. I assure you, you won't miss your meeting with Marni. And, Mr. Walker...?"

"Yeah?"

"Try not to confirm all the preconceptions I have about you. I would actually like to be proved wrong."

"Screw you, Professor Gibbons. I'll see you at nine."

I had scrambled eggs on rye and a pot of strong, black coffee. Then I walked the two miles to Bethesda Terrace through the morning sunshine, watching the joggers, the skaters, the people on bicycles and those walking quickly in business suits, some carrying attaché cases, others wearing stupid mini rucksacks on their backs. But if I saw five hundred people that morning, of all types, shapes and sizes, five hundred of them were connected in some way to a device. They were either staring at a screen or they had something plugged into their ears; at least half had both. I wondered how long it was since any of them had noticed a bird sing. But then I realized, there was probably an app for that.

You could go to Central Park, plug in, and listen to birds singing on your iPhone.

Gibbons arrived early. I'd found a place to sit in the

shade of a large hickory, and I was watching who arrived, who left, and who stayed. At that time of the morning, very few people stayed more than a couple of minutes. So it looked as though he was going to arrive alone.

At ten to nine I saw him approach through the trees, from the direction of 5th Avenue. He was about five-ten, with receding white hair and a paunch. He stopped by the side of the fountain and scanned the area. He made no attempt to be discreet or to hide the fact that he was looking for somebody. You had to wonder at these clowns, thinking that I was a liability. I stood and walked over to him, approaching from behind. When I was six inches away, I said, "Bang, bang, you're dead. Why don't you hold up a big sign saying, 'I'm looking for Lacklan Walker'?"

He turned to face me. His eyes were not friendly. "Not everybody is out to kill everybody, Mr. Walker."

"But it's the ones who are that you need to worry about. Can we go somewhere less visible? Walk and talk, we'll cross the bridge." I started walking toward Bow Bridge and he followed. I said, "So what do you want to talk to me about?"

"I want you to stop trying to contact Marni."

"That's not going to happen." I looked at him. "Why?"

He thought for a moment before answering. "I know about Omega, Marni has told me all about them, and about your father. Frankly, I don't think she is at risk from them. I think they are more interested in negotiating with her than harming her."

"And this conclusion is based on what?"

He took a deep breath, as though he was sifting through his thoughts, deciding which ones he wanted to share with me. "I have been a consultant to many governments over the years, not least the U.S. and the U.K. A long time ago, I realized that presidents and prime ministers come and go, but they serve higher masters, and I have gained some idea of who some of those masters are."

"So?"

"Like all conspirators, the men and women who run Omega fear public exposure. Conspiracy prospers in the dark, Mr. Walker. That being the case, they try to keep their assassinations to a minimum, because every high profile murder risks investigation and exposure. Add to that the fact that we have her father's research..."

I stopped. "You have it?"

He looked me over a couple of times, making no secret of the fact that he was suspicious. "That's important to you?"

"It's important to everybody, Gibbons. Omega will do anything to get their hands on that research."

He shook his head and started walking again. "No, they will do anything to suppress, and preferably destroy, that research. They will do anything to stop it coming into the public domain. And as long as they believe that Marni's death will provoke just that, they will take care not to harm her."

"That is a very dangerous game."

We had reached the bridge and he stopped to lean his elbows on the edge and look down at the water.

"Well, that's just it. I don't think it is. What I think is dangerous is this warmongering, confrontational approach you have." He frowned and shook his head, as though I had said something absurd and he was having trouble believing I'd said it. "You can never beat them, Walker. There is no way to beat them. All we can ever hope to do is influence them."

"How do you know?"

"What?" He looked at me like I was insane.

"How do you know that we can never beat them?"

"They are far too powerful! They control governments. They have entire armies at their disposal…"

"And yet they are scared stiff of Marni Gilbert, who murdered one of their senior members. And after all the damage I have caused them, here I am. You know why they are not coming after me?"

He turned back to look at the lake. "I can hazard a shrewd guess."

"They hope that they can get to Marni through me. And they want Marni, as you pointed out, because they are scared of what she can do with her father's research."

He didn't say anything, but he nodded.

I pressed the point. "That kind of fear does not come from being invincible. They can be beaten! You should not be afraid of them."

"I am not afraid. I am pragmatic. I am a realist."

"So was Neville Chamberlain."

His face constricted with irritation. "Don't be absurd. There is no comparison!"

"I disagree. These people are ruthless. They're beyond ruthless. I know. My father was one of them. Did she tell you that they had my father kill hers?"

"She told me, yes."

"Did she tell you why they chose him for the job?"

He eyed me a moment and told me no with his face.

I told him why. "They chose my father because Frank Gilbert, Marni's father, was his best friend."

He turned away. "I find that hard to believe."

"That's your choice. He told me the whole story when he asked me to find Marni after she disappeared. The price for refusing to kill him would have been the death of his own family, as well as Marni and her parents." I paused a moment, then asked him, "Are you able, fully, to see what they did to him?"

He frowned. "What do you mean?"

"They offered him a choice, but it wasn't really a choice, because only one of the two options was even conceivable. And the conceivable option meant the destruction of his own soul. It meant murdering his best friend, doing something so horrific that he would detest himself for the rest of his life."

I reached in my pocket and pulled out a pack of Camels. I lit up with my battered old brass Zippo and blew smoke across the morning air. Then I went on.

"Having forced him to make that choice, to kill his best friend, they then rewarded him. They elevated him to a position of inconceivable wealth and power. Can you begin to imagine what that did to his mind? They showed him two things. One, that there was no depth they would not sink to to achieve their ends; and two, that they owned him completely." I gave him a moment to assimilate the full horror of what I had told him. "You are like Chamberlain, Gibbons, wanting to negotiate peace in our time with people who have no conscience and no inhibitions. There is no limit to what they will do to another human being, or eight billion human beings, in order to consolidate their power. If you believe you can reach a compromise with these people, you are already dead."

His face flushed and he turned on me. "*And your solution is to kill them all?*"

I held his eye for a slow count of three. "Yes."

He threw his hands in the air. "You see! This is why it's impossible! Have you *any*..." He screwed up his face like he had brain constipation and put his fingertips to his forehead. "Have you *any* conception of the *enormity* of what you are suggesting? The *logistics*...!"

"I don't know, I spent ten years in the SAS, what do you think?"

"This is the real world, Walker! This isn't a bunch of overgrown schoolboys running around the desert shooting at each other! We are talking about people's *lives!*"

For a moment I considered picking him up and throwing him over the bridge into the lake. Instead, I snarled, "What the hell are you talking about?"

He sighed, "I'm sorry, Walker, but you and your chums in Hereford live in your own rarified world where things are solved by shooting people. That might work in Afghanistan, but in London, New York, and Beijing, things are done differently. It is a very delicate balancing of power and you simply *cannot* go in just shooting people and blowing them up!"

I sucked on my cigarette and inhaled deeply, then let out the smoke slow. "Gibbons, my father was a lawyer. He got his degree from Harvard. He was a very intelligent man, and if anybody understood power, he did. He used to say, 'Murder is the most serious of all crimes, not because it is the most heinous offence against the person, but because the

State reserves to itself the authority to inflict violence and take life. This is because the ability to inflict violence and take life is the root of all power.'"

He closed his eyes and groaned loudly. "Heaven preserve us! A philosophizing thug!"

I studied the burning tip of my cigarette for a moment. "OK, Gibbons, I've been patient, but I have had about enough of your arrogance and your insults. I'm not going to try to convince you that you're wrong. You're stupid and you can't help it. I figure soon enough Omega will convince you of that. Now, I want to see Marni, and I am not going to take no for an answer."

He looked at me as though my poodle had just shat on his doorstep. "Fortunately it is not up to me. She does not want to see you, Walker. She asked me to come here and convince you to leave us alone."

"I don't believe you."

"That's your choice. But she believes, as I do, that you are a loose cannon. You are a danger to everybody. You are out of control. You have no discipline..."

I shook my head. "Discipline is not about obeying orders, Gibbons, it's about staying cool and taking the right steps to achieve your ends. Believe me, I have discipline. Now you are going to listen to me, and you are going to listen with care."

His eyes were resentful, but there was a hint of fear there, too. "Don't try to bully me, Walker."

"Shut up and listen. You are right about one thing, I am dangerous, and I am all that stands between you and torture and death at the hands of Omega. The moment they realize that Marni won't come to me, they will destroy you, or worse. Now tell me, is she going to present her father's research at her talk?"

He nodded. "Yes."

"Is it as explosive as Omega fear?"

"Yes, it is."

I sighed and flicked my cigarette butt into the water. "As soon as she presents it, you'll have played your hand and you will have no defense against them."

"No, then they will have to talk to us...!"

"Don't be stupid, Gibbons! Once she exposes their research they will have nothing to lose. They'll kill you both and create the biggest cover up since Kennedy. Think about it! If they did that to Marni's father and mine, what the hell do you think they'll do to you?"

His skin had acquired the color and texture of porridge.

"You have to convince Marni to talk to me, Gibbons."

I reached out and took hold of his tie. I pulled his face close to mine. His eyes were wide and I let him see death in mine. "She is committing suicide, Gibbons. She knows it, but she figures your life and hers are a fair price to pay for bringing down Omega. But her death will be in vain. She'll hurt them, but she won't destroy them. Talk to her. Make her talk to me."

I let him go when I saw in his eyes that I had got through to him. Then I watched him hurry away toward Bethesda and 5th Avenue. It was odd, I told myself, how a man could be brilliant and brave, like Gibbons, and at the same time be so stupid and cowardly.

I smoked another cigarette, watching the dark water beneath me and wondering what to do next. I didn't have much time. Omega knew that Marni and I were both in the same city. Despite my stunt the morning before, they would be watching me. They'd be watching us both like hawks. And it wouldn't take long for them to realize that Marni didn't want to see me. When that happened, when they realized that I was no use to them in getting to her, two got you twenty they would kill us both. They were rats, and Marni and Gibbons, in their emotional stupidity, had put them in a corner. A rat in a corner is not a good thing.

I started walking back through the park, taking my time, and wondering if my time had come; if everything, my unhappy years in prep school; the fights, the girls, and the drinking in high school; the endless battles with my father; loving my cool, distant, unreachable mother at a distance; and then the ten years of relentless killing and surviving, living always with Death at my shoulder, if all of that now resolved itself into a single, breathless, shocking moment, when I too died.

For a moment I wanted to take it all in, every car, every tree, every pretty girl, every bird, every birdsong, every note on the blue summer air. I wanted to take it in and hold it and live it for eternity.

But that's not how it works. You live each moment as it comes. And then you die.

He was waiting for me at the 97th Street exit, leaning against the 'Do Not Enter' sign, watching me. He looked lean, healthy, and cruel. I wasn't surprised to see him. I had half-expected it.

"Hello, Ben."

"Hello, Lacklan."

I went and stood at the crossing, waiting for the lights to

change. He stood beside me. "Have you got anything to report?"

"I don't report to you, Ben. I keep telling you, but you don't hear."

He ignored me. "Why was it Gibbons and not Marni?"

I looked into his face. "Mind your own business."

The lights changed and we started to walk. "I've been patient, Lacklan. I need a result and I need it now, or I can't keep protecting you."

"I don't need your protection. You need mine and you know it."

He eyed my face as we walked, trying to read my expression. "Is she going to reveal her father's research at the conference?"

I shrugged. "I haven't spoken to her."

"What did Gibbons tell you?"

"He said he wants to negotiate with Omega. He believes he can influence you and reach some kind of agreement."

We reached the far side of the road and I stopped. He faced me. "What did you tell him?"

"I told him he was stupid. I told him the only solution was to kill you all." He frowned at me. I didn't smile. "I told him the truth, that the only thing standing between him and Marni and death was me, and that I needed to talk to Marni."

His eyes made little darting movements over my features, like he was trying to read them. Finally, he said, "What did he say?"

"He said he'd try to persuade her."

"Where is she?"

I smiled, then gave a single, humorless laugh. "I don't

know, Ben. And if you try and torture it out of him I guarantee she won't be there by the time he talks." I sighed. "He wants guarantees, Ben. He believes, and so does she, that there is common ground between you and them, and some kind of compromise can be reached."

He nodded. "I am sure they are right. I keep telling you that, Lacklan. Isn't it time you started listening?" He jerked his head in a northerly direction and said, "Have a drink with me."

He led me to Columbus Avenue by way of 105th Street, to a bar with bare red brick walls and rough wooden tables. He ordered two martinis and we sat. Neither of us drank. He leaned back in his chair to study me for a moment.

"Lacklan, we are at a stalemate. You and Marni, and Professor Gibbons, can do Omega a lot of harm if she publishes her father's research. You know that, we know that. You also know that we have the power to hurt all of you very badly. You know that we won't flinch, and you know that we can and will kill you, without hesitation. Right there is the stalemate."

"What's your point?"

"That if we play chicken, if we keep on this course toward a head-on collision, you will die—all of you. We will be very badly hurt, but we will survive. And in time we will recover."

It was, in so many words, what I had told Gibbons. I sipped my martini. "I'd rather die fighting you, Ben, than live serving you. I know what that did to my father, remember?"

He nodded. "Maybe there's a third alternative."

I told him with my smile that I didn't believe him, but I said, "Go ahead, I'm listening."

"We, the members of Omega, Lacklan, are just people. We are not evil aliens from a parallel dimension, and we are not clones of each other. We are just people, and not everybody agrees with the way things are done. I am not going to stick my neck out and put myself at risk, but I will tell you that there are people, among the twenty-seven leaders, who would be willing to listen. For God's sake, Lacklan, your own father was Gamma, and it was no secret that he had his doubts. We have one objective, and only one. That is to preserve the little of good that humanity has created, when the end comes. But how we achieve this end, we are open to new ideas about that. And I genuinely believe that the Twenty-Seven would listen to you and Marni, and Gibbons."

I sighed, letting him know that I was bored. "Words."

"OK. Let's go one step at a time. Tonight, there is a cocktail party at the residence of Prince Mohamed bin Awad, in honor of the delegates and speakers at the UN conference."

I frowned. "Why?"

"Because he is the New York consul for the Awadi Arabian Kingdom, and his family have a vested interest in the outcome of the conference. The Middle East stands to lose a lot if the planet keeps getting hotter." He shrugged. "Everybody south of parallel forty-five does, but let's face it, nobody stands to lose more than a bunch of billionaires living in a desert and making money from oil. Climate change is not good news for them, right?"

"OK, I see that."

"So they have an interest in this conference, at the very

least as observers, but more likely as attempting to influence the speakers and the delegates."

I shrugged. "So why are you telling me this?"

"Because Marni will be at the party, and I can get you on the guest list. I want you to go. Ambush her. Make her talk to you. Let us at least have a dialogue. We all have things to lose, and we all have things to gain."

He reached into his inside pocket and pulled out an invitation which he slid across the table to me. I stared at it and felt a hot pellet of excitement in my gut. I was going to see her, talk to her, and touch her, after all this time. I was going to see her that night.

THREE

THERE ARE NOT A HUGE NUMBER OF HOUSES IN THE
immediate vicinity of Central Park. This one was a neo-
gothic monstrosity on East 79th Street that looked as though
it had once belonged to Dr. Frankenstein. It had too many
arches and gabled roofs, and Central Park as a back yard. I'd
bought an expensive evening suit that afternoon, with satin
lapels and a bowtie, and decided to arrive fashionably late, at
twenty minutes to nine. But when I got there, there were
still gleaming limos arriving out front and disgorging glittering people onto the sidewalk and the broad, stone steps
that led up to the grotesque pseudo-Tudor arch over the
doorway.

There was a man at the door dressed up like Jeeves. He
regarded me with a special kind of contempt he reserved for
people who were not famous or billionaires. I showed him
my invitation and he looked at it without touching it, like he
might catch vulgarity from it. He gestured me toward the

door with something that should have been courtesy but wasn't, and I stepped inside.

The inside was carpeted in red and paneled in oak, and populated by more of the same glittering people I had seen outside. I took a glass of champagne from a passing tray and moved through a set of double oak doors, half expecting a portcullis to drop on me from above. I figured there were at least a hundred people there, possibly twice that many. Most were in their fifties or sixties and many had the look of senior academics, or those strange creatures that hover in the gray area between academia, politics, and the military-industrial complex. They stood in small groups, smiling urbanely at each other, preening themselves, discussing exhibitions, concerts, and plays, accidentally dropping names, letting slip connections, like peacocks with important friends stuck up their asses, instead of tail feathers.

Somewhere I could hear a chamber orchestra playing Mozart, and I headed in that direction. Nobody seemed to notice me, which suited me fine. I crossed one large room and entered another. By the size of it, and the checkerboard floor, I figured it was a ballroom. A small stage at one end held a string quartet with a clarinet and an oboe, all in traditional eighteenth century clothes. They were busily playing a selection of Mozart and Handel which made you want to grab the nearest woman and break into a crazy minuet. The crowd was more dense here, and I stood on the periphery a while, watching. But I couldn't see any sign of Gibbons or Marni.

I spotted a waiter approaching with another tray of champagne and signaled him over.

"Is there a bar where I can get a real drink?"

He smiled. "Sure, other end of the ballroom, they got all the beer and spirits you want."

I put my glass down by a palm and negotiated my way through the throng to a long table covered in a white linen cloth, silver buckets of ice, white wine, and champagne. There was also a reassuringly large range of spirits. The guy in the white dinner jacket behind the table smiled. I said, "Give me a Bushmills, straight up."

While he poured it, I looked around. That was when I saw her. She was in a mauve satin evening dress and had her dark hair lifted into a knot at the back of her neck. She had a glass of champagne in her hand and was listening to Gibbons talk. There was a small group around them. A couple of the men looked Middle Eastern.

I felt a jolt of cold anger inside. I ignored it and strolled over to join the group. Marni was the first to see me. She went pale and her eyes stared. I smiled down at her.

"Hello, Marni. It's been a long time. How are you keeping?"

Her voice was barely a whisper. "Lacklan..."

I was aware of Gibbons staring at me. The group had gone silent, smiling pleasantly, expectantly. I smiled back. "Professor Gibbons, how are you? Please don't let me interrupt. Do carry on."

He stammered. "Yes, I...Walker. I didn't expect to see you here."

"And yet, here I am!"

The groomed and polished guy standing next to me held out his hand. "Salman bin Awad, how do you do?"

I shook his hand. "Lacklan Walker."

"Professor Gibbons was giving us a most fascinating talk on political philosophy."

I smiled with my mouth while my eyes did something else. "He's very good at that. He gets a lot of practice, don't you, Philip?" He scowled at me and I took Marni's elbow. "Please, carry on, I am just going to borrow Marni for a second. I promise to return her in one piece."

Gibbons flashed a look at her and she sighed. "I'll be right back."

We stepped over to the wall and she glared at me. "What the hell do you think you're playing at, Lacklan? What are you doing here?"

I raised an eyebrow. "It's nice to see you, too. What am I playing at? Well, you know what? I've been wanting to ask you a question. You see, there was this cabin outside Turret, where you kissed me, and where you were so worried that I had been hurt after I destroyed the sun beetle farm. Then I blinked, and next moment you disappeared and showed up negotiating for a seat at the Omega high table. I blinked again and, after I'd helped you escape, you killed my father. Now, however boring and inconvenient it might be for you and your academic colleagues, I think at the very least you owe me an explanation."

She closed her eyes and took a deep breath. When she opened them again, the anger had gone out of her face. I noticed absently that the deep blue of her eyes looked deeper because of the color of her dress. She looked beautiful and for a moment, I was overwhelmed by a feeling of loss.

"I'm sorry, Lacklan. The part of your story that you omitted was where you told me that your father had murdered mine. You hated your father, but I loved Daddy.

He was my idol. And when I discovered that your father, whom I had trusted all my life, who had always been there for me and Mom, when I discovered that he had not only killed my father, but that he was a member of Omega..." She shook her head. "You can't imagine what that did to me."

"I think I can, Marni."

She looked away. "I'm sorry, that was a stupid thing to say. Of course you can."

"I am no stranger to betrayal."

She raised her eyes to meet mine.

"I have been betrayed by just about everybody I have loved."

"Don't say that, Lacklan."

"Why are you cutting me out?"

She stepped close and placed her hand on my chest. "Please believe me, you are too dangerous."

"What does that mean?"

"You don't realize the power our enemies wield."

"I think I do. I think I know them a damn sight better than you do. How do you think I got into this party?"

She frowned. "What are you saying?"

"I'm saying that we need to talk. *You* don't understand the danger you're in, or what will happen if you release your father's research at the conference. They will kill you, Marni, and they will kill Gibbons and they will kill me. We need to join forces. You have to stop running from me."

She was still frowning. "How did you get into the party?"

"You remember Ben, my father's personal assistant?"

She nodded.

"He is with Omega. I don't know what his position is, but he carries weight."

Her frown had deepened. "But why did they want you to come... To talk to me? They wanted you to talk to me?"

There was something like panic in her eyes. I gave her a moment, then said, "Look at me, Marni. Look at me." Her eyes met mine. "As long as they think that I am looking for you, as long as they think we have a bond, your life is safe. The minute they decide that I cannot reach you, we are both dead. Do you understand that? You need to assimilate that fact. Because it's the only thing keeping us both alive."

She nodded. "Yes, I see."

"They want you on board, but above all, what they really want is your father's research." I shook my head and narrowed my eyes at her. "What the hell did he discover, Marni? Why is his research so important to them?"

She didn't answer for a moment, examining my face. "You don't know?" She sighed and shook her head. "I can't tell you."

"How would I know? Why can't you tell me?"

"Not here. Lacklan, have you gone over to them?"

She must have seen the anger in my face because she closed her eyes and raised a hand. "All right, I'm sorry!"

"Marni, you're accusing me of being a loose cannon, but you are panicking and you are out of control. You need to get a grip, realize who you can trust. And we need to start making a plan together, coordinating our efforts."

She nodded again. "Yes, you're right. I have been so scared. I've missed you, but Lacklan, you scare me sometimes."

"Come home with me tonight."

"I..." She glanced at Gibbons. "I don't know..."

"Marni?" She looked back at me. "Come home with me tonight."

She hesitated, then nodded. "Yes, all right."

"We'll join them, chat for a while, then we'll walk out together."

"What if they are waiting for us?"

"They won't be."

"How do you know?"

"Because they know I would kill them."

"Jesus!"

"And that would attract too much publicity. They want to do this subtle and quiet. We'll play on that."

She was staring at me with horrified eyes. "What happened to you in England?"

"It wasn't in England. It was in Afghanistan, in Iraq, in a hundred other places. If you stop running away from me, maybe one day I'll tell you about it."

"What about Gibbons?"

"He can come along if he wants to."

She hesitated. "OK..."

"Come on, let's go and be sociable for a while. And Marni?"

"Yes?"

"Be nice to me, OK?"

She nodded. "I know, so we don't draw attention."

"No, because I'm tired of being brushed off by you, and I like it when you're nice."

She sighed and repressed a smile. We made our way back to the group. Gibbons was taking a break from lecturing, and Salman was speaking with an earnest look on his slim, handsome face.

"With the greatest respect, Professor, despite everything that has been said about politics, the many volumes that have been written on the subject—it has been defined as both an art and a science—in reality what it boils down to in the end is that it is a simple practice. And the practice is no more than the acquisition and retention of power. That is *all* politics is—'how can I acquire more power, and how can I retain the power I have?' And for both of these ends we need two conditions..." He paused and held up two long, delicate brown fingers. "One, the people over whom we exercise power must be divided, and two, they must fear some outside threat. It may be the Jews, or the Muslims, it may be the Communists or the decadent west, it may be the aliens..." He paused, holding his audience suspended from his arched left eyebrow. "...or it may be the *environment!* But as long as people live in fear of an outside threat, they will give their political leaders a good deal of latitude in how they are governed." He smiled. "In how they are *controlled!*"

A large man in a brocade waistcoat and a deep purple dinner jacket had moved up to us like a Spanish galleon in full sail, parting the sea of people as he went. He had a huge, leonine head, silver hair brushed back and a complacent smile on his face.

"What you say is absolutely true, Salman. But it is merely the circus part of bread and circus. The virtue of the circus is to keep people's attention focused on something other than the fact that their leaders are making free with their possessions and their liberties. There is no special virtue in a terrified populace. All you really need is a distracted one." He turned his complacent smile on Gibbons and then Marni. "Professor Gibbons, Dr. Gilbert. Speaking of circuses and distractions, I believe you have some entertainment in store for us."

I felt Marni stiffen and gave her arm a gentle squeeze. Gibbons curled his lip. "Your Excellency, what a pleasant surprise to see you at a conference of this type. The rate at which your country's rainforests are being depleted, one would be forgiven for thinking your government had no interest in climate change at all."

His Excellency chuckled the way a mountain might chuckle. "Climate change! Reds under the bed. We have other things to frighten our people with. But I'll tell you what I *am* interested in..." He looked around at us one after another. "Screens!" He announced it as though he expected us to gasp. "Screens," he said again. "You know, in 1955, the Generalissimo Francisco Franco, the last great fascist, was being conducted around the brand new studios of Television Española, due to be inaugurated the following year. Franco had been the supreme, authoritarian leader of Spain for some sixteen years by then. The fascist regimes of Italy and Germany had collapsed, the Allies had won the war, and there was a new mood of hope and liberalism in the world. So Franco was under a lot of pressure from his so-called technocrats to liberalize his regime. They wanted reforms, but Franco had been holding out, resisting their pressure.

"But on this day, he was shown around the brand new television studios at Prado del Rey, in Madrid, and it was explained to him how every village would have a television in the church hall, and with time, every home in Spain would own a television. And naturally, the government, and ultimately Franco himself, would control the content of the programs." His Excellency laughed out loud. "At the end of his tour, as they were leaving the studios, he turned to the leading advocate for reform in his government and said to him, 'You can have your reforms, *I* have Television Española!'"

There was much laughter around the group, except that Gibbons did not laugh. He looked sour. "The man was a swine, but he was prophetic. Today, practically every brain in the western world is controlled by a screen. Not even Orwell foresaw that we would willingly carry the damned things around with us."

Salman was nodding as he finished laughing. "As I say, politics is merely the practice of acquiring and retaining power, by whatever means. Franco was a past master at it, and he understood well the power of the screen in controlling people's minds. And let's be honest, ultimate power is the power to control people's thinking."

Gibbons scowled at him. "More than that, Salman, much more than that. The power of information technology, delivered via ubiquitous screens, is to mesh, by means of an information matrix, all minds into one single mind, controlled from one single source."

Salman and His Excellency smiled at the floor. Salman muttered, "A little extreme, science fiction, surely, Professor Gibbons."

Gibbons grunted ill-humoredly and I thought this was probably a good time to go. So I spoke up.

"Well, gentlemen, I think we'll be pushing off."

Gibbon's head snapped around.

I smiled blandly and went on. "It has been fascinating.

We must do it again." I turned to the professor. "Gibbons, are you coming or are you going to stay?"

He opened his mouth, looked at Marni, and said, "I...um..."

Marni turned to me. "Just give me a moment to fix my hair, will you?"

I searched her eyes behind a smile. "Sure." I grinned. "I think I'll fix mine too." I looked at the group. "Gentlemen, it's been a pleasure."

We moved across the ballroom toward the exit. The entrance hall was empty, save for the doorman, who had now moved inside and watched us with incurious eyes. Marni glanced at me. "The restrooms are upstairs." I followed her up a broad, mahogany staircase to the next floor, and then down a passage. She smiled, but there was an edge to her voice. "You going to come in with me?"

"No, but don't do a disappearing act on me again, Marni."

She stopped outside a door with a brass plaque that bore the legend *Ladies* on it in French script. She looked up into my eyes. "I won't. Just wait for me a moment."

I nodded and she pushed through the door. I strolled back to the landing and stood leaning on the banister, looking down into the entrance hall. After a moment, a man in a dinner jacket came into view and stopped to talk quietly to the doorman. I went cold inside. I knew him, but it couldn't be.

I watched him pull out a silver case, extract a cigarette, and put it in his mouth. He lit it with a gold lighter, made a comment, laughed, and went to step outside. Then Gibbons came strutting into view and asked the doorman something.

The doorman answered and jerked his head at the stairs. The guy with the cigarette turned to look at Gibbons and when he did, I saw his face. Hot rage welled up in my gut. It was him. It was Abdul Abbassi, nicknamed by his pals the Butcher of Helmand. It had been five years, but I would never forget that face as long as I lived. But the question that was burning inside me right then was, what the hell was he doing at this party?

I stepped back and watched Gibbons come stomping up the stairs. I moved down the passage and he followed after me with anger burning in his cheeks and his eyes. As he drew breath to give me one of his lectures I stepped close to him and drove my fist, not too hard—just enough to shut him up —into his solar plexus. He gasped and wheezed and I pulled him down the corridor toward the cans. There I slammed him against the wall and thrust my face close to his.

"Now you listen to me, Gibbons, and you listen carefully. There is a man at this party called Abdul Abbassi. His nickname is the Butcher. I have watched him murder an entire village and kill women and children with his own hands, just to make an example of them. If he is at this party, it is for one reason and one reason only, and that is to kill Marni.

"Marni is coming to my place, *now*, where I can protect her. You can come along if you want. But get in my way and I swear, Gibbons, I will gut you like a fish and I will not hesitate. Do you understand me?"

There was rage and contempt in his face, but no fear. He was too damned stupid to be afraid. "You damned fool!" he said. "*You are going to ruin everything!*"

I reached behind my back and slipped my Fairbairn &

Sykes commando knife from my waistband. I held it to his throat.

"Your call, Professor."

The door to the ladies' room opened. Marni stood staring at me, a mixture of horror and disbelief on her face.

"What in the name of God...?"

I snapped. "I can't explain now. Just trust me!"

"*Trust* you?"

I snarled, "Gibbons...?"

He spat the words at me, "*You're insane!*" Then he turned his head toward Marni. "*Get out of here! Go!*"

And she was running along the passage toward the stairs. I shouted, "*Marni! No! Don't!*" and made to go after her, but Gibbons was clinging to me, dragging me back, shouting after her, "*Run! Run!*"

I turned and gave him a savage back-hander with my left fist. His eyes rolled and his legs went to jell-O. He dropped to the floor and I slid the knife back into my belt as I ran after her. As I reached the top of the stairs she was running out onto the street. I took the steps three at a time and went to go out after her, but the doorman stepped in front of me, his left hand on my chest.

I didn't think. I didn't look at him. I took his wrist in my left hand and twisted. His arm locked. I jabbed my right savagely into his exposed floating ribs and stepped over him as he went down, wheezing. I wrenched open the door and ran into the night. She was there. Ten paces away, climbing into a yellow cab. I shouted, "*Marni! Wait!*" But the door slammed and she was away, moving down 79th Street and left onto Madison Avenue.

There was a dangerous rage inside me. I turned to go

back, get Gibbons, and beat him until he told me where she had gone, but the doorman was staggering out with a purple face, pointing at me, gasping. "I call the cops! They are coming for you! You in *big* trouble!" Next to him, watching us, was Abbassi, with one hand in his pocket and the other holding a cigarette. I swore violently under my breath and ran across the road to the parking garage to get my car.

Two minutes later, I was struggling to stay within the speed limit as I cruised down Park Avenue toward Union Square and Broadway. As I drove, I dialed the number for the FBI.

"Federal Bureau of Investigation. How may I direct your call?"

"I need to talk to somebody in the Counter Terrorism Division."

FOUR

I was in an interview room on the 23RD floor of number 26, Federal Plaza, the New York field office of the FBI. Special Agent Harrison Mclean was sitting across from me and observing me through slightly narrowed eyes, like he couldn't make up his mind whether I was a clown or a jackass. His partner, Special Agent Daren Jones, had just left the room on a pretext, but I was pretty sure he was checking their database to see what, if anything, they had on me.

"I'm having some difficulty getting a handle on this, Mr. Walker. You say you were at a party thrown by..." He checked his notes. "Prince Mohamed bin Awad, at his house on 79th Street. The party was in honor of the speakers and the delegates at the UN conference on climate change. So..." He gave his head a little shake. "How did you come to be at this party?"

"That's not important."

"With all due respect, Mr. Walker, I'll decide what's important. How did you come to be there?"

I sighed. "I was accompanying Dr. Marni Gilbert, who will be talking at the conference. In fact, she's one of the key speakers."

He nodded and made a note. "You her boyfriend?"

I sighed. "No. We're old friends. We grew up together."

He nodded again, like my answer was confirming some suspicion he had. Then he went on, "So while you were there you saw..." He looked down at his pad. "Abdul Abbassi, 'The Butcher of Helmand', and you recognized him."

I was struggling to hold on to my patience. "Yes."

"And you recognized him...how?"

"I was stationed in Afghanistan for a while."

His eyes narrowed further. "Who with?"

"The British SAS."

A thin smile, a raised eyebrow. His eyes took in my evening suit. "Next you'll be telling me your name is Bond, James Bond."

I didn't smile. "My name is Lacklan Walker."

He nodded. "I know it is." He eyed me a moment, still smiling. "Our Marines too tough for you?"

"Excuse me?"

"You're an American, how did you wind up in a British outfit?"

I took a deep breath. "I had personal reasons for leaving home. My mother is English. I joined the SAS. It's not a soft option."

"Personal reason?"

"Yeah. I couldn't stomach my father. Look, Special Agent Mclean, I don't mean to be rude or disrespectful, but I am trying to report the presence of a terrorist at a party that was exclusively for delegates to the UN Conference..."

"And their childhood friends..."

I frowned at him. "Are you not interested?"

He didn't answer for a while. Finally, he sat forward and looked at his notepad again. "See, here's my problem. Our Operational Branch has no Abdul Abbassi, Butcher of Helmand, on its wanted list." He shrugged. "I think it's a name you made up." He smiled almost apologetically. "Let's face it." He gestured at my clothes with his open hand. "Your whole story, your costume... It's fantastical."

I sat forward and leaned my arms on the desk, mirroring his posture. "Listen to me, Mclean..."

"Special Agent Mclean, Mr. Walker."

"Listen to me. I watched that man butcher an entire village. I saw it with my own eyes. There is only one reason why he would be at that party..."

He spread his hands. "Why would the Taliban want to bomb a United Nations conference on climate change, Mr. Walker?"

"I don't know..."

The door opened and Special Agent Jones came in. He handed Mclean a couple of sheets of paper and sat down. "Mr. Walker, I can see you have no record, and I can see that you were a captain in the British Special Air Service. But we have nobody on our wanted list answering to the name Abdul Abbassi, and I'm afraid that even if you did recognize this man, and he has committed wartime atrocities in Afghanistan, that is not reason enough for our Operation Branch to start an investigation, or take any other action for that matter. He is not on a wanted list."

I held his eye for a long moment. "That man is going to perpetrate a terror attack at that conference. Whatever your lists and databases tell you, *I* am telling you that he is going to strike at the conference."

Mclean spread his hands. "Well, thank you for coming in, Mr. Walker. We've made a note of your observations and we will look into it."

I couldn't keep the irony from my voice. "You'll look into it?"

Harrison matched my tone. "Sure, we have nothing better to do, have we, Special Agent Jones?"

Jones smiled. "Nothing that won't keep."

I stood. "Thanks for your time, gentlemen. I won't waste any more of it. See you around."

Back on Broadway, I stopped and pulled my pack of Camels from my jacket pocket and lit up. I drew the smoke down deep and blew it in a stream up at the starless sky. I stood thinking. I had a problem. I had lost Marni, in more senses than one. I needed to find her and make her understand about Abbassi, but what little chance I had of getting Gibbons to cooperate with me, I had shot to pieces when I threatened him with my knife. Now, as soon as Ben discovered that I had lost her, I'd have him gunning for me. He was running out of patience with me, and I knew it.

And if all that wasn't enough on its own, now I also needed to find out what Abbassi was planning, why he was at that party.

I started walking toward my car. I couldn't do all of it. There was only one of me. I needed to prioritize. I reached the Zombie and leaned on the roof, thinking and smoking, gazing at the sleepless, lamp lit street with its endless streams of people and traffic. The chances were that Marni and Gibbons had some kind of safe place, and that was where she'd gone. The way he'd told her to go, to run—it hadn't been a cry of panic, telling her to get the hell out of there. It had conveyed more. It had conveyed that they both knew where she was going to go, somewhere prearranged. I had no precise reason for believing that, except a gut feeling based on my reading of their body language, and the tone of his voice.

So if she was safe, at least for now, then I should focus on Abbassi, because right then I was pretty sure he was the major threat to her. To her and maybe to hundreds of other people. I looked at my watch. An hour had passed since I'd left the party. Abbassi had been smoking a cigarette outside. He hadn't had the look of a man who was about to leave. There was an at least even chance that he would still be there. I climbed into the Zombie and made my way back up Centre Street toward Union Square and Park Avenue.

It wasn't much of a plan, but right then it was all I had. I'd wait for Abbassi to leave, tail him, and see where he went, who he saw, what he did. Sooner or later he would give me some clue as to his reason for being there. Meanwhile, I would think about how to deal with Marni and Gibbons when the time came. If I had to, I'd abduct her and force her to listen to me. And I might well have to. I needed time to think and plan, but time was one thing I had very little of.

I pulled into 79th Street and parked a hundred yards down the road from the house, across from the Serafina. It was almost eleven o'clock and there was a desultory flow of cars driving up to the door and collecting couples and small groups of people who were glittering a little less than when they had arrived, but laughing a little more.

I waited half an hour and saw a red Ferrari V12 Superfast pull up. A guy in a suit climbed out and spoke to the doorman, who was still holding his side. The doorman spoke into a radio and after ten minutes, Abbassi came out and had a word with the guy from the Ferrari, who handed him some keys. I fired up the Zombie. Abbassi climbed into the Ferrari, did a U-turn, and took off. I went after him. He turned left on Madison Avenue and kept going north.

I let him get well ahead. A bright red Ferrari is not easy to lose. He eventually crossed the Madison Avenue bridge into the Bronx. He kept going north, up 3rd Avenue and Boston Road toward the Bronx Park area. At 180th he turned right and crossed under the railway bridge.

You couldn't get much further from East 79th Street. Everywhere you looked there was decay and graffiti, desolation, poverty and hopelessness. His Ferrari stood out like a strippergram at a wake. He moved up Morris Park Avenue, turned into Amethyst Street and pulled up outside an ugly, detached, white clapboard house with iron railings on the windows and the door. It was three stories and had a flat roof. I drove past like I knew where I was going and watched him get out, unlock the door and go inside. I parked at the end of the road, lit a Camel, and sat watching the house in my mirror.

A couple of things were clear to me by now. The first was that Abbassi was not worried about being spotted. You have to be either very confident or very stupid to bring a Ferrari 812 into an area like Van Nest. Or both. I could buy that he was both.

The other thing was, if he was hanging out with the prince and driving a three-hundred grand Ferrari, clearly this shack wasn't his house. So if he didn't live here, what was this place? It had three stories and it wasn't small, so it was reasonable to assume there were people inside it. If that was correct, then he was visiting. Whoever he was visiting, I was pretty sure it wasn't another Arabian prince, or his in-laws. I needed to know who they were.

That led me to thinking I needed to look inside and bug the place. For that I needed to know how many of them there were, and when the house would be empty. To find that out I either needed to sit on the place for a week, or bug it. It was a vicious circle—and I didn't have a week.

I waited another hour, mulling things over, and saw the lights go out in the windows. After that, I cruised around the neighborhood for a bit, thinking and smoking. That was when I discovered there was a small mosque, or *mushalla*, three or four hundred yards away on Rheinlander Avenue. If they were Muslims, the chances were pretty good they would go to the mosque on Friday. That was tomorrow. It didn't give me much time, but it might just be enough. I tried to remember what I had in my kit bag in the trunk. I had replenished it after Burgundy.[1]

I had my Smith & Wesson 500, my two Sig Sauer p226s, the take down bow and six aluminum arrows. The night goggles were there and there were a couple of cakes of C4, and half a dozen detonators. And bugs. I'd gotten Kenny to send me some bugs and trackers. Since I'd been chasing Marni, I had come to realize how useful they could be.

---

1. See *The Storm*

I headed south toward Manhattan. I planned to grab four hours sleep and be back before dawn, to wait for my opportunity. Then I'd find out exactly what Abdul Abbassi and his pals were about.

It was almost one AM when I left my car in the parking garage and took the elevator to my apartment. I knew something was wrong as I put the key in the lock. It's a sixth sense you develop. It's as though your skin prickles, like you can smell something on the air, but it has no aroma.

I turned the key and stepped aside as I pushed the door open. Nothing happened, but I could see the lights were on. Whoever it was wasn't shy or didn't expect me back. I cursed myself for leaving my 9 mm in the kitbag in the trunk, but slipped my knife from my waistband and stepped in. Ben's voice came to me from the living room.

"It's only me, Lacklan. You can close the door and put your weapon away. I hope you don't mind, I helped myself to some of your Irish whiskey."

He was sitting in my armchair with a Glock 19 on his lap. I still had my knife in my hand. He looked at it and said, "Are you going to kill me?"

I jerked my head at his gun. "What's that for?"

"Insurance. You are unpredictable. I thought if you found somebody in your apartment you might go all ninja on my ass, so to speak. I left the lights on so you would be forewarned."

"Are you here to execute me?"

He dismissed the idea with a small laugh. "No."

I checked the kitchen, the bathrooms, and the bedrooms. They were clear. I came back and looked down at him. "Take out the magazine and put your weapon away, or I'll cut your throat."

He started to laugh and shook his head. He released the magazine, put it on the table, showed me the chamber was empty and put the weapon in his holster. I sheathed the knife, poured myself a whiskey, and sat on the sofa. "What do you want?"

"What happened at the ball? Cinderella got away."

I sighed. I wanted to sleep. "We have a problem. She was coming with me. We were on our way. She wanted to go to the can before we left. While she was in there, I saw an old friend."

He frowned. "Who?"

"Abdul Abbassi. He's a jihadist, worked for the Taliban. He was at the party, in full tux and driving a Ferrari."

Ben frowned. "Abdul Abbassi? The Butcher of Helmand?"

"You know him?"

"I know of him. He's a very dangerous man."

"If he's here, as a guest of the prince, it means they are planning an attack, and in all probability on the conference."

"I wouldn't jump to conclusions, Lacklan."

"Well, he isn't here for the hot dogs, Ben."

He thought for a moment. Sipped his whiskey and studied my face. "He's not your concern. Leave him to us. We'll deal with him."

"Deal with him how? He's a threat to Marni. I want him neutralized."

"We'll deal with it. I want you to focus on Marni. Bring her in."

"You don't give me orders, Ben."

He sighed. "I am not giving you orders, Lacklan, but this is the best use of our resources. Bring her in, make her safe. Arrange a meeting. We'll deal with Abbassi."

I stared at him for a long moment. Then I asked, "Tell me something, Ben. Why don't you go after Gibbons? Wouldn't it be easier for you to get to her through Gibbons than through me?"

He shook his head. "We can't go after Gibbons. Don't ask why, I can't tell you. You understand a fraction of what goes on. If you would see sense and join us, I could tell you so much more. And believe me, we could use a man like you to fill your father's shoes." He shrugged, drained his glass, and stood. "Just get Marni on board before it's too late, Lacklan. Thanks for the whiskey."

I heard the door close and sat a long while staring at my glass, thinking about Gibbons, about how he had been willing to sacrifice his own life to allow her to get away. That took real commitment. A man like that was a real danger to Omega, and yet they couldn't go after him. How, I wondered, does an Oxford Don like Gibbons get that kind of protection from an organization like Omega?

I went to my room, set the alarm for five AM, and fell into a restless sleep.

FIVE

Forty minutes after five found me sitting at the end of Amethyst Street drinking black coffee from a flask while pre-dawn touched the edges of the sky with a sleepy gray. Twenty minutes after that, lights started coming on in the windows of the house, touching the red Ferrari with shiny amber highlights. Another hour and the sky seemed to stir and stretch. Beyond a giant cypress tree, where some guy had turned his yard into an orchard, the sun warped over the horizon, spilling molten light and turning the dawn into morning. Down the street, windows slid open, front doors began to bang, and car doors like volleys of rifle shots scattered the birds from the trees into the yawning sky. And the machinery of the great city started to grind into action, sending streams of people, its lifeblood, flowing through the streets, the arteries of the vast cyborg: men and women to work, to generate wealth for their masters and revenue for the state, children to school to learn to be like their parents and generate wealth for their masters and revenue for the state. Collectively essential, each one, each individual was a replaceable, expendable cell in the body of the beast.

By eight thirty, the street was quiet again, and half an hour after that, Abbassi's front door opened and four men stepped out. They were talking and laughing as they made their way up the road toward Rhinelander Avenue, headed for the mosque. They passed within eight feet of the Zombie. The tinted glass meant I could see them but they could not see me. Abbassi was slightly ahead of them, staying aloof. Two of the others were clean shaven and looked as though they were in their early twenties, with short hair, sweatshirts, jeans, and sneakers. The other was older, maybe thirty, with longer hair and a beard. He wore an Afghan hat and a long jacket over baggy pants. It was easy to see the set up. Abbassi was the commander, the Afghan was the sergeant. Two got you twenty he had combat and field experience. The other two were grunts, new recruits, probably from the West.

I let them get around the corner and gave them five minutes. At an approximate speed of one and a half yards per second, that put them almost five hundred yards away. Then I started the silent engine and slipped down the road to park across from the Ferrari. I cocked my Sig and slipped it in my waistband. Then I walked across the road, fishing my lock picks from my pocket like they were a bunch of keys. I didn't expect a real active neighborhood watch on this street, but it pays to be careful. It took me a few seconds, the lock yielded, and I stepped in, closed the door, and pulled the Sig.

I knew the chances were they had all gone to the mosque, but there was still a possibility somebody had stayed behind. I moved to the living room. The furnishings were sparse, basic, and cheap. There was a couple of old sofas and a dining table with four chairs. There was no TV and there were no bookcases. An open door led to the kitchen. I placed the first bug on the top of the door frame. In a house occupied by four guys, you can be pretty sure it's the least touched place in the house. Another went in the same spot on the kitchen side. A kitchen is a place where people do a lot of talking.

I ran silently up the stairs. There were four bedrooms. They were unremarkable. Like the rest of the house, they were sparsely and cheaply furnished, with IKEA beds and melamine wardrobes. I placed a bug in each room.

They were essentially voice-activated, micro-cell-phones that were pre-dialed into my laptop. If anybody started talking, the sound of their voice would activate the cells and whatever they said would be automatically saved into a file on my hard drive.

I wasn't sure how long I had, so I made only a cursory inspection of the house, searching the wardrobes, suitcases under the beds, and the cupboards under the stairs. I didn't find any bomb-making equipment or explosives. That didn't mean they weren't there. It just means they weren't easy to find. What I did find was three passports in the sideboard in the living room. The Afghan guy was Aatifa Ghafoor. The other two were a Pakistani, Ali Kamboh, and a British national of Pakistani origin, Hassan Barr. I photographed all three with my cell. I checked my watch. I'd been in the house for just over half an hour. I closed my eyes and went through everything I had done since I'd entered the place, checking if I had left any sign of my presence. I was pretty sure I hadn't.

I let myself out, went to my car, and got in. I lit a cigarette and sat thinking about what I had to do next. I had to make peace with Gibbons somehow. I had questions for him that I needed answered immediately, like why was Omega so afraid of him? And, above all, where was Marni?

I pulled my cell from my pocket, selected the three photographs of the passports, attached them to a text message, and wrote, "These three men, plus Abdul Abbassi, the Butcher of Helmand, are the reason I needed to get Marni out of the party. They are here in New York. I had no time to argue or explain. We need to talk. I'll call you."

I pressed 'send', then fired up the engine and pulled away. I crossed via 3rd Avenue Bridge and made my way to Morningside Park. There I strolled by the pond and called Gibbons.

"What do you want, Walker?"

"I understand you're mad at me. But that isn't important now. I am getting tired of saying this, but you really need to talk to me, and above all, you really need to listen."

"Give me one good reason why I should."

"I just sent you three damned good reasons, but I'll give you a lot more than that if you will just give me the chance."

"That's exactly what I am doing, against my better judgment. Talk."

"OK, first, what happened last night would never have happened if you and Marni had listened to me from the start."

"What the bloody hell are you talking about?"

"I'm talking about Abdul Abbassi, a terrorist commander who, five years ago, was attached to the Taliban. I won't waste time now giving you his CV, but believe me when I tell you I have seen him do things that would make a hard man weep. He was at the party last night, and whether you take it from me or not, Gibbons, you have to ask yourself what he was doing there."

I gave him a moment. He didn't say anything but I could sense he was thinking. I went on.

"You and Marni were driving me crazy. I had finally got her to agree to come with me. I knew you were going to cause trouble, and just as you were coming up the stairs, that was when I saw Abbassi. He was the guy stepping out for a smoke, remember? I had no time, Gibbons, I couldn't risk a ruckus. I had to shut you up and get her out."

I was half-expecting him to ask what made me think she was Abbassi's target. He didn't. Instead, he asked, "Who are these other men?"

"I don't know any of them. I followed him last night after the party. He has a run-down house in Van Nest. These other three are living there."

He was quiet again, then asked, almost to himself, "What does it mean?"

"Listen, we have to get off this line. For the hundredth time, we need to talk and we need to unite forces. Let's meet."

"All right. Do you know The Parlour, on West 86th?"

"The Irish pub? Sure."

"It's not far from you. We'll meet there in an hour and have some lunch."

I nodded, even though he couldn't see me. "Sounds like a good idea. See you then."

THE PARLOUR IS A BIG PLACE, and at that time it was practically empty. He arrived punctually, ignored me even though I was the only person sitting at a table and he must have seen me, and went to the bar and ordered a pint of Guinness. He waited for it to be pulled and finally brought it over to the table where I was sitting, watching him. I decided he was obnoxious because that was his intrinsic nature. He couldn't help it. There was also the swollen bruise on the side of his face, and that might have had something to do with it.

As he sat, he said, "I've been thinking it over on the way here, and it is fraught with all sorts of problems. Tell me what you have to say anyway, but be aware, I think any kind of cooperation is almost impossible."

I sat studying his face, trying to suppress the desire to reach over and give him a matching bruise on the other side. Finally, I sighed and said, "Are you a pain in the ass on purpose or by accident?"

"That kind of thing won't help."

"And your strutting in with that kind of hostile, negative attitude will?"

"I am simply being practical and telling you how things stand."

"OK, Gibbons, have it your way. Now let me tell you how I see it. Either ISIS or Al-Qaeda are planning an attack on the UN. If I am right, they will time the attack for the high point of the conference. That will be your talk and Marni's..."

He interrupted me. "Why would Al-Qaeda or ISIS have any interest in bombing the conference? It doesn't make any sense."

I tried not to snarl but failed. "Just because you can't see it, it doesn't mean it isn't there, Gibbons. You can't see my foot, but believe me, it's within striking distance."

"More gratuitous violence, Lacklan?"

I sighed and carried on. "I don't know what their purpose might be. It might be simply that there will be a lot of western leaders there. It might be a blow against a United Nations that they perceive as biased toward western interests. It might have something to do with the fact that if global warming and droughts escalate as Omega foresee they will, the Muslim heartland in the Middle East will be all but wiped out." I shook my head. "These people are fanatics, Gibbons. I am not sure they need a coherent reason for the fucked up things they do." I sat back in my chair and sighed. "Whether we understand their reasons or not, the fact is that in a party thrown by an Arab prince for the speakers and delegates at the conference, Abdul Abbassi was present as a guest. When he left the party, he went to a house that had all the appearance of a terrorist cell." I held up my thumb. "Why was he invited to the party?" I raised my index to join it. "He was dressed in a two thousand dollar evening suit and driving a three hundred grand Ferrari, what was he doing shacking up in Van Nest with three down and outs?" I raised my middle finger to make a trio. "What have Abdul Abbassi, an Afghan, a Pakistani, and a British Pakistani got to bring them together, with Prince Mohamed bin Awad?"

He grunted and took a long pull on his Guinness. As he set it down, he smacked his lips and wiped his mouth with the back of his hand. "We don't know."

I shook my head. "Wrong. We don't know precisely. But we can assert with a degree of confidence that they are not practicing for a spelling bee. We can be certain that if Abdul Abbassi is involved, it is related to jihad."

He nodded. "Yes. You're right."

"And in my opinion, it is too much of a coincidence that it coincides so closely with the conference. Whether we can see it right now or not, there is a connection, Gibbons."

He made a face of reluctant acceptance. "Yes, you're right. You're right."

I waited a moment, then said, "So...?"

He shrugged. "What do you want?"

"For a start, I want to be able to protect Marni."

He sighed. "That just can't happen, Lacklan."

"Why?"

He gave a small, exasperated laugh. "Well, for a start, because you're so bloody dangerous. You attract violence. You're like a walking war zone. People go their entire lives without seeing a bar brawl. Five minutes in your company and somebody get a broken bone, or their face pushed in."

"That's ridiculous."

"I agree. It also happens to be true."

"She would be safe with me and you know it. What protection has she right now?"

"She is safe."

"This is a decision she should make. Why are you making these decisions for her?"

"This is her decision, Lacklan. For your information, she

thinks you're insane, and so do I. She believes something happened to you during your time with the SAS, and you are not quite normal. Your absurd behavior at the party only served to confirm it."

"I explained that to you."

"Even so…"

I was learning that putting Gibbons under pressure just made him more obstinate, so I changed the subject.

"Explain something to me."

He eyed me and waited.

"Why is Omega afraid of you?"

A barely perceptible smile. He thought for a long moment. "Omega is not the only organization that is aware we are on the brink of catastrophic change. There are others. You might be surprised if you knew who they were, or who was involved. Let me put a question to you. If the SAS decided to prepare for a coming holocaust, how do you think they would prepare? What would their focus be?"

I frowned. I had never considered it in that way. "I guess they would focus on survival techniques, appropriate armament, technologies, and materials to be able to make effective weapons in the new, changed environment…"

"Precisely. But now imagine that Harvard made contingency plans for such a catastrophic change. What would *their* focus be?"

I sat back in my chair, curious about where he was going. "I guess they would focus on preserving their libraries, their store of knowledge…"

"Exactly. We all want to preserve the things that we think are important. Who constitute Omega? I'll tell you, bankers, lawyers, politicians, billionaires—the people who own the

Federal Reserve. They are not all that scared of you, Lacklan, because you can kill a hundred of their men and they will just keep buying new ones, until they buy one who is bigger and more dangerous than you are. But they are terrified of me because I *know*. I have knowledge that can really hurt them."

"Frank Gilbert's research..."

"Partly."

I leaned forward on the table. "Philip, divided we play into their hands. United we could be much more powerful, we could really hurt them. I have caused them a lot of trouble so far, on my own. With you and Marni, we could really make a difference.."

"I'll tell you why not, Lacklan. On the one hand, as I have already told you *ad nauseum*, I believe you are too volatile, and dangerously unpredictable. On the other hand..." He took a deep breath and sighed loudly. "I am still not one hundred percent satisfied that you are not in Omega's pocket."

"*What?*"

"You are awfully close with Benjamin Brown."

"Ben?"

He nodded.

I said, "He keeps offering me a place in Omega and I keep telling him no."

"You may well be telling the truth, but I can't be one hundred percent sure, and my instincts tell me to steer clear of you, Walker. Whichever way you look at it, you are a dangerous man. And I don't want to be involved with you."

"Marni does."

"So you say, but that isn't what she tells me."

"Where is she?"

He shook his head. "No. I've listened to what you have to say, Walker. I grant you are probably sincere, but I am afraid I don't—I *can't*—trust you. Do whatever you have to do, but stay away from Marni."

He stood and I let him walk out of the bar. Then I got up and followed. On the street I ran the few yards to catch up with him, reached out, and grabbed his shoulder. "Gibbons! Wait a moment!"

He stopped and turned to face me. We almost collided and I staggered a couple of steps grabbing hold of him. He looked mad and snapped, "Good grief, Walker! What is it now?"

"I'm sorry. I just wanted to ask you, will you please ask Marni to call me? I want to apologize and explain."

He rolled his eyes. "Don't you ever give up? Very well, I'll tell her, but don't expect her to call. Now, goodbye, Lacklan!"

I watched him walk away with his pompous little strut, and smiled. Then I made my way back to my car, where I had left it on Broadway. I climbed in, slammed the door, and took the tracking device receiver out of the glove compartment. I switched it on and there he was, striding down 86th Street toward Central Park. His bleep stopped for fifteen or twenty seconds and then started moving faster. I figured he'd got into a taxi. The cab took him all the way down to the Civic Center and then across the Brooklyn Bridge. On the other side of the river, they came off at Anchorage Plaza and went, via Middagh Street, to Colombia Heights and finally stopped outside number 75. There he went inside.

You have to have a plan B in life. My plan A had been to

try to persuade him we should be allies. But I had been sure from the start that he was going to be either hard or impossible to convince. So plan B had been to drop a microtracking device into his jacket pocket. Now I knew where he was, and chances were good that Marni was with him. If she wasn't, it wouldn't be long before he led me to her.

SIX

GIBBONS STARTED TO MOVE AT FIVE THIRTY THAT evening. I was parked a hundred and fifty yards down the road, waiting for him to do something. I saw the bleep had been activated and after a moment, I saw him exit the house carrying a couple of suitcases. Marni was just behind him. They climbed into a Ford Focus and took off up the road toward the bridge. I let them get a mile away and then followed.

Over the bridge, he kept going west through heavy traffic until he reached St. John's University. There he turned north up West Street. For a moment, I wondered if he was headed for the Upper West Side, if Marni had had a change of heart and he was going to deliver her to my place. But at Canal Park, he turned suddenly right and started moving southeast again, down Canal Street, like he was going back to Brooklyn. I thought perhaps they were having an argument in the car and couldn't decide what they were doing, but before I'd had a chance to think much about what the hell he was doing, he'd turned north again up Avenue of the Americas. Then he turned west, through Greenwich Village and West Village. And after that, he turned right into Bank Street and then south again on Greenwich Avenue. He was like a headless chicken on speed. I slowed and pulled over.

Gibbons didn't strike me as the type to suddenly take leave of his senses. He was as obstinate as a burro with a grudge, but he was about as grounded as you could get without growing roots. It made a lot more sense that he was either trying to shake a tail, or he was trying to make sure he didn't pick one up. That meant wherever he was going was important.

He eventually came to 6th Avenue and turned north. He passed the Hennessy Foundation and kept going. I started to follow again. He cut through the park a couple of times and then came out on Madison Avenue and I knew he was going to cross into the Bronx. After a couple more twists and turns, he did just that.

Once over the water, he made for Goose Island in the east, via Van Cortland Lake in the north and Throgs Neck in the south, traversing the entire Bronx in the process. In the growing darkness, he crossed Pelham Bridge and we headed through parkland and woodland toward Woodside and New Rochelle, and finally, after more than three hours of driving back and forth across New York, he pulled off Pelham Road onto Hudson Park Road, wound down some dark, empty paths and stopped outside a brace of large, iron gates set in a fifteen foot stone wall. I killed the lights and slipped silently into a small parking lot set nearby, in what looked like a village green.

There I sat and watched while he waited. After a

moment, the gates swung open and the car moved into the grounds of a large, gabled house that sat on the shores of Echo Bay, on the East River. The gates clanged closed behind him and the car's glowing red taillights disappeared from sight.

I lit a cigarette and settled to wait and think. Gibbons was not stupid and he had felt threatened by my insistence on seeing Marni, so he had decided to move her to what he considered a safe location. Judging by the size and grandeur of the house—at least what I could see of it in the dark—he was either very rich or very well connected. I figured it was most likely the latter, and some rich pal was lending him his riverside pad. His sympathetic views and his powerful connections were probably why Marni had hooked up with him in the first place.

I thought about the elaborate, roundabout route he'd taken to get there. It could be just a symptom of an excessively cautious, meticulous nature, but I didn't think so. Remembering how he had turned up at the Bethesda Fountain, and how he had walked in to the Parlour, he didn't strike me as an excessively cautious man. If anything, the opposite was true. So the pains he had taken to shake off any possible tail suggested to me that the security and alarm systems in the house were not exactly cutting edge; that its advantage lay in its being remote and out of the way, rather than high-tech secure. Not so much a fortress where to meet an enemy in combat, but a bolt hole where to go to ground and hide.

I took my infrared binoculars from the glove compartment, got out, and had a look at the gate and the wall. I couldn't see any CCTV cameras. That didn't mean there weren't any, and, perhaps more important than that, it didn't mean there were no dogs either. Give me a CCTV any day over a pissed Rottweiler.

I took a walk by the side of the wall to see where it would lead. It led over a rough stretch of green down to a beach on the shore of the river. There it climbed a small cliff and came to an end at a precipitous drop into the water. I didn't think twice about it. It was too obvious. I took off my shoes and my socks and waded into the dark, icy water. I swam, shivering and spluttering, around the rocks and into a private cove where the beach led to a well-tended lawn. From there, handsome stone steps rose to a terrace and a set of French windows that gave onto a brightly lit drawing room in a large, pseudo-Jacobean house with tall gables and chimney-pots. I could see all this clearly because the garden was floodlit by spotlights concealed in the trees.

The current this close to the shore was not dangerous, but it was strong enough for me to feel it trying to drag me into the deeper water. So I struck out for the shore. In a few strokes I found my feet and, keeping close to the rocks, I waded onto the sand. I found a nook between the small cliff and the base of the wall, settled there, and scanned the house with my binoculars. The image was smudged by the wet lenses, but it was clear enough. Marni was sitting at a table on the terrace, staring at the water and the lights of Glen Cove. Gibbons was behind her, framed in the doorway. It was hard to make out whether they were talking, but if they were, it wasn't warm and fuzzy. Neither of them looked very happy.

I waited a while to see if any dogs picked up my scent, but nothing happened. So, staying close by the wall, I crawled on my belly to the cover of some bushes on the lawn, closer to the house. There I stopped and watched Gibbons step out and sit at the table as a girl in a maid's uniform brought out a tray with drinks. I thought of some of the safe houses I'd been in over the years—take out pizza and you were lucky to get a TV. I guessed it paid to be connected.

I kept inching closer until I was able to pick up snatches of their conversation, or what there was of it. Mostly what I could make out was the odd unhappy comment from Marni, and Gibbons' hectoring, nagging tones. I crawled a little closer. Marni was saying, "I am really not happy about this, Philip. It feels wrong."

"Don't be absurd, Marni. You are a scientist. You can't be guided by feelings. You must apply rational thought. Would you rather be holed up with that barbarian?"

"I have known him all my life, Philip. We were very close at one time, and he has always been very loyal. He's a good man. He's just..."

"A barbarian. He is just a *barbarian!*"

"We should have him on our side, not against us."

"We don't need him. He is irrelevant."

She gave a small laugh. "No, Philip. He is not irrelevant. He is very relevant."

He looked across the table at her for a long moment. "You're still infatuated with him, aren't you?"

"Don't be ridiculous. I just know, a lot better than you do, what kind of man he is—and what he is capable of. We have our hands full with Omega, we don't want Lacklan working against us, too. And aside from that, he could be a very powerful ally. You've seen what he did in Colorado and

Arizona." She paused a moment and added, "Single-handed!"

He shook his head. "You're letting your feelings cloud your judgment. He's a liability. And believe me, after the debate tomorrow, things will be very different. Tomorrow will be a game changer. They don't know what they have got themselves into."

I frowned, wondering what was going to happen the next day. It was the first I had heard about any debate. She turned to look at him with no real expression, then shook her head. "I hope you're right, Philip. I worry that you're overconfident. I think you're underestimating Omega, and Lacklan. I think this whole thing could blow up in our faces."

"Trust me. I've been working towards this my whole career. I know Omega. They are blinded by their own arrogance and greed. Tomorrow we will drop our first bombshell. They won't be expecting it and the battle will shift in our favor. You'll see."

He reached over and patted her hand. After a while, he stood and went indoors. She sat for a while, alone, looking into the floodlit garden. For a moment, I was tempted to go to her and tell her that all her doubts were right; to come with me and I would protect her and look after her. Maybe I should have done that. But before I could make up my mind, she stood and followed Philip Gibbons inside, and closed the French windows.

I have wondered many times since then what would have happened if I had just walked in and confronted them, forced a showdown, even taken her by force if necessary. But something stayed my hand and I didn't do it.

The temperature had dropped and a cold breeze was coming off the river. I realized I had started to shiver and decided to head for home. I crouch-ran back to the shore, waded into the dark, icy water and swam, against the current this time, back toward where I had left my shoes and socks. I pulled them on with numb, trembling fingers, ran back to the car, clambered inside, and switched on the hot air. Then I fired up the powerful twin engines and started back toward Manhattan, taking a more direct route this time than we had followed to get here.

I followed Boston Road as far as Morissania, where I turned onto 3rd Avenue. At the lights on 3rd and East 158th, I watched in my rear-view mirror as a cop patrol car pulled up behind me. There was nothing special about that and I had no reason to be worried, but for some reason, some sixth sense made me aware of him. After a moment, he put on his indicator, pulled out, and drew up alongside me. I didn't look. I kept my eyes on the lights. But in my peripheral vision, I was aware that the driver and his partner were both looking at me.

My mind ran through the possible reasons. There was nothing special about the car except it was a '68 classic. If that was it, they'd be looking at the car, not me. So what made them interested in me? The lights changed to green and I pulled away. They stayed with me till East 149th and then turned west. I carried on south toward the 3rd Avenue Bridge and Manhattan.

I picked up the unmarked Dodge Charger on the other side of the bridge, just past Harlem River Park. It stayed four or five cars behind me all the way to my apartment block, and as I decelerated to pull into my parking garage, I saw it slow behind me, like it was looking for a space to stop.

On my way up in the elevator I wondered if it was Ben, but that didn't seem to make much sense. Why would he be following me? Besides, it wasn't his style. It was too crude. Say what you like about Ben, but he wasn't crude.

If not Ben, who then? Maybe I'd have to go and ask them, but that could wait. First I had more pressing jobs. I let myself in to my apartment, closed and locked the door, checked the rooms for visitors, and had a long, hot shower.

After that, I put a pizza in the oven and opened my laptop. I found the audio file for the bugs. There was a total of four hours of it. I switched it on and poured myself a generous glass of Bushmills. I listened for a minute or two to familiarize myself with the voices. The common language was English. The British guy's Arabic was basic and the Pakistani guy's English was better than his Arabic. But as I had expected, mostly it was just grunts and sporadic comments. What little conversation there was was the kind of garbage that most people talk about when they share a house. "Has anyone seen my cell phone?" "The girl in the grocery store is hot. I think she likes me." "Man, I need to buy some new pants." And so on.

Occasionally the Afghan guy would call them to order and bark at them in Arabic. I had learnt enough in my time with the Regiment to know that he was reminding them to stay focused. They were jihadists, warriors of God, they would get all the women they wanted when they joined Allah. But as long as they were fighting the holy war, it didn't help anyone if they started thinking about girls.

Girls meant sex, sex could lead to love, love meant

marriage, kids, and home. That was not the warrior's way. There was no room for women and love in the warrior's life. I smiled, but it wasn't a happy smile.

"Tell me about it, Aatifa."

Once I had familiarized myself with their voices I was able to have the file playing in the background. One part of my brain registered the steady flow of domestic noises and comments, alert for buzzwords or extended conversations, while the rest of my mind was able to focus on other things, like pizza, and wondering what Gibbons had meant about the next day being a game changer.

I switched on the news and stood staring out at the terrace, sipping my whiskey and listening to the drone of familiar half-lies and half-truths. America needed a wall to protect her from illegal Mexican immigrants. America did not need a wall to protect her from illegal Mexican immigrants. Islam was a religion of peace, those who feared it were jingoistic reactionaries and fascists. Islam was nothing but a call to arms, a call to jihad against the whole world. Islam was the greatest threat civilization had faced since Hitler. Climate change was a hoax, a conspiracy of the Left. Climate change was the biggest threat to life on Earth since the comet that wiped out the dinosaurs, sixty-five million years ago.

And then suddenly a woman was talking and I was listening.

"...in a surprise development that has had conference organizers scrambling to adjust their schedules, Professor Philip Gibbons, of Green College in Oxford, issued this morning a challenge to former president Dick Hennessy, to debate with him, tomorrow evening, in a public forum at the conference, his role and the role of the Hennessy Foundation, in preparing the world for the inevitable changes that global warming will bring..."

I moved to look at the TV. Zain Asher was on the screen with a picture of the UN building behind her.

"We tried to talk to Professor Gibbons earlier today but he was not available for comment. However, he did issue this brief statement through his secretary..." She read from a slip of paper. "While Democrats and Republicans present the world with an ever more grotesque circus of the absurd, and rally an ever more gullible public behind their banners, hurling abuse and accusations at each other, the world slides towards catastrophic near-annihilation. The Hennessys, through their cynical foundation, present themselves as champions of the poor, the weak and the marginalized, yet they are among the richest and most powerful people on Earth. Well, I have challenged Dick Hennessy to stand before the American people, before the people of the world, and defend his indefensible lack of action in the face of a threat that will, if left unchecked, wipe out the most vulnerable and the weakest people on the planet. This is a man who, during his tenure in office, spent two point four billion dollars bombing a single Arab nation, but consistently failed, despite his Democrat rhetoric, to put a single initiative in place to address the threat of climate change. Well I challenge him, and his foundation, to answer these charges tomorrow in open debate before the world."

So this was it, this was his game changer. I sat on the arm of the sofa and continued to listen.

"We asked former President Dick Hennessy what he had to say to Professor Gibbons' allegations, and, to many people's astonishment, and the open distress of the conference organizers, Dick Hennessy good humouredly accepted Professor Gibbons' challenge. Here is what he had to say."

The screen cut from Zain Asher to a shot of Hennessy at the offices of the Hennessy Foundation. He looked relaxed and amused. He was talking into a microphone that was being held in front of him. "I have always been a great admirer of Professor Gibbons and I am sorry that he takes that view of the efforts of the Hennessy Foundation. I think he needs to have a word with his researchers because they clearly haven't been doing their homework. The Hennessy Foundation has invested many, many millions of dollars in helping developing communities to grow and prepare for the world's changing environment."

Asher's voice was heard asking, "What do you say to the allegation that you were able to find two and a half billion dollars to bomb a foreign nation because it was a threat to American economic interests, but you never started a single initiative to counter climate change?"

He laughed. "Obviously I haven't got the figures at my fingertips. I will have tomorrow evening when I meet with Professor Gibbons. But I will say this, when we bombed Irastan, the U.S. and her allies were facing a direct threat and Congress was virtually united in a bipartisan condemnation of Irastan's development of weapons of mass destruction. However, climate change is a threat that affects the entire planet, and the U.S. cannot act alone. For all sorts of reasons..."

He smiled, excused himself and walked away.

It cut back to Zain Asher in the studio.

"Dick Hennessy's response there to Professor Gibbons'

challenge. And we have been informed by Mr. David Staines, the chief UN organizer of the Conference, that last minute alterations have been made to the conference schedule to accommodate this impromptu debate, called by the professor. It will be attended by the world press and media and it will be free to the general public on a first come, first served basis. It is worth stressing that this is probably a first in UN conference history, and certainly I have never come across anything like it in my experience..."

I muted the TV and sat thinking, smoking, sipping my whiskey and listening to the small, inarticulate sounds issuing from my laptop. The implications of what I had just seen and heard were almost too huge to comprehend. Gibbons was taking on a former President of the U.S.; taking him on as a first step in exposing the government within a government.

Taking him on as though he was a member of Omega.

I picked up the phone and called Ben. He answered straight away with a question.

"Are you watching it?"

I nodded. "Yeah, what does it mean?"

"Join us and I'll tell you."

"I need a ticket."

"I have one for you. I'll courier it over."

SEVEN

In slightly more than twenty-four hours, the unprecedented debate had generated so much publicity that by the time I got there at fifteen minutes after five, First Avenue was crammed with people, there were cops trying to clear a path for the traffic, and the UN had taken the unusual step of letting people into the plaza and setting up a giant screen to broadcast the event to the onlookers.

I forced my way through the crowd, showed my ticket, and was admitted to the main building. There were signs saying that the conference had been moved from Conference Room 12 to the much larger Conference Room 4. Arrows pointed the way to the first basement, where all the conference rooms were.

When I got down, the place was milling with people. There was tension in the air and the mood was taut with expectation. People were clustered in small groups and the conversations were animated and loud. I looked around for

Ben, but he wasn't there, so I made my way into the conference room and found my seat.

The room was more of a traditional lecture theater than the amphitheater design of the smaller conference rooms. Two lecterns had been set up, facing each other across a stage, as though it were a presidential debate. Gradually, the seats began to fill as the crowds drifted in from the lobby outside. As the hands of the clock moved toward six, the lights dimmed and a man I recognized as David Staines walked onto the stage. The room hushed.

"I can think of few occasions in the history of our organization when a conference has caused so much expectation, and such a stir beyond the confines of the group having an immediate interest in the subject of the conference. But from the start, this event has proved, if proof were needed, that the general public is deeply concerned with climate change and the issues of overpopulation. This is not, by any means, a subject exclusively for climatologists. It is a subject that affects every man, every woman, and every child on the planet.

"However, the dramatic, unexpected developments of the last twenty-four hours have placed this conference firmly in the public eye, as has been demonstrated by the fact that we are today packed to capacity, both inside and out! I am informed by the New York Police Department that traffic has had to be diverted away from First Avenue, to allow for the overspill from the United Nations Plaza.

"Ladies and gentlemen, we have before us a week of fascinating events, talks, and debates. The highlight will be next Friday, as you know, when Professor Gibbons and Dr. Marni Gilbert will present to us research which, in their words, will transform the world's view of climate change, and galvanize governments worldwide into positive action. But tonight, to open the conference, will you please welcome Professor Philip Gibbons and former President Dick Hennessy!"

There was animated applause as Hennessy, tall and urbane with his thick, silver hair, strolled onto the stage in his understated Saville Row suit. Opposite him, on the left, Gibbons strutted out in his tweed jacket, with his short legs and his pugnacious expression. After the applause had died down, Staines said, "Professor Gibbons, will you please open the debate."

Gibbons nodded. "Thank you, Mr. Chairman."

As the Oxford Don that he was, rooted in the modern world's oldest and finest tradition of debating, he orated with power and confidence. He seemed to grow in stature as he spoke, and his conviction seemed to inform every statement he made with weight and credibility.

"It must surely," he started, "have crossed everybody's mind at some point, to ask the question, how is it possible that the governments of the U.K. and the U.S. can mobilize a million troops, billions of dollars worth of weaponry and hardware, and incalculable sums of money in food, medication, and ammunition—all in order to wage war on a third world regime that threatens to take control of crude oil reserves..." He paused, looking around the room, then went on, "How is it possible that these two governments can mount a huge international diplomatic offensive, putting pressure on every nation on Earth to support that military offensive, *all within the space of a few months...* then go ahead with that military offensive *in spite of the lack of international support*—and yet, after *thirty years* they are *incapable* of coming up with one single initiative that works to confront climate change? *How is it possible?*"

He thrust his hands in his pockets, stared down at his feet, and took three slow steps toward the center of the stage then. Then he turned and walked back again. He was like a stand up comic and some people in the audience had started to laugh. He came back to the lectern and leaned on it. He was laughing himself.

"In three months, they lobbied the United Nation, the Security Council, and every major government on Earth. From the President," he gestured over at Hennessy, "and the Vice President, down to the lowliest White House aide, they were all engaged in a frenzied, single-minded campaign to make that war work. In the U.K. it was a similar, unedifying spectacle at Number Ten, with the Prime Minister and his cabinet falling over themselves, each other, and their various illicit affairs, to find money and influence to wage that war. The cost of that war to the U.S. is close to *seven trillion dollars*. Just to the U.S. alone." He held up his hand and laughed. "But wait! I haven't come to the punch line yet! Seven trillion dollars of *borrowed money*! Because that war was fought with *borrowed money!*" He paused, staring at the audience. "Now here's a question for you. Don't worry, it's a simple one. You'll know the answer." He laughed again. "I guarantee it. Who benefits when you borrow money?" He looked around, like he was waiting for an answer in a classroom. "Anyone? Who benefits when you borrow money?" He stopped, nodding. "Yes, that's right, the banks. Specifically, the banks that lent you the money." He grinned. "Duh! So, I wonder, I wonder, I wonder, who were the banks that supplied the money for the war in question? Well, you'll have to wait till Friday for the names, though I do invite you to go and do some research for yourselves in the meantime. You might start by perusing the Federal Reserve. You might find that very enlightening.

"Meanwhile, getting back to the subject of tonight's debate, my point is that here is a government, here is a president, who is not just willing, but able, to spend some seven trillion dollars for the purpose of waging war in order to protect oil interests. And yet, in thirty years, has been unable and unwilling to start a single, serious initiative, either as president of the U.S. or president of his foundation, to deal with climate change and overpopulation. Why?

"Is it because climate change is not real? You have heard all the lobbyists crying out that climate change is a left wing conspiracy. But where were all these sleuths when the CIA and MI5 found all those weapons of mass destruction, that weren't there? No, climate change is real. The reason for their inaction is a different one.

"Let me tell you, the only possible explanation for the lack of motivation in tackling climate change and overpopulation, is that these people have a vested interest in allowing it to run its course. What kind of vested interest? A very simple one, a financial one. And the reason I have challenged former President Dick Hennessy to this debate today is because he, his wife, and his foundation are central to the *conspiracy* by which they and others will profit from this catastrophic change."

There was a collective gasp. Gibbons grinned. "You don't believe me? I shall give you facts and figures and name names on Friday—I promise you we will deliver documentary proof. But for now, let me just return to the interesting question of the government's borrowing for the war. Exactly whom they borrowed the money from is very hard to establish, because it is hidden under a paper trail that would drive most accountants to suicide. But we are diligent and we worked our way through it, so let me sum it up for you. The government borrowed one point five *billion* dollars to fund the war, indirectly, through pension funds and similar, from a number of banks, both national and foreign..." He paused, stared at the audience, and then glared at Hennessy. Then he bellowed in a huge voice, *"Every single one of whom is either owned by Hennessy Investments or have directors sitting on the board of the Hennessy Foundation!"*

There was total silence in the room. I saw Hennessy lean over and speak to somebody in the shadows. Then Gibbons was bellowing again.

"And the seven trillion balance is profit! Interest! Interest paid to Hennessy and his cohorts through the Hennessy Foundation! Interest sucked from the blood of fallen soldiers!" His face was flushed and you could see he was barely controlling his rage, but when he spoke again, his voice was quiet. "If the necessary steps were taken to address climate change and world overpopulation, the Hennessy Foundation and the criminals who associate with them—you can find most of them in Forbes—would lose trillions, *trillions*, of dollars, and all their global influence. Their plan, which is infinitely more profitable, is to allow climate change to run its course, allow catastrophic change to happen, and when it does, make sure they are in the dominant position of top dog so that they can profit from it. And they plan to do this through an organization...."

There was a stir and a gasp in the audience. Gibbons faltered and stared. I turned and looked. There was a scuffle at the back of the room. Somebody shouted, "*Allahu akbar! Allahu akbar!*"

A woman screamed. I saw the guy shouting. He looked Middle Eastern. A couple of security guards were wrestling with him, but half a dozen other guys joined him and a fight broke out. There was more shouting of, "*Allahu akbar!*" and a voice screamed, "He has a gun!" Then pandemonium broke out. People were scrambling and running in all directions. I looked back at the stage. Gibbons was scowling at Hennessy. Hennessy was smiling back. He shrugged and left the stage.

I sat and waited for the chaos to subside. I saw Gibbons turn and walk off the stage in the opposite direction. It had been a good attempt. I was impressed by the way he spoke. It showed another side of the man, he was intelligent, charismatic and powerful. But it had been naïve. Omega were dirty fighters. They always had been and always would be. To expect to outsmart them like this was unrealistic. What he had managed to do was to damage his own reputation. He would appear in the press the next day as a deranged crank and the establishment media would have a feeding frenzy picking over his bones.

Eventually, a security guard came down and asked me to vacate the room. I followed the throng up to the first floor and into the night. There I pushed my way through the crowd and made it to First Avenue, where the people dispersed some, and I walked down to 41st, where I had left my car. I had opened the door and was about to climb in when I saw a large, black limo emerge up the ramp from the

UN parking garage. As it cruised past, I saw that it had the Awad royal family crest on it. I climbed into the Zombie and followed at a discreet distance.

I wasn't very surprised to see them take West 42nd as far as Madison Avenue, and then turn north. I followed them as far as East 79th. There I parked on the corner and watched them pull up in front of Prince Mohamed's house, where we'd had the party the night before. I watched as an Arab in his fifties, in an elegant suit, climbed out of the limo, closely followed by Ben and Dick Hennessy. They walked into the house and I drove away.

As I drove I could feel hot excitement in my belly. I couldn't see it clearly yet, but I knew the connections were there as surely as I knew that I was breathing. I needed to get Marni out of that conference. I needed to get her to safety, and I had to do it within the next couple of days or it would be too late.

I dialed Gibbons' number. It rang for thirty seconds, then stopped, and a voice told me it was either switched off or out of range. That left me just one option. I needed to go back to Echo Bay and take Marni by force. I didn't want to hurt Gibbons, but if he stood in the way, I would have to. One thing was real clear to me right then. The opponents we were up against—the problem we were up against—was vaster than even I had imagined. Whatever Gibbons and Marni intended to do, they were headed for disaster and Gibbons was refusing to see it.

I decided to go home and work out how I would take Marni, which I would execute that night. If I was lucky, Gibbons would stay in Brooklyn and Marni would be alone. I pulled my tracking device from the glove compartment and switched it on. The cell I'd dropped into Gibbons' pocket was still active and it showed him heading south toward Brooklyn Bridge. I smiled to myself. At least that was in my favor.

I left the car in the parking garage and rode the elevator to my penthouse. I went through my usual routine but the apartment was clear, so I cracked a beer and switched on the laptop. I selected the audio file for the bug at Amethyst Street and while I listened to the meaningless noises of people opening and closing cutlery drawers, coughing, spitting, and mumbling, I opened Google Earth and found Marni's safe house.

It didn't help much. The focus was poor and there was little detail. If I postponed the operation by a day, my best bet was an inflatable dingy. I could purchase that in the morning, but if I went that night I would have to swim, so I should take a change of clothes in a plastic bag. The advantage of going that night was that I would not have to deal with Gibbons.

I decided that that advantage outweighed the inconvenience of getting wet. Power and phone cables to the house were probably underground, so there was no chance of cutting them. My best plan, then, was to go in late, after she had gone to bed, find the fuse box, and disable the phones and the wifi. I would use my night-vision goggles and find her room. An unknown quantity was the staff. I had no idea how many there were or if they were live-in or went home at night. I would have to get there early and watch to see who arrived, who left, and how many upstairs lights went on and off after bedtime.

It wouldn't be hard. It would be a straightforward in-and-out operation.

That was when a new voice on the audio file made me stop and listen. There was a lot of effusive greeting and praising of Allah. Then, a strong, clear voice asked them all to sit down and listen, because he had important news.

"Today, my brothers, I can identify for you your target. You will strike at the United Nations. This will be even bigger than nine-eleven!"

There were whoops and laughter that were pathetically reminiscent of excited schoolboys. Then a voice I knew to be the Pakistani kid asked, "Abdul, Allah be praised, how will we get the bomb into the building? The security is very tight! It will not be easy!"

"Don't worry about that, Ali, that is not your concern. Trust me, that has been taken care of. I have the components here for you. You will each carry a separate part. Ali, you will carry the C4. Hassan, you will carry the detonator, Aatifa, you will carry the agent. You will arrive separately on Friday, at eleven o'clock, eleven fifteen, and eleven thirty. You will not be detected at security. Forget about that." Then again, more emphatically, "Forget about that! You go down to the basement at exactly eleven thirty-five and you meet in the gentlemen's toilets between the Public Counter and the coffee shop. There you assemble the device exactly as you have practiced it. Then you take it up to the second floor, to the General Assembly Hall. Any questions so far?"

There was a general, negative murmuring.

"OK, you will be provided with passes for Professor Gibbons and Doctor Marni Gilbert's talk. It will begin at twelve noon. You will detonate the device as the talk begins.

Your deaths will be the most glorious of heroic acts in the eyes of Allah."

Hassan said, "I have a question, Abdul."

"Yes, my brother?"

"I realize that there will be some very important delegates there..."

"Some very important men and women, representing the major governments of the western world, Hassan."

"But the death toll will be only in the hundreds..."

Abdul laughed. "Spoken like a true warrior! No, Hassan, the death toll will be in the hundreds of thousands, possibly millions. It is impossible to calculate." There was a rustle and a metal clank. "This sealed canister, my brothers, contains enough SF2 to wipe out several million people."

An awed silence, and then, "SF2?"

"The key parts of a lethal strain of influenza that in 1918 killed more than twenty million people. It has been genetically modified to make it highly resistant to known antibiotics. The blast will kill a few hundred people, maybe, Hassan, but everybody who leaves that building will be carrying this virus. And nobody will know."

"Allah is merciful!"

"Allah is great!"

"*Allahu Akbar!*"

I stared at the screen, not hearing anymore what they were saying. I was looking at the time stamp for when it was recorded. Five thirty. Two and a half hours ago. I grabbed my jacket and walked to the door. Now at least I knew what I had to do. I had to do what I was good at.

Killing.

EIGHT

I LEFT MY CAR AT THE CORNER OF RHINELANDER Avenue and Unionport Road in a pool of depressing lamp light, and walked around the corner onto Amethyst Street. I had my Sig, my Fairbairn & Sykes, and my night vision goggles. I figured it was better to be over-equipped. The echo of my feet on the blacktop and the sidewalk had a flat, dead sound. The road was a dark tunnel, with hazy patches of amber that filtered through foliage and reflected in liquid pools off the cars. Houses and cars with dead, black eyes.

There was no Ferrari today. I was pretty certain he didn't live here, with the cell. He would have an apartment in Manhattan. Maybe he was a guest of the prince. I looked up at the windows of the house. They were all dark. The boys were either out or asleep. Either one suited me.

I stepped to the door and slipped in the pick. The lock gave. I remembered from my first visit that the hinges did not squeak. I moved in and gently closed the door behind me. The house was dark and silent. I closed my eyes and remained motionless, listening. Nothing. I pulled on the goggles, turning the world into a weird, green and black nightmare. I pulled the Sig. I had cocked it in the car. Four long steps took me to the kitchen door. I knew it would be empty and it was, but it pays to be double sure.

I moved up the stairs. There were two bedrooms here. Both doors were closed. I took one long step to the nearest and gripped the handle. Quick is quiet, slow makes a noise. I pulled gently toward me and yanked down. The spring squeaked slightly. I pushed the door open with my gun leveled toward where I knew the bed was.

The sheets were a translucent green and his face was slightly luminous. His mouth was open but his eyes were closed. He was snoring softly. It looked like Ali, the kid from Pakistan. Nineteen years old and secure in the belief that all God wanted from him was that he kill people who did not believe his name was Allah. I moved in, closed the door behind me, holstered my Sig and drew the Fairbairn & Sykes. Another step took me to his bedside. I looked down at his unthinking, unquestioning face. One thing the world didn't need was more stupid people. I pressed my left hand hard on his forehead and simultaneously shoved the long, razor sharp blade through his trachea and out the back of his neck, severing his spinal cord on the way.

His eyes snapped open and stared at me while his body jerked and quivered for a second. Air hissed and bubbled out of the wound and he was gone. I gave the blood flow a second to settle and then withdrew the knife, wiped the blood on the luminous green sheet, and sheathed it.

I opened the door with the Sig in my hand and stood

listening. The house was still quiet. I took hold of the handle of the next door, pulled and yanked down as before. Nothing. I pushed it open. This was the British guy, Hassan Barr. He had his back to me. That would make the kill a little more awkward, but easy enough. I took a long silent step and clapped my left hand over his eyes and his forehead. I had the option of slipping the blade through his jugular, the carotid artery and then his trachea. If done effectively, it causes an almost instant, silent death. But it is best done standing. In this position, with him horizontal and roughly at the height of my knees, it could go wrong, and the last thing I needed was a scream and a fight, with Aatifa still alive.

Instead, I opted to ram the point of the knife hard into the vertebrae at the base of his skull, severing his brain from his body. Even if death was not instant, whatever his brain told his body to do in those last few seconds, it wouldn't do them, including scream.

His body jerked and quivered, his breath hissed out of his lungs, and he lay still. The last thing Hassan Barr ever saw was my fingers clasped over his eyes.

That left Aatifa Ghafoor upstairs. These two had been naïve amateurs, but I figured Aatifa was experienced and battle-hardened. My money was on him and Abassi being old friends from Afghanistan.

I withdrew my knife, wiped off the blood, and sheathed it. Then I drew the Sig and moved up the stairs through green luminescence and black shadows to the next floor. I didn't want Aatifa dead. I wanted him talking.

I didn't try to be quiet. I kicked open the door, holding the Sig in both hands trained on the bed. I shouted, "*OK,*

Aatifa! On your feet with your hands in the air!" But before I had finished, I'd seen that the bulk under the covers was not a man but a roll of bedding and cushions.

I swung left to where I knew he would come at me, but it was too late. He had the barrel of the gun in his left hand and was rushing me to slam the heel of his right into my elbow. His face leered at me in a weird, green grin. I let go the Sig with my right and bent my left elbow hard, pulling him to me as I slammed my right fist into his nose. He rolled with the punch and didn't let go of the gun. Instead, he gripped it with both hands, trying to lever it from my fingers. For a man fighting almost blind, he was doing OK.

When somebody grips the barrel of your piece and levers, there is only one thing you can do. I released the magazine, pulled the trigger to empty the chamber, let go, and landed three punches on the side of his head with my right fist while gripping his collar with my left; but most of the power was wasted on his hunched shoulder. Then he struck at my floating ribs with the butt of the gun. It hurt and I stepped back.

It was all he needed. He slammed on the light and lunged for the magazine on the floor. I ripped off the goggles and kicked at his head. I caught him a glancing blow, but the guy was tough. He took it, gripped my ankle, and twisted. I let myself fall, expecting him to jump me and try to pin me down. Then there would probably be a knife. It was going to get ugly.

Instead, he made a mistake. He reached again for the magazine and with scrabbling fingers, tried to ram it into the butt of the Sig. As his fingers worked feverishly, he watched me with bulging eyes and a swollen, corded neck as I rose to a squatting position, pulling the knife from my boot, and rammed it into his elbow joint. He screamed and dropped the weapon and the magazine. I left the blade in and slammed my fist into his jaw. His eyes rolled and he fell quivering to the floor as though he was in an epileptic fit.

I picked up my gun, rammed the magazine back in, and holstered it. Then I pulled the knife from his elbow, wiped off the blood, and sheathed the blade. In the wardrobe I found several wire coat hangers. I took four down and opened them up. After that, I went down the passage to the can and filled a tooth mug with water. I brought it back and threw it in his face. He spluttered, grunted, and opened his eyes to look at me. He said something in Ugly and then the pain in his elbow kicked in and he started moaning.

I showed him the business end of the Sig and said, "Stand up."

He struggled to his feet. He was shaking badly, and if he hadn't been a man planning to kill an entire city, I might have felt sorry for him. Instead, I waved the gun at the stairs and said, "The living room, get moving."

He shrugged and made a face like stupid. I pistol-whipped him and as he staggered back I stepped to the door and took the bug from the top of the frame. I showed it to him. "Lying to me is not a good idea, Aatifa. And every time you do it, it will become a worse idea. Get downstairs or I'll blow your kneecaps off right here. Go."

He swallowed and nodded, then made his way down the stairs. I followed with the coat hangers. When we were down, I said, "Grab a chair, sit."

He pulled out a chair and sat. I stood behind him. He'd

gone very pasty and he was shaking badly. "Put your right hand behind the chair."

He did and I looped one of the hangers tightly around his wrist, then twisted the other end around the top of the leg. I did the same with his other wrist and with his ankles. Plastic zip-ties and duct tape are OK, but if you know the tricks you can bust them. Wire coat hangers—there is no way out.

By the time I pulled a chair out and sat in front of him, he looked very scared. I set my cell phone to record, put it on the table, and stared into his eyes for a long time, then I said, "Aatifa, I am going to go to the kitchen now and get the big kitchen knife."

I left it at that and went into the kitchen. I took my time and selected the big cleaver from the block, then I brought it back and put it on the table. I sat down again.

"Aatifa Ghafoor, you need to understand that Ali Kamboh and Hassan Barr are both dead upstairs." I pulled the Fairbairn & Sykes from my boot and showed it to him. "I killed them with this, while they slept. I am a professional." I put the knife back and picked up the cleaver. He was shaking badly by now. "I am going to cut off your fingers, one by one."

I stood.

"*Wait!*"

"You have something to say to me?"

"What do you want?"

"You know what I want."

"Information! You want information! I give you information! I tell you!"

I sat. "I know about your plan to release SF2 into the

United Nations Assembly Hall on Friday. I know your cell commander is Abdul Abbassi. What else can you tell me?"

"Anything, anything you want know."

"Where are the components for the bomb? Where is the canister of SF2?"

His mouth started trembling and tears started running down his face. He tilted his head on one side. "Please, Abbassi have it. He does not live here. He will bring, on Thursday."

"Where does he live?"

He shook his head. "Please, I don't know."

I didn't hesitate. I took the cleaver, stepped behind him, and cut through the joint of his right thumb. The scream was horrific. I didn't like doing it, but while he screamed and sobbed I replayed in my mind the women and children that Abdul Abbassi had tortured and executed in Helmand, because he suspected one of them had helped me. When I was done thinking of that, I thought of the eight million people that this bastard was willing to murder, women, children, and babies, because they didn't believe the right things in the right way.

I went and sat in front of him again. "Where?"

He shook his head, sobbing, "He don't tell us. It is protocol. He does not tell us. Please...."

"How often does he communicate with you?"

"Fridays."

"By phone?"

"Only in emergency. He come in person."

"You have his cell number?"

He nodded. "But never call, only in emergency."

I stood and pulled my weapon. "Make peace with your god, Aatifa."

His face crumpled and he began to sob.

"This is the path you chose. Next time choose a better path."

I put a round through his forehead and it was all over for him. I holstered my gun and went up the stairs to his room. I collected my goggles from the floor and found his jacket hanging on the back of a chair. I fished around in the pockets till I found his cell phone. There was only one number in his address book, Chief. I figured that had to be Abbassi.

I had the son of a bitch.

I went downstairs, opened the front door, and stepped into the night. The houses and the cars all looked at me through the yellow haze of the streetlamps with gaping black eyes. I ignored them and started up the road in the direction of Rhinelander Avenue, where I'd left my car.

A movement across the road made me look. Two men in trench coats climbed out of a Dodge Charger. The doors slammed like two gunshots and they walked across the road toward me.

"Hold up there a minute, Mr. Walker."

I slowed but kept walking. "Agents Mclean and Jones. What are you doing out this late?"

"Just stop walking, would you?"

I kept walking. "Any reason why I should?"

Jones stepped in front of me and Mclean snarled, "Yeah. I want to ask you some questions."

I stopped and looked deep into Jones' eyes. Then I

turned to look at Mclean. "Really? Aren't you afraid my replies will be some elaborate James Bond fantasy?"

"Yeah, maybe, but I'm curious anyway."

"I'm sorry, boys, I don't have time to talk to you tonight. Phone Miss Moneypenny at MI6 and make an appointment."

"Cute. What were you doing in that house?"

"Your job."

Jones scowled. "What's that supposed to mean?"

I leaned toward him and stared into his face. "It means I was in that house doing your job, Special Agent Jones. Now please step aside."

Mclean hitched back his coat to reveal the butt of an automatic. "Take it easy there, Walker. Don't do anything you're liable to regret. Now I'm going to ask you again, what were you doing in that house?"

I sighed. "If I tell you, can I go on my way?"

Now Mclean frowned, like I'd asked a stupid question. "Well, that depends on what you were doing in there."

I looked him straight in the eye with no expression at all and spoke in a dead voice. "I killed two young terrorists, Ali Kamboh and Hassan Barr, by stabbing them in the neck while they slept. I pulled a third, an Afghan by the name of Aatifa Ghafoor, from his bed, tortured him to find out where the bomb was, and then shot him in the head."

They both struggled for a moment to make sense of whether I was telling the truth or being a wiseass. Then Mclean said, "Jesus...!"

"Agent Mclean, have you ever heard of SF2?"

"*What?*"

"After this, look it up."

"After what?"

Bruce Lee said the abdomen and the hips were the most important parts of the body when you were fighting. He was right. If you use your abdominals and your hips to drive a punch, instead of your arms, you can multiply the speed by a factor of three or four. I smacked Jones on the tip of his chin and while Mclean was still wondering what the hell was happening to his partner I rammed my elbow into the side of his jaw. The whole thing took maybe a second. Jones sank down where he stood and Mclean fell back against a battered old Ford pickup. I felt bad, they were just doing their job. But I had no time to waste on them, or on getting arrested. I needed to get to Abbassi, and I needed to get to him fast.

I fished in Mclean's breast pocket and pulled out his wallet. I found a business card and kept it. I'd be sending him an email that night. I put his wallet back and jogged the rest of the way to my car.

As I pulled away and headed south, I barked at my phone, "Gantrie!"

Gantrie was a contact my father had given me before he died. He was an IT genius and had never yet let me down. His cell rang twice and a voice that could only belong to a nerd said, "Lacklan. Long time. What's happening?"

"Listen very carefully, Gantrie, all your craziest conspiracy theories and nightmares just came true. I haven't got time to explain, but I need you to locate a phone for me, and I need you to do it now."

He was quiet for a second or two. When he spoke you could hear the smile in his voice. "Are you serious?"

"Yes, Gantrie, I'm serious!"

"Disclosure? Aliens...?"

"No, Gantrie! Not aliens! Just locate this number for me, will you?"

I gave him the number and he sighed. "I assume it has GPS."

"I'm pretty sure it has."

"You realize there are websites where you can do this yourself?"

"Cool. Just do it, will you!"

"OK, I'm on it. I'll get back to you as soon as I have it."

I hung up and then called Ben.

"Yes."

"I need to see you now."

"I'll send a car for you. Where are you?"

"I'll be at my apartment in an hour and a half."

"Is everything OK? Anything I need to know?"

"No, everything is not OK. But I'll tell you when I see you."

I got back to my apartment within half an hour. I immediately sat at the computer and set about editing an audio file which included all the information about the bomb and Aatifa's statement that Abdul Abbassi had the device and the canister. I attached the file to an email, along with the earlier file where Abbassi explained the plan to them, and sent it to Mclean.

My phone rang. It was Gantrie.

"Dude..."

"What?"

"I was having trouble finding him, then I realized he was at a location where I was being jammed. I narrowed it down and I can place him within an area of about two hundred and fifty feet square."

"Good. Where?"

"Dude, you were not kidding. That area is occupied by the palace of Prince Mohamed bin Awad. And they are jamming my GPS locating software."

"Good work. Keep tracking him, Gantrie. Stay on him until I get back to you."

I hung up, closed down the computer, and the doorbell rang. I went and opened it. It was Ben.

NINE

We stood staring at each other for a moment. I was debating whether to drag him to the terrace and throw him over. I decided not to—not yet—and stepped aside.

"Come in."

He crossed the threshold and I closed the door. He said, "Have you got Marni?"

I nodded. "Yes."

"Where is she?"

I walked into the living room and poured myself a whiskey. "You want a drink?"

"Sure. Whiskey is fine, straight up."

I poured him a glass and handed it to him. I was still wondering whether to kill him. He took the glass. He was watching me with curious eyes. "Where is she, Lacklan?"

"Safe."

"What's that supposed to mean?"

"It means I am seriously debating whether to beat seven bales of shit out of you and then throw you over the terrace."

"I wouldn't recommend that."

"I imagine you wouldn't. Now how about you quit asking me questions and start answering a few of mine?"

"Shoot."

"Don't tempt me." I fished a Camel out of the box and lit up. I let the smoke out slow, taking a hold of my anger. "You said you'd take care of Abbassi."

He walked over to a chair and sat, crossed his legs, and studied my face, like he was wondering which of a number of answers to give me. Finally, he said, "So?"

"You didn't take care of him."

"What makes you say that?"

"I'm running out of patience, Ben. Answer one more question with a question of your own and I will kill you."

He nodded and sipped his drink. "I wasn't aware you had asked a question, Lacklan. It sounded like a statement to me. What is your question, exactly?"

"Why didn't you take care of Abbassi?"

"I told you to leave it to us."

"That isn't an answer."

He sighed. "They have a part to play."

"What part is that?"

"It is none of your concern."

I took a deep drag, let the smoke out, and took a pull on the whiskey. "Let me see if I can get through to you, Ben. I don't work for you. You don't get to tell me what to do." I gave a small laugh. "And you sure as hell don't get to tell me what is and isn't my concern. Now, what part does Abbassi play in this game?"

"I have no reason to tell you that, Lacklan. Join us, and you will be a party to the whole thing."

I studied his face for a while. He really believed I might do that. "Aatifa Gafoor, Ali Kamboh, Hassan Barr and Abdul Abbassi." His face went hard. I went on. "They are planning to detonate a bomb at the United Nations on Friday, during Gibbons' and Marni's talk. It will be a dirty bomb and it will infect everybody there with SF2, within weeks the casualties might be counted in hundreds of thousands, perhaps millions. Two of those casualties will be Marni and Gibbons. Now I want to know, what part of your plan is that?"

"How did you come by this information?"

"Fuck you. Answer my question."

"That is no part of our plan."

"You expect me to believe that?"

"No, Lacklan, I don't expect you to believe it. You are too stupid and obstinate to believe it. But you might try thinking. In what possible way could this further our interests? Just think about it, Lacklan! Why could we possibly want Marni and Gibbons dead? And, if we wanted them dead, do you really think it would be that difficult for us?"

I felt the anger welling up inside me. "Then why the hell didn't you act on Abbassi when I told you about him?"

"We did. We were watching him. He has hardly moved out of Prince Awad's house!"

I moved to the other armchair and sat. "When Gibbons challenged Hennessy, at the UN."

"What about it?"

"You and Hennessy used Muslim activists to disrupt the debate." I waited. He didn't answer. I went on, "Then you and Hennessy were taken in Prince Awad's car back to his house." I shook my head. "I don't believe you. I don't believe you did anything at all about Abbassi, because I think you knew about him all along. I think you're in bed with Awad."

He sighed again. "Lacklan, you are a problem. You are becoming a problem. I like you, I am trying to help you, but you are becoming a problem."

"Just answer the goddamn question, Ben. Is Omega in bed with Awad?"

"You are asking me questions that I cannot answer for somebody who is outside of Omega, and you know it." He sat forward, earnest and eager. "Just take up your father's position and I can answer all of these questions for you, and more! Join us! And anything you want can be yours: wealth, information, power—Marni! But as long as you persist in this absurd, lone wolf position, you are doomed to failure." I didn't answer and he sat back in his chair. "Do you really think you hurt us at Turret? Do you really think that the setback at the Biosphere in Arizona harmed us at all? Not even this conference, with Marni and Gibbons threatening to disclose her father's research—not even this is a serious threat. It's an inconvenience." He shook his head again. "You are swimming against the tide, Lacklan. More, you are beating your head against a brick wall, and all the blood you see is your own. You are hurting no one but yourself."

I thought about it for a long moment. Finally, I said, "Bullshit. You're a liar."

"How did you find out about the attack on the conference?"

I raised an eyebrow at him. "That's not your concern. Join me, Ben, and I will tell you everything."

He smiled, drained his glass, and looked at mine. It was empty, too. He said "May I? You have excellent whiskey."

I gave a sour nod. "Sure."

He stood and held out his hand. "Can I get you a refill?"

I gave him my glass and he went to the sideboard to refill them both. While he was there he asked me, "Have you killed Aatifa, Ali, and Hassan?"

I thought for a moment, then said, "Yes."

He came back and gave me my drink. "Is that your solution for everything, Lacklan? If somebody is a problem, just kill them?"

I sipped, savored the malt, and swallowed, feeling the pleasant burn as it went down. "If it were, Ben, you'd be dead by now. You may not have noticed, but I am trying to cooperate with you. You say you don't want Marni and Gibbons dead. If Abbassi goes ahead with his plan, Marni, Gibbons, and maybe a million more souls will die."

"You've answered your own question, haven't you? If that is the case, why would we be in bed with Awad?"

"I don't know. That's what I am trying to find out. You seem awful cozy with people who should be your enemies."

He smiled. It was a tolerant, patronizing smile. "Like you? Here we are, drinking whiskey and chatting like old friends. But am I cooperating with you?" Before I could answer he went on, "So you saw the cell as a threat, you tracked them down, and you killed them?"

I nodded, "Yeah, but I tortured Aatifa first."

"For what purpose?"

"To find out where Abbassi was, and where the bomb was."

"And did he tell you?"

Did he tell me? It wasn't an easy question to answer right then. I frowned. I felt very tired. I saw the glass between my fingers slip and fall on the carpet, and wondered if that mattered at all, if it was important, if anything was important anymore. My breath was heavy and warm with alcohol. I frowned at Ben and sighed a big sigh. "No," I said. "No, he didn't know. It's a cell. A need to know basis."

"So you killed him."

"Yeah. I killed him."

He was hazy and kind of far away, but I could see he was shaking his head. "You are a problem, Lacklan," he was saying. "I try to help you, like your father asked me to, but you make it so hard. You're a problem, a real problem..."

And then I blacked out.

———

I WOKE up with a bad hangover in a room I did not recognize. I wasn't so much thirsty as dehydrated. My mouth tasted as though a medium-sized rodent had gone in there to die, and my stomach felt as though its mother was decomposing in my bowels. My head, on the other hand, felt as though they had both impaled blunt axes in my skull before they scurried off to die.

I shielded my eyes from the glare that was shouting at me from the open window. As I adjusted, I became aware of green hills and forests that did not correspond to Riverside Drive. I levered myself onto one elbow and waited for a wave of nausea to wash over me and pass. Then I levered myself the rest of the way up. There was a glass jug of water on my bedside table. Beside it there was a glass. I managed to spill half of the water into it with a hand that hadn't shaken so badly since Mindy Sinclair took me behind the bike shed when I was fifteen.

I sipped some of the water and looked around the room, trying to link up random, unhappy thoughts. There was a bathroom en suite. The walls were off-white. The door had an institution look which was enhanced by the presence of some kind of chart on a clipboard hanging on it. There was a sage green vinyl chair with wooden arms between my bed and the window, angled so that anybody sitting in it could look at me and feel sorry for me. To complete the picture, there was another clipboard attached to the foot of my bed. The bed was made of metal tubing painted white.

I was in hospital. I looked out the window again. I was in hospital outside New York. I tried to remember. I tried to remember what I remembered and I didn't remember much.

I swung my legs out of bed and realized I was wearing one of those hospital gowns that expose your ass to ridicule. As I realized that, my stomach lurched toward my mouth and I staggered to the john just in time to vomit convulsively, but to little effect. After a couple of minutes I rinsed my mouth, drank a little more water, and returned to fall on the bed. I began to shiver and covered myself with the sheets.

Shortly after that, the door opened and a pretty nurse in her late twenties came in and smiled at me.

"Aha," she said. "We're awake!"

"What, both of us?" Even when I'm sick I can be a wiseass if I have to.

She ignored me and asked, "How are we feeling?"

I repeated my joke, hoping she'd get it this time. "What, both of us?"

She winked. "Well you can't be that bad if you're being a pain in the ass, can you?"

"What, now it's only me? We're not both pains in the ass?"

"I'll let Dr. Banks know you're awake. Can I get you anything?"

"Yeah, something to stop me feeling sick."

"I'll leave that to the doctor."

She opened the door. I said, "What's your name?"

"Nurse Rogers."

"You free after work, Nurse Rogers?"

She raised an eyebrow at me. "In your condition? I do enough nursing while I'm on duty, tough guy. After work, I like to be nursed."

I smiled and she left. I lay back and closed my eyes. I wondered for a moment if I even knew who I was. I did. I was Lacklan, Lacklan Walker. I was rich because I had inherited a fortune from my father. He had died. I hated him and he had died. Because Marni had killed him. She had killed him because...

The door opened and I opened my eyes. There was a black woman in a white coat. She looked oddly like Oprah. She had her hands in her pockets and her head cocked on one side. "How are we feeling?"

I managed to raise an eyebrow. "You too? What's with the we? Everyone in this hospital has blue blood or what?"

She smiled on the right side of her face, where it looked both tolerant and ironic. "Oooh kaaay, how are *you* feeling?"

"Like shit. Can you give me something to stop vomiting?"

She nodded. "Sure. I came prepared."

She stepped closer, popped a pill from a plastic sheet, and handed it to me with a glass of water. I pushed myself up again and took the pill and the water. As I swallowed both, she started talking again.

"The nausea will pass quickly. It's the after effect of the drug you took."

I frowned. "What drug?"

"Yeah, you probably don't remember much. It will affect your memory for a bit too. That'll pass."

"Where am I? What happened? Who are you?"

She crossed her arms and watched me for a moment. "In reverse order, I am Dr. Banks, you took a large dose of Benzoacetalokine. It knocked you out for a good few hours, but it has side effects, like making you feel like shit and wiping out your memory." She waited a moment while I frowned at her and tried to remember. Then she added, "The pills will reduce the inflammation in your stomach and your intestines fairly quickly. The rest of it will take time."

I shook my head. "I have never even heard of Benzo..."

"Acetalokine. Probably not. But you took it."

"Hang on... I was at home. Ben. I was with Ben. Did he call you?"

She nodded, but not in the affirmative, more like she was agreeing with her own thoughts. Then she said, "Try to get some rest. Can you manage some food? It's the best thing you can do, if you can keep it down."

I answered absently, telling her yes, but not really listening to what she was saying.

She left and I lay back and tried to search in the amorphous grayness that was my mind for details of where I was and how I had got here. But my thoughts drifted into vague irrational sequences and without realizing, they became dreams in a world of sleep. I don't know how long I slept, but I awoke feeling better and stronger, though still confused.

Nurse Rogers was there. She had pushed up the overbed table and placed a plate of scrambled eggs, bacon, and pork sausages on it, with a large mug of coffee and a side plate of toast. She smiled and winked in a weird replay of the way she'd left last time I saw her. "Good morning, sleepy head."

I pushed myself up and she adjusted the cushions behind me. "Do you patronize all your patients, Nurse Rogers, or only the ones who want to sleep with you?"

"Now why would you want to sleep with me, silly?" She asked it with a big, friendly smile. "Surely it would be more fun if we were awake."

"You didn't answer my question."

"All of them."

"What day is it?"

"Monday."

"Date?"

"14th of May. Anything else, Herr Walker?"

I smiled at her. "Yeah, wiseass. Where are my clothes?"

"Somewhere safe, where you can't get them."

I cut into a sausage and she made her way to the door. I said, "Nurse, I took a sleeping pill. Why am I in hospital?"

She stopped and turned back. "I'll let Dr. Banks explain that. She'll be 'round to see you soon."

She left and I ate hungrily, then drained the mug of coffee and felt good. As soon as I felt good, I felt impatient. I wanted my clothes and I wanted to be up and out of there. I got up and opened the door to look out. There wasn't much to see. A corridor that on the left made a right angle and on the right led to a desk with what seemed to be a reception area. Dr. Banks was leaning on the desk reading some papers and looked up when I stepped out. She put down the papers and came toward me.

"You're looking better."

"Yeah. I don't know why I'm here. I need some answers and I need my clothes."

"Of course you do." She put her hand on my shoulder. "Let's step inside and get you sorted. You have a visitor."

I yielded to her pressure and moved back into the room. "A visitor? Who?"

"Your nephew."

I shook my head. "That's a mistake. I haven't got a nephew." A small ache in my head and a memory. "I only had one brother. He's dead. He never had kids."

She smiled. "Well, that's what he said. Now you just rest while I get you something to wear, and then we'll take you down to the garden."

I felt a stab of anger. "I don't want something to wear, Dr. Banks. I want my clothes. And you don't need to take me anywhere. Just tell me where it is and I'll go. And then I'm out of here."

She gave a little nod. "That's not a problem, Mr. Walker. Nurse Rogers will bring you something to wear right away."

"Something to wear...What happened to my clothes?"

"She'll be right here. Try not to get upset. Everything is going to be fine."

I went and stood by the window, looking out. I barely registered the view. I was remembering. Ben. I had been drinking with Ben, discussing something... I had fallen asleep. Ben had said it was a problem. There was a problem, but I couldn't remember what the problem was. Marni? Had Marni been the problem?

Then there was a face, a sobbing face with a large beard. I shot him in the head, even though he was bound. Bound with coat hangers. And bodies, dead bodies upstairs, with their throats cut. I was aware my heart was pounding. The door opened and I turned to see Nurse Rogers, still smiling. Over one arm she had a toweling dressing gown. "I got you something to put on while we sort out your clothes."

I growled, "What the hell do you mean, sort out my clothes? What do you need to sort out?"

She didn't falter. "Well, we had to wash them when you were brought in, didn't we? Now, do you want some help to change?" She winked.

I snarled. "No, get the hell out of here."

"Rude! Just call when you're ready and I'll take you to see your nephew."

"I don't have a nephew!"

She laughed. "Well, you'd better tell him that!"

She left. I stripped off the nightgown and put on the dressing gown. I looked for some slippers or shoes, but there weren't any. I yanked open the door and shouted, "*Nurse Rogers!*" She peered around from the desk down the corridor. "What am I supposed to put on my feet?"

She disappeared and reappeared a moment later with a wheelchair and a pair of fluffy slippers. I stared at her. "You have got to be kidding."

"Sorry, Mr. Walker, it's hospital policy. Our insurance company insists upon it."

"You can tell your insurance company that they can

shove that chair and the slippers right up their corporate ass. Now where is this guy who claims to be my nephew?"

She shook her head. "I can't tell you. I can take you there."

"Then take me."

She indicated the chair with her eyes and her head. I sighed and she handed me the slippers. I sat in the chair and threw the slippers on the floor.

She made a *tsc!* sound and sighed back at me. "How old are you? Four?"

TEN

SHE WHEELED ME PAST THE DESK TO A BANK OF elevators. A couple of people passed and smiled at me. We boarded one of the elevators and rode it down to the first floor, which consisted of large, open spaces and plate glass walls overlooking lush gardens and sweeping parkland. There were a lot of people. All of them were dressed in normal clothes. Some had white coats. They all seemed busy. She pushed me across the lobby, past a reception desk, and out a set of automatic doors onto a path. That path wound its way through hydrangea bushes to a broad lawn that sloped down to a dense hedgerow running beside a stream. She wheeled me onto the grass and down to a bench where there was a man sitting cross-legged in an expensive suit, watching me. It was Ben.

Nurse Rogers stopped a few feet away from him and said, "Well, I'm sure you two have a lot to catch up on. I'll leave you to it. If you could just bring him to reception when you're finished?"

Ben looked up at her and nodded. She walked away.

"How much do you remember, Lacklan?"

"Everything."

He made a face that said he was almost impressed. "That's good. That's a quick recovery."

"Now I want my clothes back and I want to go back to my apartment."

He gave a small smile and a small snort to go with it. "Let's not rush things, Lacklan. Let's see first if we have come to understand each other yet." I didn't answer. I just watched him. "Your mistake, from the start, was to think that we needed you." He spread his hands. "You were convenient. You were *very* convenient. And you are very good at what you do. But, let's be clear, Lacklan, Omega does not need you."

"OK. Lesson learned."

"Your other mistake: you kept telling me, 'I don't work for you.'" He shook his head. "Wrong. You do, Lacklan. From the day you came to my office at the Pentagon, you have worked for me. You see, just because you don't want to, doesn't mean you don't. I own you, Lacklan."

"Fuck you."

He gestured at me with his hand. "Look at you! Half naked, barefoot, in a wheelchair!" He laughed out loud. "A prisoner of your own obstinate stupidity. And look at me. I am wearing a two thousand dollar suit, five hundred dollar leather shoes, my Jaguar is waiting out front, I have the freedom and the power to do whatever I please. And that includes letting you go, forcing you to stay, letting you live, or killing you off. Assimilate it, Lacklan. I own you."

"What is this place?"

"I'm glad you asked. It's the Richard John Erickson Institute. It is a research center that studies psycho-social dynamics."

"Mind control."

"You sound like a 1950 radio horror show."

"Do I? Am I wrong?"

He shrugged. "Only in so far as the term is impossibly simplistic. What is 'mind', Lacklan? What makes your mind yours and my mind mine? Have you ever asked yourself that question?"

"No."

"Mind..." He shook his head, biting his lip. "It's a whole range of *processes*! Hunger, thirst, libido, anger, joy, excitement, *analysis*... And somehow you know that your joy is not the same as my joy, your anger is not the same as mine. When you analyze something, somehow you *know* that I am not making that analysis, it's you. That sense of 'I' is also a part of Mind. But, what if, Lacklan, what if that separation was an illusion?"

I yawned. "Yeah, what about that?"

"What if your mind and my mind, and Nurse Roger's mind, were all the same mind?"

"You know what, Nephew Ben? People who didn't have anything better to do have been asking themselves that same question for about ten thousand years. And for all their philosophizing and asking of *stupid* questions, every baby that is born still knows that it's an individual, and when it craps it doesn't crap your crap, it craps its own crap. And when it laughs it laughs its own laugh, not yours. You can get Stanford University to do as many experiments as you like, and you can fund as many psycho institutes as you like, the bottom line is, I am me and you are you. So get off your fucking ego-god trip, because you don't own shit."

He narrowed his eyes into an unpleasant smile. "And yet here we are. And with every passing decade since 1960, people in the west have felt themselves increasingly connected, due, in no small part, to the television's power to homogenize culture. And since the late 1980s, due to the explosion in information technology. There is a matrix of thought and information, Lacklan, with a nexus within the World Wide Web, that is steadily exerting an ever stronger influence over the collective thought and the collective emotions of the world. Journalists are murdered in Paris and the people weep in Sao Paulo, New York, and Tokyo. A child is shot in Cape Town and people demand justice in London, Paris, and San Francisco. Trump is elected president in the U.S.A. and people demonstrate in Moscow, Madrid, and Munich. There are great streams of consciousness, information, and emotion flowing around the planet in a way that is not dissimilar to the streams of electrons flowing through your brain. I am here to tell you, Lacklan, that the destiny of humanity is to have a collective consciousness."

"Ben, there is an Islamic terrorist cell threatening to bomb the United Nations General Assembly hall on Friday. They will not only kill several hundred people present, they will spread a genetically engineered virus, SF2, all across New York. Quit talking shit, and get me out of this damned hospital."

"Institute."

"I am going to come over there and break your fucking legs."

"Move an inch and I will have you shot."

I flopped back in my chair and closed my eyes. "What do you want, Ben? You want New York wiped out? Why? What for? If you wanted Marni and Gibbons dead you could have done it long ago, without this four ring circus. What do you want?"

He nodded. "That's a lot better."

I scowled at him. "You arrogant piece of shit."

"Arrogant, yes. Piece of shit, not by a long chalk." He pointed at me. "You, in your ridiculous bathrobe, in your wheelchair. You, you are a piece of shit. I am not."

I repeated, "What do you want?"

He stared at me for a long while. "I *want* you to bring me Marni."

"That's what I was doing, Ben."

He shook his head. "No, you were going off half-cock —*again*—murdering terrorists, uncovering bomb-plots..."

"They were going to kill Marni, goddammit!"

"Not if you had got her to us."

I stared at him, incredulous. "They were going to kill thousands, possibly millions of people! Doesn't that *mean* anything to you, Ben?"

"Lacklan, there are almost eight thousand million people on this planet, and they are *all* going to die. It's what people do. They live, and then they die. The vast, *vast* majority will have insignificant lives. A very, very few will do something useful in their time. Let's help those few, and let the many die where and when they will." He stood. "Wake up, Lacklan. Time to wake up."

"What are you going to do with me?"

He smiled and looked around, like he found my question amusingly stupid. "This is an institute that studies psycho-social dynamics, Lacklan. They are going to help you to adjust, psycho-socially."

"You can't do this to me. You have no authority..."

"On the contrary, Uncle, as your only surviving relative, and given your recent attempted suicide, I have the authority. Like I said, I own you." He laughed and took hold of the back of the chair. "Now, shall I wheel you back, Uncle?"

Dr. Banks was waiting for us at the reception desk. She and Ben barely acknowledged each other. He patted my shoulder and said, "I'll see you again soon, Uncle," and walked out to his dark blue Jaguar.

I watched him go. Banks smiled at me and said, "Well, how are we getting on? Did we enjoy our little visit?"

I raised an eyebrow at her and repeated, tediously, "What, both of us?"

She took hold of the handles of the chair and started to push me down a passage. People passed and smiled at me. She chuckled. "You're going to be an interesting case, Mr. Walker, I can tell."

"He's not my nephew. You know that, right?"

"Is that so? Well, you can tell me all about it in just a moment."

We came to a door and she backed through it into a spacious, modern office with broad windows overlooking a garden with a lily pond. She pulled me in after her, then wheeled me up to the desk. There, she dropped into a large, black leather chair and sat smiling at me. Everybody smiled at the Richard John Erickson Institute for Psycho-Social Studies.

I said, "So, are we going to pretend that you are a regular

psychiatrist and I am a potential suicide case? And that Ben is my nephew, even though we are practically the same age?"

"So what do *you* think is going on, Lacklan?"

"I'm not Mr. Walker anymore, Banks?"

"Are you going to answer all my questions with a question of your own?"

"Are *you?*" She pulled over a pad and made a note. I jerked my head at it. "Is that supposed to intimidate me?"

She didn't look up. "Does it?"

"Should it?"

She finished making her note, set the pad on the desk and looked at me. This time she wasn't smiling. "Do you know why your nephew registered you with us, Mr. Walker?"

"Yeah, do you?"

She obviously didn't want to play the question game anymore because she said, "Yes, of course I do. Why do *you* think he registered you with us?"

I smiled on the right side of my face, where it's most ironic. "So that I would stop killing Islamic terrorists."

"Is that what you do?"

I nodded. "Yeah, it's one of the things I do."

"Would it be accurate to describe you as a lone warrior fighting against a vast conspiracy?"

"That would be accurate, Dr. Banks, yes. Does that make me paranoid?"

She gave a small laugh. "I wouldn't be much of a psychiatrist if I came to a diagnosis like that on the basis of a short exchange like this, would I, Mr. Walker?" I didn't answer. She took a breath and added, "Besides, at the Richard John Erickson Institute, we try to take a broader view. We don't really think in terms of disorders or syndromes..." She shook her head. "Psychosis, neurosis, schizophrenia, paranoia... even normality! They are all very limited views of the mind."

I made my voice dull to reflect my lack of interest. "Really?"

"We prefer to look at the relationship between the so-called individual's mind, and the collective mind of society. Where a person is socially integrated, conflict naturally disappears and there can be no paranoia. Does that make sense?"

"Well, Doc, I'll tell you what, it sounds to me like you're all out to get me and make me one of you." I smiled. "The Invasion of the Mind Snatchers."

"Are you not already one of us, Lacklan? What makes you different?"

I yawned loudly. When I'd finished, I rubbed my face and looked at her with an expression that said she was boring me intensely. "Mainly, Doc, I guess, the fact that I am a paranoid schizophrenic homicidal maniac."

"Do you consider yourself dangerous?"

"Very. Where are my clothes?"

"They are being laundered."

"No, Banks, they're not. You are keeping me in this robe, in this wheelchair, in a pathetic attempt to make me feel humiliated and rejected by the society around me. It's undergraduate social psychology, and while you are playing your stupid games, people's lives are at stake out in the real world."

"And they need you to save them. Is that how you integrate, Lacklan? As a hero? You must either be an outcast psychopath, or a hero."

"Smart."

"How long do you think you are going to be here, Mr. Walker?"

"Do you know how transparent you are? When you want me to feel alienated you call me Mr. Walker. When you want to offer me integration you call me Lacklan."

"How long do you think you are going to be in here?"

"I don't know, but I have to be out before Friday."

She leaned her elbows on the desk and rested her chin on her hands. "You'll be lucky to leave here in ten years, Lacklan. More likely, you'll be here for the rest of your life. If I were you, I would start adjusting."

I gazed at her for a long moment, thinking. Finally, I said, "OK. If there is one thing I do understand, it's power. Just tell me what I have to do, and I will do it."

"Unfortunately, it's not that easy, Mr. Walker."

"It isn't?"

"No, you see—and this is why it might take the rest of your life—you have to want it."

"I have to want to become part of your society?"

She nodded. "That's right. We will, of course, help you in every way."

"Help?"

"With courses, mental training, meditation, hypnosis, group activities..." She paused and smiled. "...medication, electronic aids. We have some very advanced technology."

I gave a single nod. "I understand. Well, Doctor Banks, I feel very motivated to fall in with your program and make lots of progress very quickly."

She sat back in her chair and laughed. "Oh, Mr. Walker, I don't believe that for one moment. I think you are being devious and manipulative, and I know just the cure for that."

She pressed a button on her desk and, after a moment, four very large male nurses stepped in. The biggest one, a Russian-looking giant with a bald head, said, "You gonna come quiet, or we have to pacify you?"

I looked at him, and then the other three: a black guy with a mustache, an Aryan with real short hair and a guy who looked like Stallone with a lobotomy. They all looked like wrestlers, and I figured there were ten more where these had come from. I shook my head. "No, I'll come quiet." I looked at Dr. Banks and gestured at the wheelchair. "May I stand or am I going to be wheeled?"

She raised an eyebrow. "You may stand."

I stood, and my only excuse for what happened next is that it caught me totally by surprise. Perhaps it shouldn't have, but it did. The big Russian nurse plunged a huge fist into the pit of my stomach. I folded and sank to the floor, retching. And that was when they started kicking me and stamping on me. It wasn't hard enough to do permanent damage. They didn't want to break my bones or rupture my organs. They just wanted to teach me that I wasn't such a tough guy. It hurt. It hurt a lot.

I don't know how long it went on. It felt like a couple of hours, but it was probably not more than a minute or two. I adopted the fetal position and tried to ignore the pain by thinking about what I was going to do to each one of them when it was my turn. I fixed their images in my mind so I would not forget.

During the beating, I heard Dr. Banks get up and walk

over. I couldn't see her because I had my head covered, but I knew she was watching. I had her fixed in my mind, too.

By the time they had finished, I was partially unconscious and unable to walk. They lifted me back into the wheelchair, took me back to my room, and dumped me into my bed. After they had left, Nurse Rogers came in with a bowl of hot water and a cloth. She sounded as perky as ever.

"What have *we* been up to, then? You are a naughty boy! Let's have a look at these cuts and bruises."

She cleaned me up as I drifted in and out of consciousness. At one point I felt a sharp prick on the inside of my elbow, and a moment after that I was enfolded by darkness. As I sank into oblivion, Sergeant Bradley's New Zealand voice inside my head kept saying, "Well, a fine bloody mess we've got ourselves into, lad, haven't we?"

———

WHEN I AWOKE I did not feel hung-over, but I did feel completely devoid of any kind of motivation. I knew I could move my arms and my legs, but I couldn't be bothered to try. I shifted my eyes and noted without much interest that I was in a different room. It was identical, and everything was in the same place, down to the jug of water, but the view through the window was different. I was not looking down on trees, I was looking into them. I was on the ground floor.

I considered my condition and knew it was the effect of the injection Nurse Rogers had given me. It was like being deeply depressed, only without the sadness. It was actually quite pleasant. It occurred to me that they were watching me and monitoring me. They must know by now that I was awake, and pretty soon somebody would come in to take me to the next stage of the process where they broke me down and destroyed my identity. This pleasurable, drug induced apathy would be the haven I was allowed to return to, after they subjected me to regular bouts of hell. A hell I would be blamed for, a hell I would bring upon myself by resisting them. And all I would have to do to get back to this blissful apathy, would be surrender my mind and my will to them.

As I thought that, the door opened and Nurse Rogers walked in, smiling as ever.

For the few moments she had the door open I saw a large room, like a lounge, with nests of tables and armchairs, and beyond them two sets of glass doors that opened onto lawns and gardens.

"So, how are we feeling?"

In my mind I told her, "What, both of us? Fuck you, Nurse Rogers!" But for the cameras I smiled weakly and said, "We're feeling kind of good. Have I told you how pretty you are, Nurse Rogers?"

She grinned. "No, but it's nice to hear. We all like to be told nice things, don't we?"

She came and helped me to sit up. I gave a comfortable chuckle. "I guess we do. Nurse Rogers...?"

"Yes, Mr. Walker?"

"Have you got a soul?"

She patted my pillows. "Now what kind of question is that?" She winked. "That's the drugs talking!"

"Do you think we all have the same soul? Like Manitou?"

"Well, I wouldn't know about that, but it's a very comforting thought, isn't it?"

"It sure is. Am I going to see the doctor today?""

She came close to me and leaned forward, with her hands placed against her thighs, just above her knees, so I could see her cleavage. It was a nice cleavage, but it didn't do anything to me. She smiled into my face and spoke to me like I was ninety.

"First we'll have some breakfast, then we'll take you to sit in the sunshine for a bit, and then maybe this afternoon, Dr. Banks will have another chat with you."

I winced. "Do you think she will have me beaten again this time?"

She cocked her head on one side with the same, bright smile. "Not if you behave yourself! Do we think we can behave ourselves this time?"

"Yes, I think so."

She didn't say, "Good boy!" but she may as well have. She left the room and I closed my eyes. I explored my body with my mind. There was a complete absence of desire. All I wanted was to remain motionless and be in the moment. It was almost like Zen meditation. The window was open and I could hear the sporadic song of the birds in the gardens, the sigh of the breeze through the pine trees, and the occasional touch of the cool air on my cheek. I felt my ego dissolve, and I was all of those sensations. The moment wasn't going anywhere, it wasn't leading to anything. It just was, and I was it. It was peaceful and it was beautiful, and I wanted it to last forever.

I smiled.

One of the stupidest questions gurus, life-coaches and therapists will ever ask you—and they will ask you all the time—is, "What do you want?" And they will stress the last word as though they are conveying some especially profound meaning: "What do you *want?*"

It's a stupid question because what you want will change every time your circumstances and your body chemistry change. If I ate two hours ago, I want to use the can. If I haven't eaten for three or four hours I want to eat. If Nurse Rogers hadn't been feeding me a cocktail of drugs, I would probably want to explain graphically to her and her cleavage exactly what 'we' wanted, and after that I'd want a long cold beer. Since Marni had gone missing I had wanted to find and protect her. But right now, because of the cocktail of drugs Nurse Rogers and Dr. Banks were feeding me, I wanted nothing. Literally. Nothing was the thing that I wanted. What you want changes all the time. That's why it's a stupid question.

The smart question is: what do you intend? Because where your desires can fluctuate, your intention can stay constant—if you're made of the right stuff. I reached deep down inside myself and found the last voice that had spoken to me as I had sunk into unconsciousness. Sergeant Bradley, from the Regiment, the hardest, toughest son of a bitch I had ever met. A Kiwi built like a brick shithouse with a grin that would turn your blood to ice. I heard his voice, with his rich New Zealand accent, leering at me. "A fine bloody mess you've got yourself into, Captain Walker! Haven't you? And what, may I ask, do you *intend* to do about it?"

And his eyes told me exactly what I intended to do about it.

ELEVEN

I WAS GIVEN BREAKFAST AND THEN TAKEN TO THE lounge where I sat and stared out at the garden, the sunshine, and the birds. I used the opportunity to do some meditation. Anyone who has done martial arts seriously has learned to meditate, and in my drug-induced state it was very easy to achieve a deep trance.

After an hour or so I was taken to Dr. Banks' office. This time I was allowed to walk, though I still wore the bathrobe I had been given earlier. Nurse Rogers opened the door for me and smiled as I went in. I smiled back. I had learned that, as we were 'we' and not you and 'I', it was always important to respond in kind. That is a big part of belonging. You smile, I smile, we all smile.

I stood looking down at Dr. Banks, as Nurse Rogers closed the door behind me. The doctor gestured to the chair across from where she was sitting, behind her desk, and said, "Please, sit." I sat. "How are we feeling today?"

I nodded. "We're feeling very peaceful. I know the feeling is drug induced, but it feels good."

She studied my face for a moment and leaned back in her chair, holding a fountain pen like it was a twig she was about to snap.

"I have to say, Lacklan, I am surprised at the speed with which you have adapted. I am a little suspicious."

I smiled in a way you could call rueful and gave a rueful little snort to go with it. "What day is it?"

"Why is that important?"

"Because I don't know how quickly I have adapted. All I know..." I paused, as though I had realized that I knew more than I thought. Then shrugged and went on. "When those guys gave me that beating. That has never happened to me before. Normally I would have killed them all, and it would have taken a few seconds. Less than a minute. Being on the receiving end like that..." I paused again, staring at the silent trees beyond the double-glazed windows. "I realized how tired I am of killing, how tired I am of fighting." I looked her in the eyes, like I'd had a sudden thought. "I don't know if you are genuinely providing therapy, or whether you are simply here to condition me..."

I left it like that. It was not a question, but it invited an answer. She smiled, "Maybe the two are not so different, Lacklan. Had you thought of that?"

I smiled like I was impressed by her intelligence. "No," I said. "I had not. Maybe you're right. Can I tell you something about my childhood?"

"That's why we are here. There *is* a Freudian element to the work we do."

"I didn't know this as a kid, but my father was one of the

senior members of Omega. By the time he died, he was Gamma. There were only two members who were senior to him."

She checked her notes. "This is the organization you claim is the government within the government."

I knew I had never told her that, but I played along. "Yes. He was a harsh, brutal man, with very little compassion. At least that was how I saw him. He always favored my brother, because my brother was always willing to comply, and go along with my father's wishes—to be an extension of my father's will. I rebelled. The more I rebelled, the more he favored Robert. The more he favored Robert, the more I rebelled."

"How about your mother..."

I gave her that, "You're good" look. "My mother is English, minor aristocracy. Highly intelligent, well educated, cold as ice and tough as nails."

"Those are two very powerful similes, Lacklan, ice and nails."

"That's her. She hated my father, and so did I. We formed a kind of alliance against him and Robert. It was a secret alliance, but we were there for each other."

The most effective lies are the ones based on truth. I was aware of that, and I was also aware that as I was telling her these things, in my drug-induced semi-trance, it was having a cathartic effect. I was seeing and understanding things about myself, about my relationship with my parents and with Marni, that I had not realized before.

Banks said, "She was an ally whom you trusted, even though she was not physically there for you. You were forever chasing her, though you never caught her."

"That's exactly it. I left home and joined the SAS. They trained me in many things, but what I learned best was to fight. Never to give up. However powerful or invincible the enemy may seem, you never give up. You find the weak spot and you bring them down. You kill them." I smiled. "But that was a lesson I had learned already. I had taught it to myself with my father." I laughed. "I guess that's an unresolved Oedipal complex, huh? My father should have won, but he didn't. I did. My mother left him and returned to England. I won."

"So you never introjected your father as your superego. You never became one with your father, never integrated with society."

"I guess not."

She stared at me a while, "And...?"

I took a deep breath. "With Marni..."

Again she checked her notes. "This was the daughter of your father's best friend, whom you say he was instructed to kill..."

I nodded. "Yes, that's right. She wanted me to give up the Regiment and marry her. I was in love with her. I still am, I guess. But instead of accepting what life was giving me, I said no. And now I understand why."

"That's interesting. Tell me why."

I shrugged like it was obvious and I had been stupid and blind not to see it before. "I didn't know how to be her husband. All I knew was how to fight, how to kill. It was what I had done for my mother, and it was all I knew how to do for Marni." I shook my head. "I cast her in the role of my mother: distant, unattainable, somebody I could love and adulate from a distance, while I fought to protect her. And I cast the whole, damned world in the role of my father, and myself as the invincible Oedipus."

I felt a tear on my cheek. I was surprised to find it there. I wiped it away with the sleeve of my bathrobe, and when I spoke again I was astonished to hear a crack in my voice.

"I am *tired* of fighting, Dr. Banks. I am exhausted. I am sick of killing. The other day I bound a man with wire coat hangers, I cut off his thumb, and then I shot him in the head..." I gave my head several rapid shakes. "I don't want to be that man anymore. And when..." I gestured at the floor where the four gorillas hade given me my kicking. "When those guys beat me up, you know what? It felt good to surrender at last. If I have changed quickly, I forget how you phrased it, maybe it's because at heart I was ready. Maybe it hasn't been quick. Maybe you just got me at the end of a long, long process. I am *tired*."

For the last minute or so, while I'd been talking, she had been making notes. Now she raised an eyebrow without looking at me, and asked, "And what do you want as a reward?"

I frowned, taken aback by the question. "Reward?" I shook my head again. "I don't want any reward. All I want is to rest. Like I said, I am tired. I *need* to rest."

She put down her pad and considered me for a moment. "When you came in, you asked what day it was. What would you say if I told you it was Friday the 18th?"

I smiled. "Is it?"

She nodded. "You have been unconscious for over three days. Today is the day of the conference that you were talking so much about. Marni and Professor Gibbons will give their talk. Abbassi will detonate the bomb."

I shrugged, closed my eyes and smiled. "If—*if*—that is the case, then I am pretty sure that Ben has it in hand. I don't want this fight anymore."

She gave a single nod and pursed her lips. "How about if I told you it was Monday? Monday 21st?"

I sighed. "I don't know what you want me to say, Dr. Banks." I spread my hands. "It's not my fight anymore."

She leaned forward and turned her laptop to face me. In the bottom right-hand corner of the screen I saw the time and date. It said it was the 21st of May, 2018. I stared at it a long time, assimilating what it meant. Eventually I gave a single, slow nod and said, "What happened?"

"Why do you want to know?"

I narrowed my eyes, thinking about the question and the answer. Finally, I said, "Closure?" Then I nodded. "Yeah, closure."

"There was no bomb, either physical or metaphorical. The papers and the TV are full of the damp-squib of Dr. Gilbert and Professor Gibbons' revelations. There was really nothing that any reasonably informed person wouldn't already have known."

I restored my rueful smile and stared for a long time at my hands in my lap. "Ain't it always the way," I said. "It is the destiny of your idols to let you down."

She nodded. "Their destiny, and perhaps their most important purpose."

I frowned at her. "How's that?"

"Because as individuals, we are all flawed and fallible. It is only when we pull together as a family, as a society, that we can truly overcome our weaknesses."

I sighed deeply. "I hear you, Dr. Banks. But that is a very

big pill to swallow for me. I'm going to need a bit of time. All my life it has been me, alone against the dragon."

An ironic smile, but a kind one. "And how's that working for you?"

I responded with a small laugh. "Not so good. But please, give me a little time. It hurts to realize that everything you have lived by, and depended on, is false."

"I know. Take the time you need. The drugs should help. You're making good progress, Lacklan."

I nodded. "Thanks." I hesitated. "Maybe it's the drugs talking, but I mean it. Thank you."

"Sure."

I made my way back to the lounge and sat for a while gazing out at the gardens. Then I took a walk through the grounds around the house. I was aware that I was being watched, but I was still in that blissful state of unconcern. Nothing mattered, because nothing was capable of triggering my adrenal glands and increasing my blood pressure. Everything was cool, man. I would have fit right in in the summer of love of '67.

I wandered down by the stream and saw that it was actually a small river, maybe eighteen or twenty feet across. It was hard to gauge the depth, but judging by the reeds that were poking up out of it, it was at least four or five feet. The position of the sun told me it was flowing due south.

I turned and walked away. I came eventually to a small copse where there was a group of four young men and three women sitting in a circle around an older man on a chair. In the shade of the trees there was a comfortable recliner, and in the recliner there was a young woman lying back with her eyes closed. The older guy was talking incessantly, in a strange, undulating cadence, while the others watched and listened. At first, what he said seemed to be gibberish, to make no sense at all, but then I listened more closely.

"...and naturally your unconscious all the way down knows perfectly how to make deep changes are occurring even now as you listen to my voice sinking deep down all the way down into your unconscious and ever more unconscious than you were before is behind you and a part of the past that you are letting go away as far as it is possible to become so small that it disappears completely and you feel peaceful and happy as you observe how it becomes black and white like an old newspaper that has burned to ashes and you can turn and walk away because your unconscious knows exactly how to turn and walk away into a state of perfect peace and happiness..."

I paused to watch and listen. There was something deeply hypnotic about the rhythm of his voice, and I realized that that was what he was doing. He was hypnotizing the girl, probably as a master class for his students.

I moved on and eventually came to a rear entrance to the building. I moved into a long, tiled corridor with a series of doors set on either side opposite each other, maybe twenty five feet apart. Each door had a small window in it and I peered through the glass in the first on my right. There were young men and women sitting in a horseshoe around a woman in her forties, in jeans and a sweatshirt, had her ass on a small desk, talking to what I assumed were her students. I opened the door and stepped in. They all looked up at me, and the woman smiled.

"Hello..."

"Hi. I'd just like to hear what you're talking about, if that's OK."

"Sure," She gestured to a chair. "Join us?"

I shook my head. "I'm not sure if I am ready yet. I'd like to just listen."

"Sure." She turned back to her class. "So, guys, can you think of any kind of thought that is *not* a picture or a sound or a feeling?"

A guy with a blond ponytail and something that would be a beard when it grew up, raised his hand.

"Art?"

"What about smells and tastes? We can have them as thoughts, memories..."

"But remember, as we discussed earlier, smell, taste, and touch all come under the same group of kinesthetic, because taste and smell are actually physical feelings. So, is there any thought you can have, that is not a picture or a sound or a feeling?" They all agreed that there wasn't. So she went on, "So our next step is to realize that sounds, pictures, and feelings all trigger each other in our minds."

Art raised his hand again. "Can you give us an example?"

"Of course. If I say to you the words 'violent car crash' what happens in your imagination?"

They all gazed into the middle distance and Art shrugged. "I see a red sports coupe hitting another car and going off the road, smashing into a tree and bursting into flames..."

"Did I show you a picture of a red car?"

"No..."

"So the sound of my voice triggered not just a picture but a whole movie in your head." They laughed and grinned at Art. She went on, "Now let me ask you this. I want you all to play Art's movie in your heads..."

They all closed their eyes and she waited. Eventually they started to open them again. She said, "What did you experience...?"

Art said, "I heard the grating of metal, the screech of the brakes..."

A Chinese-looking girl held up her hand. "I felt the jarring impact when the car hit the tree."

The woman nodded. "We have three systems of thinking, and each one triggers the other two. Now, let me ask you *this*, in which category do emotions fall?"

The Chinese girl said, "Kinesthetic, because emotions are feelings triggered by electrochemical and biochemical changes in the body, and the brain."

"Exactly, so if I know what pictures and what sounds to present to you, I can remotely control, and alter, your body and brain chemistry..."

I thought of the man sitting in the copse with his pupils, the strange cadence of his voice and the odd syntax, with one sentence flowing into the next. I thought then of the billions of people, all attached to their screens, their telephones, their tablets, and their laptops, receiving an endless flow of images and sounds, all from the great matrix. What was it Ben had said? "There is a matrix of thought and information, with a nexus within the World Wide Web ..."

A matrix of pictures and sounds with a nexus in the World Wide Web, all triggering biochemical and electrochemical changes in our brains and our bodies, to make us feel emotionally connected to each other, and terrified of our enemies. It was science fiction, but then again, so were cell phones. So was ninety-nine percent of information technology. The future was not now—we had left the future behind.

I left the class and wandered around for a while until I found the lounge again, and from there I wandered back to Dr. Banks' office. I knocked on her door and waited for her reply. When she called for me to enter, I opened the door and moved to her desk.

"Hello, Lacklan. What can I do for you?"

"I've been for a walk around the grounds. I saw a man teaching a class in hypnosis, and a woman teaching what I think was neuro-linguistic programming, or something similar."

"Yes, that is all part of what we do here."

I shrugged. "I was thinking, if I am going to be here for a long time, possibly the rest of my life, I would like to take some of those classes, if it was possible. It might help me to integrate my experiences, come to terms with them. They have been pretty horrific, but I am not alone in that. Soldiers, cops, criminals, victims of violence—all of these people have had experiences similar to mine. Maybe, in time, I could learn to help other people to become better integrated."

She frowned at me for a long while. Finally, she said, "Integrated...?"

I searched for a word to better describe what I meant. I fumbled, "With other people... Not to be an eternal enemy, at war with the world, but..." I spread my hands, "To *integrate*..."

She raised her eyebrows high, "Into society, Lacklan! Into *society!*"

I laughed out loud. "Yes, exactly, into society...."

"Sooner or later, Lacklan, we all have to learn to share in a common experience, a common *consciousness*."

I nodded. "Yes, I am becoming aware of that." I hesitated. "In ancient Japan, the samurai, after a lifetime of war and violence, would often become Buddhist monks. They would seek to let their egos go, silence their minds and become one with...*it*. I think I am ready for something like that."

She smiled. "Yes, you know, I think you may be, at that."

TWELVE

I SPENT THE AFTERNOON WANDERING AROUND with a stupid smile on my face, and receiving stupid smiles in return. In my rambles I noted where Nurse Roberts had her little clinic and I popped in to say hello a couple of times. It was a small office with a couple of chairs and two store-rooms. On my third visit, I sat in one of the two chairs while she carried out a stock take. While she worked, I told her about my visit to Dr. Banks. She seemed to think my spaced-out state of mind was amusing and told me, "I think we may need to reduce your dosage!"

I smiled at her. "Aw, don't do that. I haven't felt this good since..." I shook my head. "...*ever!* You know, drugs affect healthy people faster, and I am really, *really* healthy."

"Well there is more to positive change than feeling good, Mr. Walker, you know?"

"Lacklan. I'd like you to call me Lacklan. Hey, Nurse Rogers...?"

She glanced up at me from her clipboard.

"Well?"

"Do you think, if I wasn't high on drugs, and if I was properly dressed, do you think you could fancy me?"

She raised an eyebrow. "Now that is *not* appropriate, Mr. Walker! But..." she winked. "As a matter of fact, I think I could."

I grinned at her with sleepy eyes. "You're cute."

She spoke to her clipboard. "You have no idea..."

"Can I close my eyes for a bit and just sit here?"

"Sure, honey."

She went about her business, working her way through the store rooms, and I sat there in my state of bliss, listening to her. When she moved into the second store room I stood and followed after her, taking my time, scanning the cabinets. When I found the Epinephrine I took one, slipped the bottle out of the box, closed the box and replaced it at the back of the shelf. Then I palmed a syringe and stepped into the second room, still smiling like an idiot.

"I'm going to go now."

She gave me one of her cute winks. "OK, honey."

"Do you film me in my room?"

"Not anymore, sugar, that was just in the beginning."

"Then maybe tonight you can give me a kiss before I go to sleep."

She grinned. "Well sure I will, honey! Now you run along and let me work, and I'll see you later."

"OK."

The rest of the day continued in that same strange, peaceful state of mind. I knew it was drug-induced and I kept expecting it to start wearing off, but it didn't.

Lunch was at one thirty in the dining room. The dining

room—at least the one where I ate in my bathrobe—was a large space with a foam-tiled ceiling and plate glass walls all along one side. The tables were round and seated eight people at each. I noticed that none of the students I had seen earlier, or their teachers, ate with us. The people who did eat in that dining room were all like me, really peaceful, and smiled a lot. It dawned on me then that the water, or the food, was drugged. But I didn't mind. It was all part of the peaceful, integrated matrix.

As I ate and drank, I was aware that I didn't especially want to do what I was going to do. In fact I would have been very happy to stay in that place, in that integrated state. It was very enjoyable. I had not lied to Nurse Rogers. This was the best I had felt as far back as I could remember. It was a real nice state to be in.

The only reason I was going to do what I was going to do, was because I had formed an intention. I intended it. And you always see through your intentions. That is why they are intentions.

After lunch I spent the afternoon meditating in the garden. I had a very special meditation technique that originated in Tibetan Buddhism, which was used widely in martial arts. You visualized a person—or sometimes a god—doing a movement or an action that you wanted to master. You watched them do it perfectly over and over again, however complex, and then you closed in on them and joined with them until you were actually looking through their eyes. And then you performed the movements as though you were that person, or that god.

And that was how I spent the afternoon. The semi-trance state, though drug-induced, was very helpful for that.

At six PM we were called for supper, and then we all went to watch a movie together, and then we all went to brush our teeth and go to bed. But before going to bed, while I was still in the bathroom, I took the vial of Epinephrine, which is basically adrenaline, drew 5 ml into the syringe, and injected myself with it.

My heart began to pound and I felt a twist of anxiety in my belly, followed by a rush of excitement when I thought about what I was going to do. It was the result I had been hoping for. I'd figured that, whatever cocktail they'd been feeding me, there was a good chance adrenaline would counter the effect. I took my bathrobe off and climbed into bed to wait for Nurse Rogers.

She came in about half an hour later with a glass of water and some pills. I kept my eyes closed but smiled. I heard her say, "Are we ready for our medicine?"

I opened one eye. "First the kiss you promised me."

"Now, now, first the medicine and then the kiss. Open wide."

"OK."

I opened my mouth and she leaned forward to pop in the first of the pills. I gently took hold of her wrist with my left hand and smiled at her, then I seized her throat with my right and sat up, forcing her down on her back. She dropped the pills. Her eyes were wide. She was getting enough air to breathe, but not to scream. I leered at her. "Guess who's been a very bad boy, Nurse Rogers..."

I stood up, stark naked, holding her up by her throat, and forced her to lie on the bed. Then I sat astride her. Her cheeks were flushed and her eyes were bright. I leaned over her and spoke quietly.

"Did they tell you what I do for a living?" She nodded. "I kill people for a living. I am a very, very bad person, Nurse Rogers. Now I want you to ask yourself, do you think I would have any problem at all killing you, considering the fact that you have been actively trying to destroy my mind? Please think about that for a moment."

She took her time, then gave a single nod. I said, "I am going to let go of your throat, Nurse Rogers. If you scream I will put your head in an arm lock and break your neck. Are we clear?"

Another nod. I released her throat. She gave a ragged gasp and whispered, "What do you want from me?"

"First, I want information. Where are we, and what is the real date?"

She swallowed, then whispered, "We are two miles northeast of Maplecrest, two and a half hours north of New York. Today is Thursday, 17th May."

I smiled. "Aren't we a good girl?"

She nodded.

"Now, clothes and a car."

"Next to my clinic is the nurses' changing room. You'll find nurses' uniforms in there, and the clothes of the nurses on duty..." She reached in her uniform pocket and pulled out some keys. "Cream Ford Focus, parked out front."

I took them and our eyes locked. I said, "Now, take your stockings off. I need them to tie you up."

Her chest was rising and falling fast and there was a strange expression on her face.

"Lacklan ..."

"What...?"

"I am so hot right now..."

I looked down at her, and after a moment I smiled.

An hour later, scratched and bruised, but smiling, with a pocket full of various narcotics, I made my way in my bathrobe toward the nurses' changing rooms. The place was still and silent. The lights had been dimmed, the doors were locked, and the main reception area was empty. Banks' office was closed and no light showed under the door. The next passage along took me to the small clinic, and next to it the changing rooms. They were not locked and I let myself in. I closed the door before putting on the lights. There were a dozen lockers, wooden benches, and, against the far wall, a row of showers. There was also a row of hooks against the wall where jeans, shirts, and jackets had been hung. I selected some clothes that were more or less my size, got dressed, transferred the medication to the jacket, on the basis that you never know when you're going to need to dope somebody, and stepped into the corridor again.

To my left was the reception area. To my right there was a T-junction. Coming from that general direction I could hear the soft murmur of voices with the occasional burst of canned laughter. It was the unmistakable sound of a common room or a night watchman's room.

I moved silently to the corner and peered around. I saw what I had hoped I would see. A door ajar, and through it the ape who'd knocked me down in Banks' office. I wondered if his three pals were there. I hoped they were.

I crossed the passage, went in and closed the door behind me. They were there, all four of them. It was like when you were a kid and you got that battery operated machine gun, and they remembered to include the batteries.

I smiled nicely. "Hello, boys."

The big Russian-looking guy was on the left, by the coffee machine, in the kitchen area. The other three were sitting around a coffee table. A small, portable TV was playing reruns of sitcoms. The Aryan guy was reading *Guns'n'Ammo* and the other two, the black guy with the mustache and the lobotomized Stallone, were playing cards. The lobotomy had his back to me. He looked around and said, "Huh?"

I reached him in two strides, grabbed his hair in my left hand, shoved forward, and smashed my knuckles into the base of his skull. I felt the vertebra dislodge and knew he wouldn't be a problem. I let go and he slumped across the table, drooling.

Then the other three were moving. Logically, I should have disposed of the big Russian-looking guy first while the other two negotiated the coffee table, but I wanted him last. So I took a step to my left and kicked the table hard into the Aryan's shins. I know it hurt because he screamed and cursed. It also destabilized the black guy with the mustache. He stood for a moment, waving his arms. I knew Ivan the Terrible was moving at me across the room, so I took another step, grabbed the black guy's wrist in both my hands, moved under his arm and twisted savagely. He had to bend forward to avoid dislocating his shoulder, but when he did that, I kicked him hard in the forehead. Twice. I let go and he fell forward, to join his Stallone-Clone pal on the table. That was about four hundred and forty pounds the Aryan had to dislodge before he could get out.

By now the Russian Bear was upon me, calling me names my mother would not have approved of, and grabbing my head in both his hands. Grabbing is always a mistake because it opens your guard to your opponent, and occupies at least two of your most lethal weapons. While he held me I delivered three crosses to his jaw. He was tough and didn't go down. But he was human and he let go and staggered back. While he was still dazed, I kicked him hard in the nuts and he went down on his knees. I figured that was a good place for him and left him there.

I turned. The Aryan had managed to extricate himself from the coffee table and his two pals, and was coming at me like a Valkyrie on steroids. He wanted to grab me too. Everybody wanted to grab me that day. As he lunged, I stepped inside his guard and rammed the heel of my right hand up into the tip of his jaw. It stopped him dead and his eye rolled. As he began to fall, I took his neck in an arm lock and twisted savagely. It broke his neck and I knew he wouldn't be giving anybody a kicking ever again. That was one good thing that happened that day.

I turned back to Ivan, the Russian Bear, who was probably from Idaho or Detroit for all I knew. I signaled him to get to his feet. He stared at me. He had murder in his eyes. I said, "You're pretty good when there are four of you and you catch a guy by surprise. Let's see how good you are on a level playing field."

He wasn't very good. He roared and charged me, with his arms outstretched, to grab hold of me and take me down. I stepped to the left, my right hand went to his right wrist and my left to the elbow. I pulled on the wrist and pushed on the elbow and he sprawled on the floor. I didn't waste any more time. I slammed the blade of my foot into the back of his neck and broke it.

The debt was paid in full, with interest. I reached in his

pocket and found a large bunch of keys. I figured he would probably have one to the main entrance, otherwise I would have to resort to more primitive methods. On the way, I stopped at Banks' office and kicked in the door. I found a notepad and a pen and wrote a message for her. It just said, "I'll be back for you."

As I put down the pen, something caught my eye. It was a small, highly polished walnut box with business cards in it. I took one out and examined it. Lara Banks MD, Director of the Richard John Erickson Institute for Research in Psycho-Social Dynamics. Beneath it was the address of the clinic, and then her private address, 2501 Pennsylvania Avenue, in D.C.

I put the card in my pocket, let myself out, found Nurse Rogers' car, and set off for Echo Bay.

But I had underestimated the security at the Institute. I had assumed that they relied on the four male nurses to keep the drugged, pliant inmates quiet during the night. Obviously that wasn't the case, or maybe they had laid on special security because I was there. I would never know. The fact was that as I moved along County Road 56, through the dense forest in the pitch black, within a couple of minutes I became aware of headlamps in my rearview mirror, and they were gaining on me fast.

I yanked on the hand brake and spun the wheel, then floored the pedal and accelerated into the oncoming lights. It was a gamble, but I had no time to waste. I was on the wrong side of the road, and he was not on a suicide mission. Sooner or later he was going to veer to his left. When he did, we were going to dance.

He was chicken. He moved to the left when he was

twenty feet away. I moved to the middle of the road, yanked on the brake again and spun the wheel left. My trunk arced around and smashed into the side of the oncoming car. I could see now it was a black, foreign SUV.

There was a screaming of brakes on blacktop and the second car, a Q5, smashed into the back of the first one. I already had the door open and jumped out as the Focus skidded to a halt. I ran to the front car and wrenched open the driver's door. The airbag was deflating and the driver looked stunned. He looked more stunned when I smashed my fist into his temple. His pal was gaping at me from the passenger seat as I reached under his jacket and found his weapon. The penny dropped too late and he started fumbling for his own piece. I put a single round through his head and it was all over for him.

Meanwhile, the two guys in the Q5 had staggered out with their automatics drawn. There was no contest. They were badly shaken and concussed. I shot each one in the head. Then I approached their bodies and knelt to take their guns and one of their watches. I checked the time. It was nine PM, Thursday the 17th of May. I had fifteen hours.

I returned to the Focus. The trunk was dented and scratched, but other than that, it was undamaged.

I climbed in, fired her up, and started again for the town of Maplecrest. From there, I figured it would be south toward the Hudson, where I'd pick up the I-87. I'd make Echo Bay by eleven-thirty, with maybe thirteen hours to go.

Maplecrest was a tiny collection of houses and large lawns along a riverbank with a crossroads at the far end. At the crossroads, I turned left onto County Road 40 and burned rubber south like I had all the hounds of hell biting at my ass. Most of the way I was in thick forest. There was no moon and the only light was from my headlamps, which cast bizarre and wild shadows from the trees into the dense undergrowth. As I drove, I tried to figure out what had happened to me. Ben—Omega—wanted Marni alive, because they needed her father's research. They believed their best chance of getting hold of Marni was through me, and they needed me to do that before twelve noon the next day, because she and Gibbons were going to blow the whistle on Omega in front of the UN—and the whole world—in the General Assembly Hall.

That much was clear. What was not clear, what was giving me a headache, was why the hell he had drugged me and put me in that crazy institute. Clearly the big thing for Omega was to turn people into ants. The one theme that ran through all their research and experimentation was the minimizing of individuality to make people obedient and pliant. The sun beetles, the Biosphere 3 research, and the Richard John Erickson Institute were all about the same thing.

But with less than a week to go before she presented her paper at the conference, why the hell did he drug me and send me there when he needed me to get hold of Marni? It didn't make sense.

My mind went back to that night. I had been tired. We had been drinking whiskey and he kept repeating the same thing, "You are a problem, Lacklan..."

I was a problem, sure, but I always had been. What had made me more of a problem then? What had made him say that? My mind was still foggy, but I struggled to remember. I had killed Ali, Hassan, and Aatifa. Why would that be a problem for him? Why the hell would that be a problem for

Omega? What had he said? I struggled to recover the conversation. He'd said they had a part to play.

A part to play in what? Obviously in Omega's master plan.

The obvious conclusion for any conspiracy theorist was that Omega was behind the bombing plot. But if that was the case, why? Why use me to get Marni if they were planning to kill her at the conference? Whichever way I turned it and twisted it, it didn't make sense.

Then my mind moved on to Mclean and Jones. I could be pretty sure that I was not their favorite person in the world right then, but I had managed to send them the audio files, and I was wondering what, if anything, they would make of them. You don't get to be a Fed by being stupid, so I could only hope they would start to investigate. But if they did, how much weight did Omega carry within the Bureau? That was an unknown quantity. They were questions I could not answer, so in the end I settled down to driving.

At Saugerties I finally merged onto the I-87 and floored the pedal. It was a hundred miles to Echo Bay. I wanted to make it within the hour.

THIRTEEN

I SAT IN THE SMALL PARKING LOT LOOKING ACROSS the darkened green at the large, iron gates set in the fifteen-foot wall. To add to my problems, I had just seen a couple of guys stroll past the gates, and I was willing to bet they were armed. I was thinking about my original plan, with the rubber dingy, and muttered to myself, in a Scots accent that Rabbie Burns would probably have sneered at, "The best laid schemes o' Mice an' Men, gang aft agley."

I had missed my chance. I should have taken her that night, but I hadn't and now I'd have to make the best of what there was. The difficulty I was having was that the easiest approach was going to be from the river, as it had been the other night, but two got you twenty that they had the area floodlit and at least two guards on the back terrace covering the sweep of lawn down to the shore. On the other hand, approaching via the gate or the wall was going to involve a fifteen-foot climb and another fifteen-foot drop, right into the arms of the patrolling guards.

To complicate things further, these were probably just rent-a-cops, and I did not want to kill them. I sighed and took the two automatics I'd taken from the apes at Maplecrest and made my way toward the shore. This time, before wading into the water, I decided to examine the small cliff where the wall ended and the river began. It was maybe twenty or twenty-five feet high, and had enough holes and ledges to offer a way up, which would bring me above the wall and maybe offer a way down. I decided it would not be an easy climb, but neither would it be impossible.

I began to pick my way up. In less than a minute, I was lying flat on the top, trying not to make a silhouette against the faint glow from across the river, and peering down into the grounds of the house. From where I lay, I could see the back terrace. They had the spots on, as I had suspected, and the lawn was floodlit. There were two guys sitting at a table, smoking and playing cards. It was a balmy night and they seemed to be comfortable and un-preoccupied. That much was good. Down the side of the house, I could see a couple more guys walking, chatting to each other in low murmurs. I lay and timed them. It took them a full five minutes to go and return. As they moved away, back toward the front of the house and the gate, I crawled down to the wall, lowered myself halfway, and jumped. I landed in a crouch and waited. Nothing happened, so I sprinted to the back terrace and walked up the sidesteps like I owned the place. The two guards looked up in surprise. I showed them one of my automatics, and put a finger to my lips. They opened their mouths and went to stand, then closed them again and sat.

I moved without hesitation and without breaking my stride. I pistol-whipped the nearest and knocked him cold, put the muzzle of the pistol in the other guy's face to keep him quiet and delivered a left cross to his jaw that put him to sleep, too. I still had three minutes. I figured the French windows would be open to give the guards free and rapid access to the house if there was an emergency. I tried the handle and it was unlocked. But I needed the other two guards out of action before I did anything, so I moved quickly down the steps and ran after the other two. I made no attempt to be silent or to conceal myself. They came into view as I rounded the corner of the house. They were about level with the front door and about thirty feet ahead of me. Beyond them, I could see three cars parked in the driveway. As I ran, I called to them, "Hey, hold up, which one of you guys is Frank?"

They stopped and turned to face me as I drew level. There was an older guy in his fifties and a younger one in his thirties. They were frowning and the older one said, "Neither of us. Who the hell are you?"

I pulled my piece and said, "The guy who is going to blow your head off if you don't do exactly what I say. Give me your weapons."

They glanced at each other, and as they did that, I smacked the younger guy in the jaw with the butt of the automatic. A straight left to the chin took care of the older guy. I used their boot-laces to tie them up and their socks to gag them, and returned to the terrace, where I did the same for those two.

So far it had gone without a hitch. The next stage would not be so easy. I didn't know if Gibbons was with her or whether she was alone. I stepped inside and closed the French windows behind me.

I was in a large drawing room. It was dark, but there was a warped checkerboard of light and shadow across the Persian rug from the glass panes in the doors. I could see a fireplace, a sofa, and a couple of big chairs. Behind them there was deep shadows. On the left there was a credenza and beyond it a door stood closed.

I crossed the room, waited, listening, and then opened the door in a single, swift movement. It didn't creak. I moved into a passage. On my left the passage was lost in shadows and I assumed it led toward the kitchen at the back of the house. On my right there was a broad entrance hall, a large door with a fan of faintly glowing stained glass at the top, and a central wooden staircase leading to the upper floors.

Wooden stairs creak, and there is no effective technique for avoiding it, even if you're a ninja, unless you can memorize in advance which ones creak, and where. The only way to minimize it is to keep your weight near the edge of the steps and take two or three stairs at a stride. By the time I had reached the first floor landing, the stairs had creaked half a dozen times, not loud, but not silent. I stood motionless for a full five minutes, listening, but there was nothing to hear. It seemed nobody had heard me.

I was at the center of a long corridor that ran from east to west. On my right, the stairs continued to an upper floor. Beyond them, I could make out a dog-leg which led into a further wing of the house. To my left, the passage ended with a gabled window through which dim light from the spots in the garden filtered in.

I couldn't think of a logical reason for her to be in one place or another, and listening was telling me nothing, so I opted for the nearest rooms and decided to work through them systematically.

The first three I tried were dark, silent, and musty, and what light came in through the closed drapes showed beds and furniture covered in dust sheets. The fourth room was different. It faced the front of the house. The drapes were open and a diffuse, blue light, which I guessed was from the parking lot where I had left my car, cast dappled shadows of leaves on the glass, and on the bed. Opposite the bed there was a large wardrobe and against the far wall an armchair was angled into the corner. They were darker objects within the shadows.

The bed was occupied. The breathing was deep and slow, but it wasn't the labored breath of a corpulent, middle-aged man. It was the light breath of a young woman. All I could see of her was a mound of quilt, and a dark patch of hair against the pillows. I knew it was Marni, but I had to confirm it. Thinking about her breathing, I was aware that I could not hear any snoring in the house. I would have expected a man like Gibbons to snore.

Maybe I'd got lucky. Maybe he wasn't there.

If he was there, he wasn't asleep.

I closed the door and moved around the bed to where I could see her face. It was her. I reached down and switched on her bedside lamp. I saw her brow furrow. I hunkered down where she could see my face when she opened her eyes, and spoke softly.

"Marni, it's me, Lacklan. I need you to open your eyes and be very quiet."

Her eyelids fluttered and opened, and she lay staring at

me. She spoke without any particular emphasis. "Lacklan... you can't be here."

"And yet, here I am." I smiled and she smiled back. But after a moment, the smile faded.

"You scare me. You're out of control. You threatened to kill Gibbons. He's a good man. He didn't deserve that."

"There is so much you don't understand, Marni, that I need to explain to you. And we haven't got the time right now. I really need you to trust me."

We stayed like that for a long moment, looking at each other. Then she reached out and touched my face with her fingers. "Were you really going to kill him?"

I shook my head. "I had no time to explain to him, and even if I had, he would not have listened. Right now, we have to go, Marni. There's a bomb..."

She frowned. "Here? In this house?"

"No, tomorrow afternoon, at the UN, at noon..."

"That's during our talk."

"I know, baby. Will you please get up and come with me?"

She blinked a few times, then sat up. She stared at me. "Who?"

"Abdul Abbassi, he was Taliban. I don't know who he is with now."

Her frown deepened. "Why?"

"I don't know, but we haven't time to think about it now. Get dressed, we have to go." She didn't move for a moment, then she climbed out of bed and started dressing. I stood. "Where is Gibbons?"

"In his room."

"Here?"

She nodded.

"Will he agree to come with us?"

She drew breath to answer, but the door opened and I saw Gibbons in the doorway. He was holding a revolver and had that obstinate look on his face that told me he would use it if he had to. He stared at me, then glared at Marni. "Have you lost your mind? Don't you realize what is going on here?"

"Philip, put that gun away. What do you think you're doing?"

"He works for Omega, Marni! Can't you see he is manipulating you?"

"Philip! Put the damned gun away!"

"No!"

I spoke quietly, but I let him hear the danger in my voice. "You'd be wise to listen to her, Professor. I can give you all the proof you need. Abbassi is planning to detonate a bomb tomorrow." I checked my watch, it was twelve fifteen. "In less than twelve hours. It will rupture a canister of SF2, do you know what that is?"

He sneered at me. "Of course I know what it is. It's theoretical, that's what it is! And why on Earth would the Taliban, or any of the Muslim fundamentalists, want to bomb our talk? We are advocating helping them!"

I snarled. "Oh, you think they need a logical reason? Like when they murdered the cartoonists at Charlie Hebdo? When they behead children for watching TV? When they flew two planes into the Twin Towers?"

"I'm not getting into a political discussion with a reactionary Neanderthal like you!"

"No, you're not, because we haven't got the time. You

can either come or you can stay, but we are leaving this house in the next two minutes."

"Over my dead body!"

Marni snapped at him, "Are you *kidnapping* me, Philip?"

He stared at her and did a goldfish impression. "Well, you can't... Surely you're not going to go with this... this... *ape?*"

"Philip! Who I go with and what I do is not for you to decide! Now *put that gun down!*"

His jaw stiffened and he squared his shoulders. "He is not leaving this house. I am going to call the police. He is a burglar and a menace!" He thrust out his arm, pointing the revolver at me. His hand was steady. "Now lie on the floor with your hands behind your head!"

I could feel the anger building inside me. I gave him the dead eye and said quietly, "No." I held his eye and carried on talking. "Marni, get dressed, we are leaving."

She sighed. "Philip, you are being stupid." Then she started pulling on her clothes. I walked around the bed. His face went taut and he waved the gun at me. "Don't come near me! I'll kill you! I swear it!"

I looked hard into his eyes. "I could use your help, Professor. You are mistaken about me. I am not with Omega."

He spat his reply. "Your father was their lackey and so are you! You're a murdering fascist and you disgust me!"

Marni snapped, "Philip, if you pull that trigger, I will see you go to jail for the rest of your life! I swear it! You are out of control and you need to get a grip."

He stared at her for a long moment, then lowered the gun. "Are you going to give the talk or not?"

"I don't know. I need to see the evidence, assess the facts, and make an informed decision. It's what scientists do, Philip."

He stared a moment longer, then his face seemed to scrunch up into a ball of sullen hatred, and he hissed, "*Traitor!*"

I held out my left hand. "Give me the revolver, Professor."

"No!"

I put a right cross through his jaw. His eyes rolled up, his legs went to jell-O and he fell gracefully to the floor. I crouched, emptied the shells out of his pistol, and put them in my pocket. I looked up at Marni. She was staring at Gibbons. She looked unhappy. I said, "I'm sorry. I don't want to get shot in the back tonight. He's out of control."

She nodded. "I know."

"You got everything?" She glanced at me, then nodded again. I said, "Good, let's get out of here. You got keys to the gate?"

"In the kitchen."

As we moved down the stairs, I asked, "How about a car?"

"Yeah, I have my car." She frowned at me. "How did you get here?"

"It's a long story."

Two minutes later we were in her Jeep, the gates were swinging open, and we headed out, into the night.

As she drove along Boston Road into the heart of the Bronx, headed for Manhattan, I filled her in on everything that had happened since the prince's party, up to and including my escape from the Institute and my arrival at Echo Bay. She was quiet for a long while after I'd finished, like she was thinking over everything I had told her. Eventually she gave a small laugh. "You don't take no for an answer, do you?"

I shook my head. "Not when I know it's the wrong answer, no."

I watched the city lights wash in a slow rhythm over her face, mainly amber, but occasionally red and green. She took a deep breath and sighed loudly. "So Ben, huh? What's his story? He seems to carry a lot of weight."

I nodded. "I have a couple of theories. One is that he was assigned to my father, and now he's been assigned to me."

"It could be. We don't really know how they operate, do we?"

"No, but we do know that they will go to extreme lengths to avoid killing you and me."

"Me because I have my father's research. You because they believe they can get to me through you."

"Apparently. But that being the case, why do they plan to bomb the conference tomorrow?"

She frowned. "I don't know. For that matter, what does Prince Awad gain by bombing the conference and killing me and Gibbons?"

"I don't get that any more than you do, and what confuses me even more is that after Gibbons' debate with Hennessy was broken up by those guys shouting '*Allahu Akbar*', I followed Ben and Hennessy to the Prince's house. Somehow, in a way I don't understand, they seem to be in bed together, both enemies and allies."

We had turned onto Third Avenue and were moving through south Bronx toward the bridge. She sighed again. "Is that how they operate?" She glanced at me. "They are subtle, Lacklan. They are very subtle. Isn't that what they do with you? You are their arch enemy, along with me and Gibbons, but you visit Ben at his office in Washington, he visits you here in your apartment, you have an arrangement with him: he helps you and you lead him to me, even if you don't plan to honor that arrangement in the end." Our eyes met for a moment. "It's exactly the way you described his relationship with Prince Awad."

I stared out the window at the passing buildings in the desolate light of the streetlamps, at the people on the sidewalks, the cars driving this way and that through the sickly amber wash. All of them expendable, all of them sentenced to die for the greater glory of whom? Allah? Or Omega?

"You're probably right," I said. Then I turned to study her face. "How damaging is your father's research? Can it really hurt them that badly?"

She nodded, glanced at me a moment, and then nodded again. "They have enough enemies worldwide who would use that information to destroy them. There are also still..." She hesitated. "*People*," she said at last. "People like Philip, who are organized, loosely, who have financial power..."

She trailed off. I said, "Ben told me they could not go after Gibbons for some reason. He didn't tell me why."

"Gibbons, and some of his friends, pull strings in very high places." She smiled. "It's not like the Illuminati in fiction. They don't have absolute power. If they did, they wouldn't need to operate in the shadows. But they are powerful, and they are very dangerous."

I nodded. "I know." We were speeding over the bridge into Manhattan. I looked at her and smiled. "You believe we can break them, don't you?"

"Yes. We have to."

"Marni?"

She smiled. "Yeah?"

"Don't run away again. We can do this, but we have to do it together."

She nodded and her smile deepened. "I know. I'm not going anywhere."

FOURTEEN

My laptop was where I had left it on the table. The two whiskey tumblers had been washed and left in the rack to dry. There was no trace that Ben or his apes had ever been there. While I looked around, Marni closed the door, locked it, and slipped the deadbolt. Then she stood staring at the living room.

"It's been a long time."

I switched on the laptop to check my files. I was wondering why Ben hadn't taken it, and I wanted to see if he'd tampered with my recordings of Ali, Hassan, Aatifa, and Abbassi. While I waited for them to load, I looked at her, thinking about what my father had meant for her. "He loved you, you know. Probably more than he loved Robert and me."

She hung up her coat and came to stand beside me. She gently laid both her hands on my chest. "They're painful memories, Lacklan." She paused, hesitated. "I went a bit crazy after you told me he'd killed my dad. I idolized my father, you know that. After he died, your dad became a surrogate father for me, and I loved him and trusted him so much for that. When you told me..." She shook her head, unable to say the words. "I couldn't believe it. I hated you for it, for telling me, and I hated him for taking my dad, and for betraying me. I guess for a time I lumped you both together, father and son, you had both robbed me and betrayed me..."

I nodded. "I know, Marni. It was the last thing on Earth I wanted to do. But right now we have to face the fact that we misjudged him. He was complicated, he was a pain in the ass and in many ways he was not a good man. But neither was he the monster we thought." I shrugged and half-smiled. "You only misjudged him at the end, but I misjudged him all my life."

"I don't think anybody could blame you for that, Lacklan. He was a very hard man, hiding secrets you could not have understood."

I saw with relief that the files were still there. I listened to snatches here and there. They seemed to be intact and I forwarded them to Gantrie for safe keeping. I noticed Marni had stepped away from me and was gazing out at the night.

I said, "You want a drink?"

She nodded without looking at me. I opened a fresh bottle of Bushmills and poured us a glass each. Then we stepped onto the terrace and leaned on the parapet. Riverside Park and the vast darkness of the Hudson beyond stretched beneath us. I didn't face her, but spoke out at the city lights.

"When he was dying, in the hospital, he told me what had happened. Do you want to hear it?"

She nodded.

"Your dad was engaged in his research. I think he was beginning to discover the existence of Omega..."

"He was. He had found out about them."

"Did he know my dad was a member?"

She shook her head. "But he was getting close. He would have found out."

"They warned him off. Apparently they told him several times to desist from his investigation. But he seems to have been a brave..." I hesitated, stumbling over the word. "A brave and a very moral man. He refused." I paused, strangely and intensely aware of the night air on my face. I was surprised at how difficult it was to talk about our fathers. "They were close—very close. And that's why Omega told Bob, my dad, to kill him. He refused, but the alternative was that, if he didn't do it, they'd have a professional hit man do the job..." I paused again, staring into my whiskey. "And take out your mother and you, as well as me and my brother. When they gave him that option, he went and told your father. They discussed it and your dad accepted."

She came close and rested her head on my shoulder. I felt her small convulsions and knew that she was crying. After a while, she wiped her cheek with her fingers and took a deep breath. She said, "You're not so different to him, Lacklan. You're a very hard man. You are very ruthless and secretive. You make it hard sometimes... At least, you've made it hard in the past."

I thought for a long while about that, about how to answer. Finally, I shrugged and said, "We are what we are,

Marni." She drew breath and I stopped her with a smile. "You can say we are what we choose to be, and that's true, but it's also a cliché. Who is that that chooses? And what makes you choose the way you do? It becomes an infinite regression, and in the end you wind up right back in the same place where you started. We are what we are, and the choices we make, we make because of who we are, not who we try to be."

She heaved a big sigh and nodded. "I guess."

"When you disappeared, my father asked me to find you and look after you. He did that because of who he was, not what Omega had tried to turn him into. And I could have walked away, but I chose to go after you, and stay with you, because that's who I am." I hesitated again, then added softly, "It's something I should have done a long time ago."

She didn't answer at first, but after a moment she drew close and took hold of my hand. "We have some catching up to do."

I nodded. "I need to know what's in your father's research. I need to know why they are so scared of it. I need to know about your congressman in Washington..."

"She's a friend of Philip's." She smiled. "But that's not exactly what I meant by catching up..."

I smiled back. "I know, but I have..." I looked at my watch. "A little more than eleven hours to find that canister and the bomb, and by the look of it, I can't count on the help of the Feds. It seems they have dismissed me as a nut."

She narrowed her eyes at me and shook her head. "There are things about that, Lacklan, that don't make a lot of sense."

"I know, but we can't afford..."

She was shaking her head. "I know, but I don't mean that. I mean, what Philip said is true. SF2 is theoretical. It was never fully developed. It wasn't practical. There were just too many problems with it."

"Well, maybe Omega..." But I trailed off because I saw the flaw in my reply before I even said it. Marni put it into words.

"If it was Omega, maybe, though Omega have access to much deadlier agents than a theoretical, genetically modified Spanish flu. The point is Al-Qaeda, or ISIS, or whoever these people are, must have bought this agent on the open market —and they can't have because it doesn't exist yet. It probably never will."

I gestured in at my laptop on the table. "I have the recording of Abbassi telling the guys in his cell..."

She shook her head and put her hand on my arm. "I am not questioning that, Lacklan. I believe you. I just don't necessarily believe *them*."

I frowned. "What are you getting at?"

She sounded a little exasperated. "I don't know. I just know that *this* explanation doesn't quite hold water. I mean..." She hesitated and spread her hands. "Do we know who *supplied* them with the SF2?"

I stared at her. "No."

"But we do know that Prince Awad and Ben are cozying up..."

It was there, for a fleeting moment, and then it was gone again. I stammered, "But—but why would...?"

"I'm not offering an explanation, Lacklan, and I may be way off base. But we have been assuming that Prince Awad knows Ben is Omega—what if he doesn't?"

"When I saw them, they were with Hennessy..."

"The Hennessy Foundation has been involved in facilitating the sale of weapons to regimes that support terrorist groups. That is a fact. Now the question is, if we are right and the Hennessy Foundation brought Awad and Ben together to facilitate the sale of this canister, what does the canister really contain?"

I rubbed my eyes. My brain was aching trying to take in the magnitude of the problem. The same question kept repeating itself. "Why would Omega do that? What would Omega gain...?"

She turned to face me and placed her hands gently on my chest. "OK, baby steps. Let's start by assuming that everything that Omega—Ben—says is a lie."

I nodded. "It's a good place to start." I looked down at her as the night breeze coming off the river moved strands of hair across her face. I felt an ache of emotion that was too powerful to put into words, and forced myself to go on. "We have assumed that they want to keep you alive because they fear your father's research. But let's assume for a moment that that, also, is a lie. Let's assume that what they want is, somehow, to capitalize on your death..."

She went pale. "They want me to die, but they want me to die at the conference..."

"In a spectacular way."

We were quiet for a long time, staring at each other. Finally, she said, "We have seen this before, Lacklan. But this time it will be even bigger, and the consequences.... We have to stop them."

I nodded. "9/11. I have to find that canister."

"How?"

"Abbassi."

I went back inside, collected some things I knew I was going to need, including three sets of cuffs, grabbed my cell, and called Gantrie.

"Dude, I got the files. What happened to you? You disappeared..."

"Listen to me. We are very short of time. Did you track the cell I gave you the other day?"

"Yeah. I still have him."

"Tell me where he is right now. Is he still in the jammed area?"

"No. He's at..." There was a pause while I heard him rattle at the keyboard. Then, "He's at the 49 Club, on 49th Street, right by the Hennessy Foundation. Go figure."

"Gantrie, are you in New York?"

"No, man. Don't ask. You don't need to know where I am. Ever."

"If anyone you care about is, tell them to leave. Now."

"...shit, man!"

"Stay available for the next twelve and a half hours, Gantrie. I may need you. If the mark moves, let me know."

"I'm here, dude."

I turned to Marni. "Go to Boston, now. Get Kenny, whoever is there, tell him what's happening. Move west."

She shook her head. There were tears in her eyes. "I'll call him. But I am staying with you. There is no time to argue. I'll make my own choices. We are what we are, remember? Get going and do what you're best at."

I took her in my arms and kissed her, clinging to her fiercely, to the feeling of her body, her living warmth. I knew I would probably never have that again, and if I died that night, or if she did, I wanted to have that memory alive in my mind to the last moment.

I resisted the temptation to speed. I needed to remain inconspicuous, and I knew that when Abbassi left the club, as he must, Gantrie would let me know. So I could take my time and think things through. In the parking garage I had taken my Smith & Wesson 500 with the short barrel from the trunk of the Zombie, and slipped it into my waistband. I didn't plan to kill anyone just then, but I wanted to make an impression on Abbassi when I spoke to him. I wasn't going to go into the club after him. If my hunch about what was going to happen at the UN the next day was right, Abbassi would be leaving within the next hour or two. So I could wait for him outside, where there would be less witnesses to what went down.

I parked at a meter outside the Sushiden Restaurant, with a clear view of the 49 Club entrance in the arcade. I called Gantrie.

"Talk to me."

"There's not a lot happening, man. It's hard to tell, but I think he's been moving toward the door. He keeps stopping. He's probably talking to people. You there? You going inside?"

"No, I'm outside, waiting for him near the door."

"What's happening, dude? You should tell me..."

I gave him the bones of what I suspected and he went quiet. Eventually, he said, "Man, that is so fucked up. What is wrong with people?"

"I don't know, Gantrie. Maybe nothing. Maybe this is just what people are like."

"I don't want to believe that, dude. Wait! He's on the move. He's going for the door!"

"I'll call you."

I climbed out of the Zombie and into the milling crowds that populate the streets of the City that Never Sleeps. I crossed toward the brightly lit doorway of the 49 Club. There was no long line or throng waiting. It was invitation only and if you weren't on the list, you didn't get in. I strolled to the arcade and stopped just past the door to light a cigarette. The doorman watched me for a moment with incurious eyes, then looked away. The door opened as I inhaled. I glanced over and saw Abbassi, in an evening suit, step onto the sidewalk. He was maybe four or five long strides away, looking toward the street. I half frowned and half smiled for the benefit of the doorman. Then I stepped toward him and called out, "Hey, Abdul! How you doing, man? Long time no see!"

By the time I'd finished, I was drawing level with him and he'd turned to look at me. He frowned. I knew him well. I had studied every feature of his face, every movement and mannerism of his body. But I had done it from a distance and he had never seen me. He didn't know me. Not yet. He shook his head. I smiled.

"Don't you remember me? Yeah, man, you remember, from Baykhan!"

I saw him freeze. I shifted my jacket, pulled the Smith and Wesson with my left hand, and rammed it into his side while I put my right arm around his shoulders. I spoke quietly, still smiling broadly. "This is a Smith & Wesson 500, Abbassi. It's loaded with 700 grain ammo. If I pull the trigger, it will blow you in half. And believe me, if you give me cause, there is nothing I would rather do. So smile and laugh and walk with me, and maybe you'll get through the night alive."

We started walking toward my car. I kept talking as we went.

"Do you remember Baykhan? I was the guy you were looking for. All those old men and women and children you killed? They were all innocent. They hadn't helped me at all. I stole the water. How does it feel to have the blood of innocent children on your hands, Abbassi?"

His breathing had grown shallower and faster. I knew he was thinking of making a run. I gripped his shoulder with my hand. "I don't need to kill you, Abbassi. I can just blow your leg off. Do I need to do that?"

He shook his head. "No. Who the hell are you?"

"I am your nemesis. I am real bad news. But if you cooperate with me, we'll have a little chat, then I leave and you continue on your murderous way."

We were approaching the trunk of my car. He glanced at me sidelong. "Are you CIA? Delta?"

I snorted. "This is a private enterprise, pal. Relax. You're not going to prison. I just want to talk to you." I popped the trunk, pushed him toward it and said, "Hand me that kit bag."

Then three things happened almost simultaneously. I heard Mclean's voice shout, "*Freeze, Walker!*", I smashed Abbassi in the head with the revolver and heaved him into the trunk, and, as I slammed it shut, I looked around to locate where Mclean was.

He was halfway across the road, with Jones, and they were running toward me. By the look on their faces and the snub-nosed .38s in their hands, I guessed it wasn't with the purpose of greeting an old pal. I didn't want to get shot, and I sure as hell didn't want to start shooting Feds, so I shoved my piece back in my waistband and went to meet them with my hands raised, shouting, "*OK! OK! OK!*"

All around us, people were screaming and running, backing away and peering at us from a distance as that familiar scene from the TV was played out in real life for them. Mclean and Jones took up their stances, training their guns on me, and shouted again, "*Freeze! Get on the ground! Hands behind your head!*"

I dropped to the ground, but not as they expected. I did a fast, low, spinning sweep and knocked Mclean's feet from under him. He landed on his back with a big *whoomph!* that sounded painful. But by then I was already standing again and moving. I stepped toward Jones, who was wide-eyed and gaping down at his partner. I levered his piece out of his fingers with my left and put a straight right into his jaw. Then I ran back to the Zombie, climbed in, and moved out of there, burning rubber.

I made it to Madison Avenue and headed north at a steady pace. There was silence from the trunk, so I figured I'd knocked him unconscious. I didn't think I'd hit him hard enough to kill him. If I had, we had a real problem.

I crossed over the Madison Avenue Bridge and turned east toward Hunts Point. There was a dive there on Bryant Avenue where you could rent rooms by the hour for cash, no questions asked. Most of the screams you heard in that place were simulated pleasure, but not all of them.

Fifteen minutes later, I pulled off Randall Avenue, past the fat, half-naked girls standing on the corner in red vinyl skirts and leather pants, and crawled up toward the rooming house. I parked out front and went inside. Joe, hairy, toothless, and unshaven, was sitting behind his counter smoking. He blinked at me as I came in.

"I need a room. Top floor. Four hundred bucks says you keep quiet. I'll be back if you tell anyone I was here."

He shrugged and spat on the colorless, threadbare carpet. I handed him the money and he handed me a key. I went out to the car, opened the trunk, and dragged Abbassi out. He was awake but he was groggy and bleeding from his head. I pulled my piece, shoved it in his back, and said, "Walk!" Joe was reading a magazine as we climbed the bare, wooden stairs. He didn't see a thing.

Upstairs, I pushed him into the room. It was a seedy box with a single bare bulb, a black window, an old bed, and a chair. I locked the door and told him to strip down to his underwear. Then I dragged the chair to the middle of the floor, facing the bed, and made him sit on it. I pulled the three sets of cuffs from my jacket that I'd collected before I left my apartment. I cuffed his wrists to the back and his ankles to the legs. When I was done, I switched my cell phone to record. Then I sat opposite him and lit a cigarette. He looked scared. I figured he wasn't used to being on the receiving end of torture, but he was recognizing the lead up to it. I inhaled deeply and blew smoke up at the ceiling.

"You going to be tough, Abbassi?"

"I don't know what you mean."

"You know what happened to Aatifa, don't you?" His skin went pasty. I went on. "He talked. He was very cooperative, but I needed him to know that I was not bluffing. Do I need to prove that to you?"

He shook his head. I sighed, as though I was losing patience.

"Let's get some ground rules clear, Abbassi. When I ask you a question, you give me clear, succinct answers. I have no time for ambiguities or body language. Don't nod or shake your head at me. Talk to me. Do you understand?"

He swallowed hard. "Yes. I want to cooperate with you."

"What is contained in the canister that will be ruptured by the bomb at the UN?"

"SF2, it is a genetically modified virus..."

"I know what SF2 is. I also know that it is a theoretical biological agent. It has never been manufactured."

He nodded. "That was true until recently, but Professor Benjamin Wilde, at the Biochem Labs in Virginia, he produced a sample for us..."

I interrupted him. "Benjamin Wilde?"

"Yes..."

"Is he here now, in New York?"

"Yes."

"Was he at the Hennessy debate?"

"Yes, it was former President Dick Hennessy who introduced Professor Wilde to the Prince, knowing that they could do business. The Professor was looking for a buyer. They came to Prince Awad's house after, to discuss the disturbance..."

Ben.

Ben had sold the canister to Awad, to plant at the conference. I stood and went to the window and leaned against the frame, looking down at the filthy yard with its trash cans and limp, dingy washing hanging out to dry in the night. I said, "Why?" He didn't answer and I turned to face him. "Why?"

His bottom lip was quivering and he had tears streaming down his cheeks. He reminded me of a woman I had seen once, kneeling at his feet, weeping just that same way. I figured, absently, that that made me like him. I reached down and pulled my knife from my boot.

"Why, Abbassi?"

FIFTEEN

Maybe the question triggered some deep conditioning inside him, because a fearful, resentful anger twisted his face and he thrust his chin out at me. "You fucking Americans! You think you own the world! You and fucking Israel, marching everywhere with your tanks and your missiles, murdering Arab women and children! Killing in Palestine, killing in Syria, in Iraq! Stealing our oil and our land!"

I rested my ass on the windowsill, waiting. I could see the hysteria building in him, like the rage of a cornered rat. His voice rose to an ugly whine. "You fucking imperialists! You make war on us because you care only about our oil! You are *shaytan*! You ally with the Israeli, Jewish pigs to rape our country and steal from us! *But Allah is merciful! Allah is great! He will guide our hand in war and we will kill you all! All of you will die!*"

He rasped in his throat and spat at me. It was ineffectual and sprayed over the filthy bed. He went on.

"You can kill me! You can torture me! Like you torture our brothers in Guantanamo! But you cannot torture Allah! You cannot kill Allah!"

His voice trailed off. His eyes were wide with terror. I sucked on my cigarette again and as I let out the smoke I said, "Murdering Arab women and children..."

"Every day in Syria, in Afghanistan!"

"Like Sayad, last year, where you teamed up with ISIS and wiped out an entire village, murdering fifty women and children. Arab women and children."

He screamed, "*They were collaborators! They will burn for eternity in hell! You cannot do this to me! It is against the Geneva convention!*"

"Really? They will burn in hell for eternity? Even the kids? Like the thirty kids and the thirty-seven women you murdered because you thought one of them had given me water? And they were all innocent of the crime you accused them of."

He screamed again, hysterical with terror, "*They were collaborators! They were infidels! God has said: The unbelievers among the People of the Book and the pagans shall burn for ever in the fire of Hell, for they are the vilest of creatures! God has said, in Repentance 9:73, 'Prophet! Make war on the unbelievers and the hypocrites and deal rigorously with them. Hell shall be their home!'*"

I said quietly, "And you are the instrument of God's wrath and punishment, right?"

He stared at me a moment before answering.

"We are all the instruments of God. Allah is merciful. But only some see it. You who are blind will burn for eternity! It is written. And the angels shall laugh at your suffering, and mock you."

"And that gives you the right to massacre women and children."

"To fight the *kafir* is the greatest thing that a Muslim can do, and he will live in the grace of Allah for it! Nothing is so hateful in the sight of Allah as a *kafir*! Allah has spoken through Mohamed, 'When the sacred months are over, slay the idolaters wherever you find them!'"

"And that is why you are placing this bomb at the UN."

He spat at me again. "And because Islam is uprising. We are sick of your exploitation, of your imperialism, of your looting and raping of our countries!"

"And I guess Prince Awad feels that way too, huh?" He didn't answer. He just stared at me. I went on. "Prince Awad, who stands at around number forty in the Forbes list of the world's richest men."

"Allah is merciful! Allah has guided his hand!"

"You're full of shit, Abbassi. You know who owns Arabian oil? You know it as well as I do. Arpetco, the Arabian Petroleum Company. It's state owned, which means it's owned by the Awad family, because they are the state. If anybody is raping and pillaging the wealth of your country, it's them. Now cut the bullshit and answer my question. What does Awad gain by bombing the conference?" He drew breath, I could see he still had that crazed look in his eye so I cut him short. "One more crazy bullshit answer and I will take your thumb off. Give me a straight answer that does not involve Allah or the great *shaytan*."

He swallowed.

"The climate is changing. There are droughts coming

and crops will soon start to fail. When the crops fail, there will not be enough food for everyone. There is very little agriculture in our countries, and the people will starve." He leaned forward. "There are too many people in the world—too many unbelievers! Africa and Arabia, the Muslim world, will suffer most, because the Jews and the Christians own all the good land! The believers will starve in the streets, and the west will turn its back on us, like always! Steal what is ours and laugh! Let the Muslims die! It is not your problem!"

"Stay focused, Abbassi."

"Professor Benjamin Wilde gave the Prince information, that you fucking Americans are hoarding genetically modified seeds! Seeds that can grow in drought conditions! You can water with salt water! Grow anywhere! Denying these seeds to the Muslims so that we die of hunger and thirst when the sky burns!" He paused, staring at me with rage in his face. "So we bomb your fucking UN! Which is the fucking servant of the U.S.! To make the world wake up to the Muslim problem! We are exploited! Enslaved by the U.S.! But Allah will guide our hand in war and now, when the Earth is burning and people are dying with no food and no water, we will bring suffering to you and we will take what is ours!"

I shook my head. "You don't hear yourself, do you?"

"Eh?"

"Never mind." I frowned and scratched my head, trying to make some sense of what he said. "So the bomb is to bring the Muslim plight to the attention of the world?"

"It is the will of Allah. Allah is merciful!"

"Yeah, he's doing a great job." I stared out the window again, down at the filthy yard. I didn't think Abbassi had any more idea of why he was bombing the conference than I had. He'd been told Allah wanted him to do it, and that was all he needed to know. He'd been fed reasons he wanted to believe, that fit in with his own, twisted view of the world, and he didn't question them. I wondered for a moment if even Prince Awad knew the real reason why he was bombing the conference.

I turned back to Abbassi. He hadn't been hurt so far, not badly, he'd given me a lot of mouth and got no comeback, so he was looking defiant.

"OK, Abbassi, here's the million dollar question. Give me bullshit and I start taking you apart. Literally."

He swallowed and the defiance slipped a little from his face. "What?"

"Where is it?"

His lip started quivering again. "I don't know. Please. I don't know..."

"Who does know?"

His head went on one side and he started sobbing. "I don't know. Please. I don't know. I am just..."

I sighed. "What? Just a warrior of God? A jihadist?"

"Please, I don't know. I don't where it is, please."

"Aatifa, Ali, and Hassan were going to deliver it to the conference. Now they are dead. You must have made alternative plans."

He was shaking his head. "No, no, I'll tell you everything I know. I'll tell you. That was a distraction. They were meant to get caught. It was not the real bomb. I don't know where the real bomb is. Only one person knows..."

"That was a feint? They were meant to get caught at the entrance?"

"Yes! The canister was empty!"

"So the real bomb?"

"I am not told. This was not my mission! My mission was to prepare the false bomb!"

"Jesus Christ! The whole damned thing…!"

"I did not plan it! I did not plan it!"

I snarled at him, "Who employed you?"

"Prince Awad!"

"How did he choose you?"

He was sobbing noisily. "I don't know! I don't know! Please, be merciful! I have answered your questions! I have told you everything I know! Please! Be merciful!"

I stared at him. "Should I learn from you, Abbassi? Should I learn from you how to be merciful?"

He rolled his eyes up to the ceiling, like he'd gone into some kind of idiot trance. "*Allah! Allah!*"

"Like you were merciful with the women and children at Sayad and Baykhan?"

"*Please!*"

And that was when the door burst in, and Mclean and Jones stood silhouetted, training their guns on me. "*Freeze, Walker! Get on your face!*"

I sighed. "Jesus, Mclean! Where were you when they were handing out brains? Did you get the files I sent you?"

"*Get on your face!*"

"No. Just listen to me, will you? This man is involved in a plot to bomb the UN conference in about nine hours…"

"*I don't want to hear it! For the last time! Get on your face!*"

I raised my hands. "I am unarmed, Mclean. Even you

can't be stupid enough to shoot an unarmed man. Do you know who this guy is?"

He glanced at Abbassi, who started burbling, "I am Abdul Abbassi! I am attached to the Embassy! I have diplomatic immunity! I am an aide to Prince Mohamed bin Awad! You are required by law to release me!"

"Do not release him, Mclean! This man is a dangerous terrorist! Do *not* release him!"

Mclean jerked his head at Jones, who holstered his .38, moved to Abbassi, and inspected the cuffs. He glanced at Mclean. "They're standard cuffs." He reached in his pocket and pulled out his standard keys. I said, "Jones! For crying out loud! This man is a killer!"

Mclean shouted, "*Shut up, Walker! I've about had it with you!*"

Abbassi was standing, rubbing his wrists. Jones was kneeling at his feet, unlocking the cuffs on his ankles. I said, "Mclean, for crying out loud..."

Abbassi bent down, muttering, "Allow me to help..."

I pointed and shouted, "*Jones!*"

But it was too late. Abbassi had his gun in his hand. He turned, smiling, and fired at Mclean. I saw the red hole in his chest and the plume of red gore explode from his back. Then, in a single, fluid movement Abbassi had hammered down with the butt of the gun on Jones' head, and as the FBI man sagged and sprawled on the floor, Abbassi emptied two rounds into his heart. I was reaching for my Smith & Wesson behind my back, but he was already aiming at me, pulling the trigger. I dropped to the floor, heard two explosions and the glass shatter above me. Then he was grabbing his clothes, running down the corridor. I scrambled to my feet. Jones was dead, but Mclean was gasping.

I grabbed my cell and called 911. When they answered I said, "Shut up! Two FBI agents down, critical, Bryant Avenue, the Bronx!" Then I hung up.

Mclean was staring at me, trying to talk. I said, "I warned you. I sent you the damned files." Then I reached in his jacket and pulled out his badge. I showed it to him. "I'm going to borrow this. I may need it."

I went after Abbassi. I ran down the stairs, taking them three at a time. In reception, Joe looked worried and I went over to him and grabbed him by the scruff of his filthy neck. "You have two Feds upstairs, Joe, that you should not have let in. That guy who ran out in his shorts just now? He shot them. You are going to have a lot of trouble now, pal. But that is nothing compared to what you'll have if you mention me. Look at me. Listen to me. I will come back and I will feed you your own dick. You understand me?"

He nodded and I left, wondering how they'd found me. I climbed in my car, knowing there was probably an APB out on it. I took off north, up Bryant to Spofford Avenue and turned west as far as Tiffany Street. There I turned left again into the industrial units. They were dim and lonely. It was late and the whores had all gone home, leaving the sad, yellow light of the street lamps to wait for the gray dawn alone.

I knew I didn't have long. Pretty soon the whole of Hunts Point would be crawling with cops and Feds. I needed to move fast. I turned right onto Randall Avenue, right again into some dark alley, then sharp left and over Truxton into 156th. There I stopped outside an industrial unit with a parking lot full of trucks. It was sealed off with a steel fence and a padlock. I checked my watch. It was fifteen minutes after three. I had less than nine hours.

I climbed out and with my Swiss Army knife, I removed my plates. I vaulted the fence, wondering if I had triggered an alarm. I ignored the possibility and set to work removing the plates from a truck at the back of the lot, where it wouldn't be noticed by cops with flashlights. It took me less than five minutes. Then I clambered back over and fitted the plates to the Zombie.

As I pulled away, headed north, I could hear the sirens descending on Bryant Avenue. And somewhere above, there was a chopper circling. I kept going, taking random turns for no particular reason, going back on myself, around in circles, but always moving north and always west, until I finally came to the Alexander Hamilton Bridge, pretty sure I wasn't being tailed. There I crossed over into Washington Heights and finally, I started to head south, toward Midtown.

At three-forty AM I finally came to West 42nd and turned east in the direction of the United Nations Head-quarters. At that time the traffic had a restless, prowling, predatory look. What had F. Scott Fitzgerald called it? The long, dark night of the soul, where it is always three o'clock in the morning. But I was closing in on four o'clock, with eight hours to go. I left my car on the corner of 1st Avenue, lit a cigarette, and took a walk up as far as the Sutton Bar, which I knew was open all night.

As I walked, the horizon beyond the East River was already touched with the first gray light of pre-dawn. My footsteps were loud on the sidewalk and, far off, an accelerating car and a woman's shouts made a strange, lonely counterpoint.

I pushed through the door of the small bar into the desultory laughter and conversation of those people left at the tail end of the night. They sat, a couple of small groups at small tables, leaning in to each other, wanting to take one more laugh, one more drink, maybe one more promise of love before they went back to an empty bed, or at least a bed that felt empty.

I sat at the bar and ordered a Bushmills straight up from a barman who looked bored and tired. I tried not to think about Marni, about what she was doing right then, what she would be doing in the last moments if I failed.

If I failed.

If I failed at what? I didn't even know what I was doing there. I didn't know what my plan was, or even what its precise objective was. The number of questions that needed to be answered was overwhelming. Was it a bomb? If it was, where was it? Was it in the General Assembly Hall? Was it in the parking garage? Was it in the wasteland nearby? Was it biochemical? And that was just the tip of the iceberg.

I knew that if I considered all the questions at the same time, my mind would seize up. I needed to select one single question and work from there. And the one that was staring at me, the one that was shining bright, was, if the bomb that Abbassi and his team were supposed to plant was a fake, if that was misdirection, then what was the other hand doing? Where was the other device going to be placed?

I tried to visualize the scene. Abbassi had assured them they could get through security carrying their pieces of the bomb. I could hear the recording in my mind. "...*Don't* worry about that, Ali, that is not your concern. Trust me, that has been taken care of. I have the components here for you. You will each carry a separate part. Ali, you will carry the C4. Hassan, you will carry the detonator, Aatifa, you will carry the agent. You will arrive separately on Friday, at eleven o'clock, eleven fifteen, and eleven thirty. You will not be detected at security. Forget about that. Forget about that! You go down to the basement at exactly eleven thirty-five..."

But he had lied to them. They would be seized at security. And hard as I tried, I could not see how that would allow for the placing of a different bomb. Unless the bomb was already there.

I took a pull on my whiskey and savored it slowly. It still didn't make any sense. If this was misdirection, it meant that while everybody's attention was on Aatifa and his team, the real bomb had to be slipped in some other way; not through the main gate. Through the parking garage then? But that didn't work either, because the seizure of the three at the gate would not affect security in the garage.

Not only that, but the discovery of the bomb would in all probability trigger an immediate shutdown of the conference. Especially after the protest that broke out at the Hennessy debate. And that would rob them of their target.

All I could think of was that parts of the bomb had somehow been smuggled in already and were being assembled. With about seven thousand people working at the complex, it would not be so hard to find a handful of sympathizers to do that job. Perhaps the misdirection planned for today was to smuggle in the detonator, or some other essential part.

Or perhaps I was thinking about it all wrong. Perhaps

whatever they had planned had been scrapped because I'd killed the team. Either way, I had to get in there and try to find the device if there was one. Or, if that failed, alert security to the possibility of a bomb.

And that raised another question. How the hell was I going to get in? I fished out Mclean's badge. At a pinch, if you didn't look too close, I could pass for him. I smiled. He lacked my rugged good looks, but what the hell!

If I failed, I wouldn't have any looks at all.

SIXTEEN

My plan was: make it up as you go along.

I walked down First Avenue as dawn turned the air a grainy shade of gray, as the lights that had burned through the night died, one by one, and the seagulls cried out in despair over the mournful bray of barges and boats that plowed through the fragile light of the new day. It was thirty minutes after five AM, seven and a half hours to go, and I was making it up as I went along.

That was my plan.

I figured that from five or six in the morning, people involved one way or another in technical support would be turning up. Janitors, electricians, gas maintenance, plumbers, cleaners, you name it. They'd be turning up before the daily rush, and a lot of them would be using vans, and they'd be leaving those vans in the parking garage.

At five forty-five, as the sun warped molten over Brooklyn, I was at the top of the ramp that led to the basements beneath the UN building. Out of 42nd Street, I saw a van pull onto the avenue. It had a logo on the side that read, 'The Tech Guys', and it moved into the near lane and slowed with its indicator on as it approached the ramp. I pulled out Mclean's badge, held it up for the driver to see, and signaled him to stop. He did and I stepped around to the passenger side and opened the door. I climbed in, waved the badge at him again, and said, "Special Agent Harrison Mclean. I'm not here. Carry on."

He stared at me and his expression was skeptical. "Uh, can I see your badge again?"

I looked at him with dead eyes and pulled the revolver. "Sure. Here it is. This is a Smith & Wesson 500, loaded with seven hundred grain flat-nose hard cast. It will punch right through four layers of concrete. Will that do?"

"OK, pal. Take it easy. I don't want any trouble."

"You won't get any. Just do what you normally do every morning when you get here, and nobody will get hurt."

"OK, mister."

I jerked my head toward the garage. "They going to check your papers?"

"Yeah."

"Will he want my papers, too?"

He shook his head. "No, sometimes I bring an assistant."

"If this goes bad, I'll shoot you, you realize that?"

"Look, man. I don't know if he will or not. He never has before."

"OK, get going."

We moved down the ramp and into the dark maw of the first basement. We stopped at a barrier and a guard in uniform came out of his office. My driver showed him his papers and the guard waved him on. We wound down through two basements into the dark bowels of the building and finally came to a halt in a bay near the elevators. There he stopped and stared at me. I could see he was scared. The smart thing would have been to throw him in the back and tie him up.

But what if I failed?

"What's your name?"

"Danny."

"You married, Danny?"

He thought about it, weighing up the consequences of a guy like me having that kind of knowledge. I saw his left hand drop out of view and he shook his head.

"Nah. Not my scene."

I smiled. "How come you're wearing a wedding ring?"

He shook his head. "Ah, we broke up. I wear it out of habit."

I sighed. "Kids?"

He went pale and swallowed hard. "No!"

"OK, Danny, here's my problem. I'm the good guy. I'm going to tell you something, and you are going to think I'm crazy, but I'm not. Somewhere in this building there is a bomb. It's a dirty bomb. You know what that is?"

He nodded. "It has some kind of biochemical agent..."

I nodded. "Yeah, something like that. It will go off at shortly after noon. I have told the Feds but, like you, they think I'm crazy. So I have to find that bomb. Now, here is my problem. What do I do with you? If I tie you up and put you in the back of the van, and fail to find the bomb..."

I let the words hang. He stared at me with dawning horror on his face. "You want me to help you find the bomb?"

I laughed. "No, what I want you to do is go back to your wife, collect your kids, and make sure you are in Pennsylvania by twelve o'clock."

He gaped at me. "Seriously?"

"Yeah, seriously. But how do I know you will not go straight to security and tell them there is some nut job in the basement who is probably going to place a bomb?"

He thought about it. "Well, I guess, if you were a real nut job and your story wasn't true, you probably..." He faltered and trailed off. "You'd probably kill me."

I nodded. "Yeah, Danny. I probably would." I opened the door and climbed out. "Get out of here. Get your loved ones and go. If twelve o'clock comes and there is nothing on the news, you'll know I found it."

He stared at me for a long moment, then seemed to snap out of it, reached in his pocket, and pulled out a technician's badge and an electronic key. He handed them to me. "These will get you in most places. Obviously there are some highly restricted areas, but the chances of a bomb being in there..." He shrugged. "The PIN that goes with the key is 1776, year of independence. You better take my toolbox, too."

I took them. "Thanks."

I watched his tail lights disappear up the ramp and wondered if I had done the right thing, or if I was growing soft in my thirties.

Now that I was in, I wasn't sure what to do next. Like I said, I was making it up as I went along. I had no idea how many levels the parking garage had. With almost seven thousand employees, it could be any number. But my gut told me, if they were going for something spectacular, the bomb was more likely to be somewhere between the first basement, where conference rooms four through thirteen were, and the fourth floor. Conference room four was large and had a gallery on the first floor. The General Assembly Hall was on the second floor, but it had galleries on the third and fourth. And it made sense, if they wanted to kill Marni and Gibbons in some spectacular way, then the bomb had to be in that area.

I figured there would be metal detectors at the access points to the main building, so I put the revolver into the toolbox and left it beside a trash can, then made my way to the elevators and rode up to the first basement. I came out opposite the bookstore. It was closed. At that time of the morning, everything was closed, the coffee shop, the gift shop, the kiosk, and the bank. I turned right and walked to the johns. I inspected the ladies' first and then the men's. Every cubicle. But there was nothing.

After that, I checked the briefing room and started to work my way methodically through each of the conference rooms. Danny's key gave me access to all of them. I checked under every seat, on every stage, every dais, I scoured every inch of them, but there was nothing. A device capable of doing the kind of damage that Awad and Abbassi seemed intent on doing is not small. It is not easy to conceal. But I could not find anything at all that was even suggestive of that kind of device.

The next four floors gave me the same result, and by nine o'clock I was exhausted and out of ideas. I made my way to the vast main lobby and stared at the great, plate-glass doors, watching security open up and start to admit the steady flow of visitors from across the globe. They straggled in, passing through the big airport-style security scanners. It was nine-thirty, two and a half hours to go, and I was out of ideas, numb, and my brain was too tired to think.

I had two and a half hours, and I had nothing.

I watched a group admitted with their tour guide or, as they liked to be called, ambassador to the people. Most of the group were young, in their late teens and early twenties. Some of them looked Latin or Mediterranean, others looked Scandinavian or German. They all had the young person's uniform of jeans, anorak, and stupid, half-sized rucksack, with a bottle of water in their hands. They were all smiling, some were laughing. They were the confident heirs to the new, global world, designed by Gene Roddenberry, where everything conformed to the three 'Hs': it was wholesome, hygienic, and humanitarian.

I rubbed my face. My brain ached. I searched it for a solution. There wasn't one. A second tour was coming in, led by an attractive, well-dressed woman. There was a family, a father, a mother and three kids. Behind them was an old woman, maybe in her eighties—maybe old enough to remember the end of the war and the building of the UN HQ. She was in a wheelchair being pushed by a young man. In less than three hours, all of these people would die if I didn't do something.

I had one last card to play. It was desperate, but it was all I had left. I wanted to discuss it with Marni, so I made my way to the public telephones and called my apartment. It rang for a long while, then went to my answering service. She might have gone out for breakfast, or she might be sleeping late. I called her cell. It was switched off or unavailable. I thought for a long moment, then tried again, both numbers, with the same result.

I had to make a decision, but I was out of options, so that meant there was only one decision to make. I had to go and see David Staines. I had to convince him that I was not crazy, and that there was a plot to plant a bomb at the UN. You'd think that such an allegation, coming from somebody like me, might make them shift their asses enough to look into it, but I guess like everybody else in the great machine that is western society, they were engaged in risk assessment and risk management. What was the biggest risk? Canceling the Conference of the Century because some kook said there was a bomb, and then winding up with egg on your face and a PR disaster, or going ahead with the Conference of the Century and having it bombed?

From my perspective and the average guy on the street's, the answer might seem simple and obvious. But the higher up the ladder you climb in the termite hill that is western society, the more your perspective tends to warp. As Ben had said to me, from Omega's perspective, sooner or later, all those termites are going to die, and most of their lives will have been insignificant. So when the vast majority of people's lives become insignificant to you, what *is* important? Some abstract idea like obedience, or belonging? I didn't know the answer to that. All I knew was that I had one last shot left, and I had to take it.

I walked to the elevators and rode up to David Staines' floor. I walked down the long passage with a sense of unreality haunting me. I barely believed myself what I was going to tell him. How the hell could I expect him to believe it?

I knocked on his door and almost immediately it was yanked open. He had his coat in his hand, like he was about to hang it up. He frowned at me from his deceptively flabby face and said, "You?" Then his eyes went to my clip-on name tag, and then back to my face. "You're not Danny Heinz."

"No, I'm Lacklan Walker, and I need to talk to you. More than that, I need you to listen to me."

"Is it about Dr. Marni Gilbert?"

I shook my head. "No. It's not. I've spoken to her and to Professor Gibbons. This is much more serious, Mr. Staines. I really need you to listen to me."

He examined my face a moment, then heaved a big sigh and stepped back. "Fine, come in. Take a seat."

I went in. He closed the door and hung up his coat. Then he sat behind his desk and I sat opposite him in a strange reenactment of our first meeting.

"I haven't got a lot of time, Mr. Walker, I have to catch a flight in about an hour. So I'd appreciate it if you made this brief."

I smiled, thinking about the irony of his words. He had no idea how little time he had.

"Mr. Staines, somebody has planted a bomb, or is going to plant a bomb, to detonate during Marni Gilbert and Professor Philip Gibbons' talk. The bomb was planted by agents working for ISIS under instructions from Abdul Abbassi, formerly a member of the Taliban, now probably freelancing for ISIS." He was staring at me like I was crazy. He went to speak and I raised my hand. "Please wait. I haven't finished. I know this because I bugged the house they had in the Bronx. I can get the audio files to you. I have already forwarded them to Special Agent Harrison Mclean of the FBI. He is currently either dead or in surgery for a bullet wound to the chest inflicted by Abdul Abbassi. I have on my phone a recording of my interrogation of that man, during which he admits that there is a bomb. Now that is not everything, Mr. Staines. There is one more very important point. The bomb is a dirty bomb, and when it detonates, it will not only kill a lot of people in this building. It will probably kill tens of thousands of people in New York. Maybe more even than that. I realize that this sounds crazy. But let me ask you something. If you had been the Commander at the First Precinct on the morning of the eleventh of September, 2001, and I had come in to you and said Islamic terrorists were going to fly two airliners into the World Trade Center, would you have thought I was crazy? Well, Mr. Staines, this is considerably less crazy than that."

He stared at me for a slow count of three, then screwed up his eyes and shook his head.

"...*What?*"

I looked at my watch.

"We have just two hours. What are you going to do?"

SEVENTEEN

"First you come in here demanding to see Dr. Marni Gilbert based on some story about your childhood relationship. Now you barge in, wearing an ID badge that does not belong to you, spouting some cock and bull story about Islamic terrorists and dirty bombs! And you expect me to *cancel* what is arguably the most important conference in recent history, on the basis of this..." He was momentarily lost for words and waved his hand at me. "*Crap!* Well the answer is *no!* Mr. Walker, *absolutely not!* And furthermore, *get out!* Or I will have security throw you out!"

I raised a hand. A wave of exhaustion washed over me. "I know it sounds crazy, Mr. Staines..."

"*Sounds crazy?* No, Mr. Walker, it *is* crazy! Have you any conception of how difficult it would be to get a weapon into this building?" He shook his head. "It isn't difficult. It's not. It's *impossible!* And as for the kind of device you are talking about, it would weigh *at least* two hundred and fifty pounds. And you expect me to believe that a handful of terrorists are going to *slip* this thing past security without being noticed? You are out of your mind!"

It was what I had expected him to say. It was what I would have said if anybody had told me this story. I sighed. "Will you at least...?"

"No! I am not going to do anything!" He leaned forward with his elbows on the desk, staring at me like he couldn't decide if I was stupid or crazy or both. "The research Dr. Gilbert and Professor Gibbons are going to present this afternoon is so shattering it will change the course of history. I have a responsibility to ensure that this conference goes ahead and it will take a lot more than the insane babblings of a maniac to make me do *anything*, Mr. Walker!"

I repeated, "Will you at least listen to my interrogation of Abdul Abbassi?"

He sighed noisily, puffing out his cheeks, like I was really boring him. He glanced at his watch. "How long is it?"

"Not very long, Mr. Staines." I reached in my pocket, pulled out the phone, and found the recording. Before clicking play, I looked him in the eye. "I understand everything you say, but you also need to be asking yourself, if Marni and Professor Gibbons' talk is so important to the future of our world, do you really want to be the man who allowed them to get killed?"

I pressed 'play', there was a moment's silence, and then my voice spoke, threatening to torture Abbassi the same way I had tortured Aatifa. It wasn't a great start. When Abbassi made his references to Former President Dick Hennessy and Prince Awad in connection with the sale of SF2, Staines narrowed his eyes at me and sighed, shaking his head. But as the recording progressed, he became more serious and listened more attentively.

At one point he reached over and paused it. "Who is to say that this is authentic, Mr. Walker? Why should I believe that this is not just something that you have staged?"

I thought about it for a moment. Then I shrugged. "Because if I had staged it, I would have put myself in a much better light. I would not have presented myself as a desperate man prepared to resort to torture. And I would have made Abbassi more convincing." He stared at me, uncertain what to believe. I hesitated. "You remember the massacre at Sayad, in northern Afghanistan?"

He nodded. "Yes, of course. It was one of the rare occasions when the Taliban and ISIS cooperated."

"That was Abbassi. He was with the Taliban. And the later massacre at Baykhan, that earned him the title The Butcher of Helmand. He was hunting for me. We had been ambushed and I was separated from my unit. He suspected the villagers of helping me. They hadn't, but he wiped out the village. This man is now a guest living at Prince Mohamed bin Awad's house on East 79th Street. And I know that Hennessy and this Benjamin Wilde—I know him as Benjamin Brown—I know that they went to Prince Awad's house after the fracas at the debate. I know because I followed them."

He narrowed his eyes at me again, drew breath, shook his head, and sighed. Finally, he said, "*Why?*"

I echoed his sigh. "I can't tell you everything, Mr. Staines, not now. It is a very long, complicated story and we just haven't got the time. But just pause for a moment and think about the interests that are in play here. Think of the stakes. You know yourself that the bulk of the entire planet's wealth is shared between a tiny number of men and women, and you know very well that they have the power to shape international politics."

"You are talking about the Bilderberg conspiracy theory."

"Maybe."

I reached over and pressed play again. We sat in silence and listened to the rest of the recording. At the end, when Mclean and Jones burst in, he looked up at me and studied my face while he listened. The last words audible were mine, speaking to the 911 operator:

"*Shut up! Two FBI Agents down, critical, Bryant Avenue, the Bronx!*" Then there was silence, followed by my voice again, harsh and brief, "*I warned you. I sent you the damned files.*" Another pause, and then, "*...I'm going to borrow this. I may need it.*" Then the recording abruptly finished.

"What was that?"

"Special Agents Harrison Mclean and Daren Jones. I had tried to warn them, as I have tried to warn you. Just like you, they thought I was crazy. I had Abbassi handcuffed to a chair. Jones made the mistake of un-cuffing him. Abbassi took his weapon and shot them both. I called 911, but Jones was already dead." I reached in my pocket, pulled out Mclean's badge and threw it on the desk. "I borrowed this to help me get in here."

He stared at it a moment, then picked it up and examined it. I said, "If I were you, I would call the Bureau, you must have a contact there, and ask them about Jones and Mclean." We stared at each other a moment. I pressed him, "This is not a hoax, Mr. Staines, whether the bomb is inside the building or not, whether it is possible or not to get it in, there is a plot to bomb the conference."

"How do I know you did not shoot these agents yourself?"

My exasperation was dampened by my exhaustion. "For crying out loud, Staines! Listen to the damned thing again! I clearly warned them not to release him!"

I reached over, took the phone from his fingers, found the spot and switched it on again. "Listen to it!"

It started with Mclean's voice shouting.

"Freeze, Walker! Get on your face!"

"Jesus, Mclean! Where were you when they were handing out brains? Did you get the files I sent you?"

"Get on your face!"

"No. Just listen to me, will you? This man is involved in a plot to bomb the UN conference in about nine hours..."

"I don't want to hear it! For the last time! Get on your face!"

"I am unarmed, Mclean. Even you can't be stupid enough to shoot an unarmed man. Do you know who this guy is?"

"I am Abdul Abbassi! I am attached to the Embassy! I have diplomatic immunity! I am an aide to Prince Mohamed bin Awad! You are required by law to release me!"

"Do not release him, Mclean! This man is a dangerous terrorist! Do *not* release him!"

Some rusting, and then Jones voice: "They're standard cuffs..."

"Jones! For crying out loud! This man is a killer!"

"Shut up, Walker! I've about had it with you!"

"Mclean, for crying out loud..."

Some muttering. Then me again, shouting, "*Jones!*"

A shot followed by a grunt. Then two shots in rapid succession. Then two more shots and the sound of shattering glass. The sound of scrambling, then my voice, urgent: "Shut up! Two FBI Agents down! Critical! Bryant Avenue, the Bronx!" A brief silence, then, "I warned you. I sent you the damned files... I'm going to borrow this. I may need it."

Then silence. I watched him while he stared at my cell. Finally, I said to him, "Does that sound like I shot them...? Does it?"

He rubbed his face with his hands. "Jesus Christ..."

"We haven't got time, Staines. We have..." I checked my watch. "...Barely one and three-quarter hours. You have got to take this on board and *respond!* If I am right and you are wrong, the consequences..."

"I know! I know! You don't need to tell me." He stood. "Very well, Walker. I'll tell you what I'll do. I'll talk to the head of security and get him to talk to the FBI. After that, it's their show."

I studied his face a moment. "Tell me at least that you'll order a search of the building."

"Yes. I'll do that, and I'll have them tighten security at the entrances and the area around the building. Just stay here, will you? I'll be back."

I nodded and he left the office. I picked up the phone and called Marni again. Again there was no response from the apartment, and her phone was either off or had no signal. I swore under my breath. Maybe she had decided to go to Boston after all. Maybe the battery in her phone had died and she hadn't had the chance to charge it.

Maybe.

I stood and went to the window. I looked out at the vast, sparkling sheet of the East River, and Brooklyn across its shimmering surface. I looked at the sun rising through the blue sky toward noon. A feeling of impotence and exhaustion drained through me. I felt I would rather face an army of trained killers than the invincible stupidity of a handful of bureaucrats. I glanced at the clock. It was eleven. I tried to decide whether I had got through to Staines. It was hard to tell. He was taking his time in coming back. Maybe he was organizing a search. A chopper flew over the river, banked and headed north.

I sat and closed my eyes. I needed to sleep. I needed rest, but my brain wouldn't stop racing. I tried Marni again with the same result. When I checked the clock again, it was eleven fifteen.

The door opened behind me and a guy in a suit came in followed by two cops, a man and a woman. They had that blank look that cops reserve for people they think are going to be a problem.

I said, "What's this?"

The suit said, "I am Hans Gunther, head of security. Are you Lacklan Walker?"

"Yes. Where is Staines?"

"This is the man. Arrest him and take him in."

I stared at him. "Now wait a minute! Are you insane?"

They drew their weapons and covered me. The woman said, "Now you had better come quietly, sir! We are putting you under arrest on suspicion of murder. You do not have to say anything, but anything you do say may be taken down and used against you. Cuff him, Bill."

Bill pulled his cuffs with his left hand but kept his .38 in his right, trained on me. He said, "Turn around please, sir."

I shook my head at Gunther. "Was that Staines in the chopper? What will you do when the blast goes off, Hans? It will kill you too, you know."

He didn't answer, but Bill said, "Don't make me use force, sir."

I turned around and put my hands behind my back. I felt the cuffs bite and they pushed me into the corridor. I heard Gunther's voice saying, "Officers, please keep this as discreet as possible. This conference is important and it has to go off without a hitch."

Bill answered, "Don't worry, Mr. Gunther. We'll be discreet."

They took me to the elevators. There was little or no point in breaking free from these cops. In fact, maybe being taken into custody was the best thing I could do. Maybe an interrogation by an NYPD detective was exactly what was required. It might be my last best hope. But there was no time. I kept telling myself, there was no time.

We reached the first floor and stepped into the lobby. It wasn't crowded, but it was getting busy. Directly ahead of us was the information center. Beyond it, on the right, were the main entrance and the stairs to the upper floor. On the left was the meditation room, and just before it the entrance to the gallery overlooking conference room four. I stopped dead in my tracks. There, outside the door to the gallery, was Marni. She was talking urgently to Gibbons, who looked flushed and angry. She glanced at me, frowned for a second, then gave her head a single shake and turned back to

Gibbons. I remembered her words: "...I'll make my own choices. We are what we are, remember?"

I felt a terrible twist in my gut. This was why I loved her and admired her. But now, if I failed, as it seemed I would, I knew that she would die.

Bill gave me a shove and said, "Come on, pal, don't make this hard," and maneuvered me toward the main doors, where the security checks were being carried out on the people entering. I seemed to see it in slow motion. They had two channels set up, like the security channels you go through at an airport, only now they also had sniffer dogs. There were two long lines stretching out into the plaza. Two women wearing bhurkas, and three guys in jeans, with long, straggly beards, were arguing loudly with one of the security guards. In the other channel, people were staring and looking nervous. I saw an elderly man in a wheelchair being pushed by a young couple. They were giving disapproving looks at the group which was making the ruckus.

One of the women suddenly shouted, *Allahu Akbar! Allahu Akbar!* Then the others took up the shout. Security guards started closing on them. Others came running from other parts of the lobby. We kept moving toward the exit. The couple turned away from the ugly scene and pushed the wheelchair forward a few feet as another three or four people passed through the scanners and the metal detectors. Behind them, a group of tourists in the eternal anorak and stupid rucksack uniform, with their little bottles of water, closed in.

As we reached the exit, the five Arabs had taken hold of each other and started chanting, "*U.S. murderers! Allahu Abar! Israel murderers! Allahu Akbar! U.S. murderers! Allahu Abar! Israel murderers! Allahu Akbar!*" And other

Arabs in their line had started joining in. For a moment it looked like the security guards had more on their hands than they could cope with. The guards in the near line paused and looked over. I saw a guy on a radio talking to somebody. More guards appeared across the lobby, trying not to run. The wheelchair went through and so did the couple pushing it. It set off the metal detectors and the guards closed in. Bill opened the door and we stepped outside into the late morning sunshine.

I said to Bill, "What time is it?"

He smiled with more irony than malice. "Why? You got a date?"

"No, Bill, there is going to be a bomb detonated at the conference at twelve o'clock. I want to know how long we have left."

He grinned at his partner. "You hear that, Maria? We have a bomb."

Maria glanced at her watch. "It's eleven thirty. We have half an hour to get away. So who's going to bomb the conference? It ain't easy to do, you know." She smiled at me. "How they gonna get a bomb through that security?"

I looked back over my shoulder, at the long lines feeding in through the vast plate-glass entrance. As we moved toward their patrol car, I muttered, "I think it just got through."

"No way, pal." They opened the back door of the car and I climbed in, still staring back, playing over in my mind what I had just seen. Maria got in the driver's seat and Bill climbed in beside her. As he slammed the door, he said, "They got scanners, metal detectors, and dogs trained to sniff out all types of plastic explosive. There ain't no way anybody's gonna get a bomb in there!"

As he said it, I went cold all over and my scalp prickled. Because suddenly I understood what I had seen. Suddenly, I knew. Maria reversed, turned, and headed for the gate. I caught Bill's eye in the mirror. He frowned. "You OK, pal?"

I shook my head. "There's no time! There is no time!"

I have devoted my life, since I was a kid, to practicing martial arts and exercises designed to gain control over my mind and body, so that I could master every type of combat technique—and also escape techniques. I always assumed I would have to use them in the Middle East, or the Third World. I never expected I'd have to use them on First Avenue in New York in the back of a cop car. But that's the way life is. You just never know what's going to happen next.

I breathed out hard three times, emptied my lungs, rolled back on the seat and, sucking my stomach up into my hollowed chest cavity, pulled my knees up to my chin and curled in on myself. I heard Bill say, "What the hell...!"

It was hard, and I thought I was going to dislocate my shoulders, but I managed to drag my wrists past my ass and then over my ankles. Bill shouted, "*Holy shit!*"

But it was too late. I sucked air back into my lungs, said, "Sorry, pal!" and slammed my two fists into his temple. He slumped, unconscious, and I reached down by his side and grabbed his .38 service revolver. I pointed it at the back of Maria's head and spoke calmly and deliberately.

"I do not want to hurt anybody, Maria, but there is a bomb in that conference hall. It went in as we were coming out. It is going to detonate in half an hour and I have got to get back in there, because if I don't, hundreds of thousands of people will die. Now don't make me choose between you and them."

EIGHTEEN

"OK, MISTER, TAKE IT EASY. WE'RE GOING BACK. Just stay cool, OK?"

"No. Don't bank on it. Put your fucking sirens on and get me back in there!"

She put her sirens on, did a U-turn, and floored the pedal back toward the UN complex while I rummaged in Bill's pockets and found the key to my cuffs. While she drove, she was saying, "I'm telling you it is impossible to get a bomb through..."

I cut across her, speaking savagely. "Conventional explosives, Maria! But did you ever hear of a tactical demolition nuclear device?"

She stared at me in the mirror as we screamed through the gates toward the crowds outside the main entrance. "*What?*"

I took the cuffs from my wrists. "It's the smallest warhead ever built by the U.S. It's designed to be carried in a rucksack. It weighs one hundred and ten pounds and has a

yield of one point five to two kilotons. It will flatten everything in a radius of two miles. That's from the docks in
Brooklyn to Central Park South, and it will kill hundreds of
thousands of people."

"Holy shit!"

She skidded to a halt outside the main doors and turned
in her seat, frowning at me. Her brain told her I was crazy,
but her gut was telling her I wasn't. "But how? I never saw
no hundred and ten pound rucksack! That is one big, heavy
sack!"

I snarled at her, "The damned wheelchair! It was motor-
ized, but they were pushing it!"

"Oh, dear Lord..."

I pulled Mclean's badge from my pocket and stared
fiercely into Maria's face. "You have to help me!" I looked at
my watch. "We have twenty minutes. You can't take the risk!
Think about it. What if I am right?"

She nodded. "OK. Let's do it."

I pushed open the door and we ran toward the entrance,
waving our badges and bellowing, "*Everybody out of here!
Go! Go! Go! There is a bomb in the conference hall! Go! Get
out of here!*"

They didn't run. They gaped and stared at us and at each
other, as the information slowly filtered into their brains.
This was natural selection in action. But either way, it made
no difference. They could not possibly get far enough away
in the time they had. I waded through them, shoving and
pushing them aside, and burst through the doors with Maria
beside me, bellowing at the security guards, "*Evacuate the
area! Evacuate the area! There is a bomb in the General
Assembly Hall!*"

The reaction was the same as it had been outside, with everybody gaping and staring at us and each other. Outside, people were beginning to turn and run, and the panic I had seeded was beginning to spread. I pointed at the security guard in charge of the door and roared at Maria, "*Him! Talk to him! Make him evacuate the area!*"

And while she tackled him, I vaulted the barrier and ran for the stairs up to the second floor, where the General Assembly Hall was. I took them four at a time. Behind me, I heard shouts, but I ignored them and kept going.

The lobby was practically empty, with just a few last stragglers making their way into the conference room. I sprinted through them, past the elevators. I crashed through the crowd around the door, spilling from the Indonesian Lounge, shoving people away and bellowing at them like a sergeant on parade, "*Out of my way! Evacuate the hall! Evacuate the hall! FBI! There is a bomb in the hall! Get the hell out of here! FBI! FBI! There is a bomb! There is a bomb in this hall! Get out! Get out!*"

People started to back away. I strode toward them, pointing at the stairs. "*Go! Go! Go!*"

They started to scatter and run, making for the stairs, the escalators, and the elevators. I turned and scanned the vast, seated audience. Some people in the chamber were beginning to stand, craning, looking, trying to see what was going on. I searched among them, seeking the wheelchair. I couldn't see it. I ran down the aisle to the dais, jumped up and walked to the lectern, still searching the crowd with my eyes. I switched on the microphone and spoke clearly and deliberately, holding up Mclean's badge.

"I am Special Agent Harrison Mclean of the Federal

Bureau of Investigation. I need everybody to leave in an orderly fashion *now!* There is a bomb in this chamber!"

The effect was electric. Like a great tide, they all rose. People started scrambling like crazy, climbing over seats and swarming down the aisles. Meanwhile, I had spotted the wheelchair while I was talking. It was halfway up the central block of seats, on the left. The couple who'd been pushing it were struggling to maneuver it in the huge swarm of humanity streaming past them. The old guy looked scared.

I jumped from the stage and ran, shouldering my way through the crowd, shoving people out of the way, bellowing at them to move. Finally, I made it to where the couple were trying to make headway toward the exits. I grabbed the man's shoulder and he turned to stare at me in alarm.

"Where did you get this chair?"

He looked at me like I was out of my mind. It was a look I was getting used to seeing. "*What?*"

"There is no time. Tell me now! Where did you get it?" He stared at the woman who was with him. The old guy in the chair was craning around to see what was going on. People streamed past us, jostling and panicking. I grabbed him by the scruff of his neck and pulled him toward me. "Listen to me! You do not look like suicide bombers to me! This chair is a bomb! *So who gave it to you?*"

He went white. The girls said, "Oh my god, Dad!" and reached down to help the old man to his feet. "Come on, Papa, we have to hurry!"

The man I was holding shook his head. "Let me go with my wife, please..."

"*Who?*"

"It was donated, through a charity..."

"Along with the tickets to the conference?"

He nodded. "My father-in-law has been a campaigner for years..."

"*Who!*"

"The Muslim Fraternity for Understanding..."

I shoved him and snarled, "Get the hell out of here!"

I grabbed the chair and hurled it on its side. Underneath, where the electric motor should have been located, it was unlike any electric wheelchair I had ever seen. There was just a steel case. I looked at my watch. I had fifteen minutes. I went ice-cold inside, pulled my Swiss Army knife from my pocket, and started removing the screws that held the casing to the seat.

My hands were steady. A stillness had descended on me. I knew that I was racing death, and I knew that I would probably lose the race. All I could do was stay focused and work methodically. As the last screw came out, I was aware that the last few people had scattered from the chamber. But now new feet came running. Three or four people. I glanced up. It was Maria and three security guards. They came to a halt a few feet away, staring at me and at the chair. I noticed with the cold absurdity that comes with the proximity of death that they made a sad and strange tableau. The big, portly guy behind her, with the big moustache. His name badge said he was Olsen. It seemed important I should know his name. He was about to die with me, I should know who he was. The guy next to him who watched me with large, brown eyes filled with terror. His name was Peralta. I wondered if he had children. And the young guy next to him, with his hand on his .38, was Ortega.

They all closed in around me, unsure what to do or who

their enemy was. I ignored them and turned back to the chair. I pulled away the casing, and there it was. The shiny steel canister, almost three feet long, a foot wide, containing maybe two kilograms of compressed plutonium. And next to it, connected by a short, steel tube, the timer counting down: eleven minutes and thirty-eight seconds, thirty-seven, thirty-six, thirty-five...

A hushed, awed voice said, "What is it?"

I pulled out my cell phone, called Gantrie, and put him on speaker.

"Dude, what's happening?"

"I need to disarm a SADM. You know what that is? A Special Atomic Demolition Munitions device. I figure it probably has a W54 warhead, or something similar. It will explode in eleven minutes and probably wipe out southeast Manhattan and part of Brooklyn. Any suggestions?"

There was silence on the other end of the phone. Then his voice, calm, like I had asked him to find a telephone number, "Eleven minutes?"

"Yeah."

"We might just make it. You cool?"

"Yeah."

"OK... So tell me what you're looking at."

"There is a cylinder, about three foot long, that's where the fissile material is, probably plutonium. Then there is a short housing, which I guess holds wires that connect the cylinder to a digital clock, which is counting down."

I pulled out my cell, took a photograph, and sent it to him.

"OK, Lacklan, this is actually quite simple. What's going to happen is that the timer is going to trigger a small explosion which will drive the fissile material together. It's very unlikely to be booby trapped, because this is not a home-made bomb. This bomb was made by the U.S. for the U.S. military. So what you need to do is remove the housing for the wires and cut them all, everything you find, simultaneously."

He hadn't told me anything I didn't already know, but it was good to have it confirmed. I said, "OK..."

I stared at the small steel tube that connected the cylinder to the timer. The feeling of unreality which I'd had before became suddenly overwhelming. I could feel my heart pounding but there was a stillness inside me, like time had frozen. Ortega, the security guard, turned and fled from the room. Maria drew closer and knelt by my side. We stared together. There were no screws visible. There was no lip or seam to indicate a join. There was no way to remove the housing.

"Maria."

"Yeah?"

"I need you to run down to the parking garage. Just beside the entrance, in a tool box, you'll find a Smith & Wesson revolver. I need you to get it and bring it back..."

"I have a .38."

"No, I need this one. And you need to get it..." I flicked my eyes at the timer. We had eight minutes. "In less than five minutes."

She scrambled to her feet and ran from the room. Gantrie's voice came over the phone. "Dude, what's happening?"

"There is no point of access to the wires. It seems to be molded out of a single piece of steel."

"No, there has to be a join. You're just not seeing it. How long have we got?"

"Seven minutes."

"OK... so the housing has to connect somewhere, right? Tear the chair apart. Approach from a different angle."

I was already exploring it with my fingers. I said, "The bomb has been bolted to the seat of the chair. But the whole thing is a unit. The housing for the wires is a solid steel tube..." I peered closer. "It's been screwed into the timer and to the cylinder." I turned to Olsen. "You! Olsen! Give me your revolver!"

"What?"

"Give me your damned revolver or I'll tear your arm off!"

He stepped forward, drawing his piece. "OK!"

There were four bolts holding the entire bomb to the underside of the seat. The base of the seat had a steel frame, but the seat itself was made of plywood. I aimed at each bolt in turn, point blank, and blew it out of the seat. The bomb seemed to lever away without fully dropping off. It was still attached by the timer.

I turned to Olsen and Peralta again. "You two! Take hold of the timer. Hold it firm. I'm going to twist." They approached, looking very sick, and took hold of the clock. It read six minutes and thirty-five seconds. I seized hold of the canister with both hands and strained hard against it, trying to twist it free from the timing device. I could see the guards' faces turn crimson with the effort of resisting me. Their arms were trembling and sweat was beading on their brows.

Suddenly, Peralta gave a great shout and the canister jumped free from their hands. He fell forward, sprawled across the chair and Olsen staggered back. I felt a jolt of triumph. We might just make it. But it was short-lived. Peralta was on his knees with blood pouring from his hand, but the housing for the wires was intact, firmly connecting the timer to the bomb. Four and a half minutes and counting.

A shout and pounding feet made me look. Maria was approaching at a frantic run carrying the Smith and Wesson. She handed it to me. "How long have we got?"

"Not enough. Stand back. Everybody stand back."

The 500 is a small cannon. It will shatter two cinderblocks and keep going. I aimed and fired twice. The explosions echoed around the hall like thunder. I took a look. The coupling was dented, bent. Maria gave a little shout of joy. I hoped she was right to, because I was pretty sure I was sealing the damn thing tighter. I emptied the remaining three rounds and dented it more, but we still had no access to the wires.

Four minutes. I shouted, "An axe! Come on, guys! Wake up! Somebody get a fire axe!"

They blinked at me and scattered. I started savagely kicking the timer, stamping on it, trying to dislodge it. It wouldn't budge. A voice kept screaming at me in my head that there had to be a way in. Defeat was not an option.

Pounding feet. Peralta, panting, shaking with terrified eyes, holding out an axe to me. I went to work on the join between the housing for the wire and the timer, where it had been dented by the bullets. The steel rang out, dull and stubborn, but it would not budge. Maria shouted, "One minute!" But by the time she'd finished saying it, it was fifty-eight seconds. I roared like some demented freak and hammered savagely over and over at the coupling. A dead voice said, "Thirty seconds..."

I dropped the axe. Maria whimpered, "Don't give up... please..."

I fell on my knees and reached over to the splintered plywood seat, tearing away the pieces. I heard Maria say, "Fifteen seconds..." My heart thudded hard, once, high up in my chest. I felt sick and the room seemed to rock. I grabbed at one large sheet of ply and tore at it with both hands. It groaned and came away. I heard a crazy laughing and realized it was me. Maria said, "Five seconds..."

I reached over with my right hand, grabbed the red and the blue wires, and ripped at them savagely, stamping at the chair as I pulled. I stared at the frayed ends in my hand. There was a nanosecond that seemed to last an eternity while I waited for the vaporizing explosion. Then, trembling, I looked up at Maria. She was staring at the timer. I followed her gaze. It stood at zero. Her voice was a rasping whisper in her throat. "What did you do?"

I swallowed, breathed. "The timer was connected to the chair battery. The battery was in the seat, behind the plywood."

She started sobbing and dropped to her knees, crossing herself and crying like a child. Peralta fell on his knees next to her. Olsen sank into a chair and buried his face in his hands.

A voice in my head said, "Marni..." I stood. "Maria." She looked up at me. Her face was sodden with tears. I shook my head. "Not yet. Get a grip. Phone your station commander. Make a report. Tell the truth and stand by it. You understand me?"

She nodded and struggled to her feet. I turned to Olsen.

"You and Peralta contact the press, the TV, all the media. Tell this story. Tell this fucking story and don't let *anybody* say it's a lie!"

I ran for the stage and out through the wings on the left, bellowing for Marni and Gibbons. I searched for them, but I knew they weren't there. I knew that Ben had finally got what he wanted. I had led him to Marni, and he had taken her.

As I sprinted for the stairs down to the lobby I saw Maria on her cell, while Olsen was dialing his own. The lobby was empty, as was the plaza outside. On First Avenue, there was a cordon of cops and patrol cars. I pushed through the door and walked toward them. Two SWAT guys in body armor came running toward me. As they approached, I said, "It's OK, it's been diffused."

They took my arms and hurried me toward the cordon, shouting at me, "Are you OK? Are you injured?"

"No. The area is clear. The bomb has been diffused."

I could see the captain behind the cordon talking on his cell phone. I pointed at him. "Talk to the captain. He's on the phone to one of his officers on the inside right now."

We had arrived at the cordon and they shoved me through, between two vehicles. The captain was approaching me. Before he could ask me any questions I put my left hand on his shoulder and pointed at the building.

"The situation is contained. There was a bomb concealed in a wheelchair. It has been diffused. You have an officer in there who has just spoken to you on the phone. The area is clear, Captain. I repeat, the area is clear. You can go in." I flashed Mclean's badge at him with my finger accidentally over the picture. "Now I need to go. My suspect is getting away. I will report back to you this afternoon. Now get *in* there and secure the evidence, Captain!"

I walked away toward 42nd Street and felt his eyes on my back for a full five seconds. Then I heard a shout, but it wasn't calling me back, it was ordering his men to proceed into the UN. I glanced back and saw them on the move. That was when I started to run.

I scrambled around the corner onto 42nd, clambered into the Zombie, and wrenched the tracker from the glove compartment, praying to whatever deities deal with that kind of stuff that Gibbons still had the tracker in his pocket. I switched it on and the bleep was there. The location was obvious. Teterboro Airport, in New Jersey.

NINETEEN

I spun the Zombie and accelerated down 42ND Street, leaning on the horn as I went, and wishing for once that the twin engines made a noise. I needed the other drivers and the pedestrians to hear me coming, and I needed them to get out of the way. I moved to the center of the road and stayed at a steady forty miles per hour. The oncoming cars flashed their lights at me and the cars I left behind added their horns to mine. Pedestrians scattered and shouted abuse the way only New Yorkers know how.

When I got to 10th Avenue, I careened right, standing on the footbrake, jumped the red light, picking my way through the scattering crowds who were trying to cross the road, then hit the gas and started accelerating again, dodging from lane to lane, moving north doing fifty, reaching for sixty, with the brakes and the tires screaming as I weaved among the cars, taxis, trucks, and buses. I kept going north until I'd passed Washington Heights. Then I skidded into West 179th and hurtled across the narrow tip of the island onto the George

Washington Bridge. Once I was there, I opened her up and felt the surge crush me back in the seat as the massive twin engines delivered their one thousand eight-hundred foot-pounds of torque, instantly to the back wheels, and the beast hurtled forward, touching a hundred and twenty miles per hour in less than a second.

I followed the I-95. The other cars on the highway looked stationary as I flashed past. At Ridgefield Park, I slowed to come off onto Route Forty-Six into Teterboro. As I did, I checked the tracker. He was still there, and the voice in my head was yelling at me that this was wrong. They should have flown out before the explosion. Why had they waited? Why, when the bomb had not exploded, had they not left immediately? It didn't make any sense.

I raised smoke from the back wheels skidding from Route Forty Six onto Hollister Road, screeched to a halt outside the airport, and killed the engine. Then I sat, staring at the wheel, with no idea of what I was going to do next. I reached in my pocket and pulled out a pack of Camels. As I opened the box and extracted a cigarette, I noticed my hands were shaking. I lit up with my battered, brass Zippo and inhaled deeply. I couldn't afford to go into shock right then. If you know how to use it, shock can help you recover and heal. But it won't help you fight and win. I had to postpone it.

I put the tracker in my pocket, popped the trunk, and climbed out. I tossed the Smith & Wesson 500 back in my kit bag, pulled out my remaining Sig and stuck two magazines in my jacket pocket. Then I had a look at the airport. It was internal, business flights only, mainly small, executive jets and air taxis for businessmen. Security seemed to be minimal. There was only a five-foot iron fence between the sidewalk and the air fields; air fields which right then seemed to be completely devoid of activity.

I walked the hundred yards to the main gates and in toward the terminal building. I pushed through the glass doors and found myself in a large, empty lounge with elevator music playing through the PA system. The boards displaying the flights showed every one of them as cancelled. Clearly Homeland Security had been informed and were taking over.

There were a couple of desks with women in uniform sitting behind them, looking bored. I pulled out the tracker and checked it. He was less than a hundred yards away, out on the tarmac. I walked to the large viewing windows and saw the plane. It was a ten-seater Dassault Falcon. Gibbons was on board and Marni was almost certainly with him. Obviously Ben had special clearance to fly.

I heard heels echoing on the marble floor behind me and turned. A tall, blond woman in an Atlantic Air uniform was walking toward me, looking straight at me. She didn't smile until she was three or four feet away. Then she stopped and said, "Are you Mr. Walker?"

I nodded. "Yes."

"They are waiting for you. Will you follow me, please?"

I frowned. "They're waiting for me? Who is?"

"Your party. They are already embarked. You're cleared for takeoff. This way."

I followed her across the hall, through an emergency door, and along a narrow passage. She held open another emergency door for me and next thing, we were on the tarmac. After that, she led me the seventy or eighty paces to the steps that led up to the jet. She wished me a comfortable flight and left. I watched her walk away, back toward the terminal building, then turned and climbed the stairs up into the plane.

There was something unreal, or perhaps surreal, about the scene that met my eyes as I entered the cabin. Yet I was aware that for that small world where Ben operated, detached from the rest of humanity, this kind of thing was the norm. It was like a luxurious old world drawing room stuffed into a tube. There were leather sofas and big leather armchairs. The walls were paneled in oak and there were art deco lamps on the high-polish mahogany tables.

Ben was sitting at one of those tables reading a document. In front of him he had a martini glass with an olive in it. For a freakish moment he looked to me suddenly like a very old man. Across the aisle from him was Marni, seated in a leather armchair, staring at me from behind an expression-less mask. Beyond them both, Gibbons was lying on a couch, apparently asleep. Opposite him on another sofa were two large men holding assault rifles. Behind me the door hissed and began to rise. A steward who looked as though he'd learned to be an in-flight attendant with the Russian Mafia, approached me from the back of the plane. He put a huge hand on my shoulder and gestured toward Ben's table.

"Sir, we are about to take off, would you take a seat, please?"

Ben looked up as I approached and sat. He stared me in the eye, and for the first time since I had met him, he looked mad. His face was tight, his skin was pale and he had two red dots on his cheekbones. I raised an eyebrow at him.

"You are becoming a real pain in the ass, Lacklan."

"Really?" I looked over at Marni. I smiled and she smiled back. I turned back to Ben. "I thought my trivial actions couldn't hurt the mighty Omega."

He drew breath, hesitated, blinked slowly, and finally said, "You can't."

We began to move. He pressed a button on the side of the table and a concealed TV screen rose and winked into life. It was CNN and Alia Fadel was standing outside the UN Headquarters on First Avenue, holding a microphone and speaking. Behind her the cops, in bright yellow reflective jackets, had the road sealed off and there were half a dozen patrol cars, a SWAT van, and a couple of CSI vans all parked in the plaza inside the gates. She was frowning as she spoke.

"...nobody really *knows* what's going on, Don. Everybody you talk to has a different story. There are lots of theories, lots of opinions, but so far there are very few facts, and those that there *are*, are very jealously guarded.

"What we *do* know is that patrolman Bill Dwight and his partner Maria Portillo arrested a man on the request of Director David Staines. Now, David Staines is not at present available for comment, nobody is very sure *where* he is, however, witnesses at the scene say they saw officers Portillo and Dwight lead away a man in handcuffs, put him in a patrol car, and then drive out of the UN complex onto First Avenue. And here is where it starts to get strange, because only moments later, the patrol car returned, with its sirens on, and patrolwoman Portillo and the man she had ostensibly arrested stormed into the UN building shouting that there was a bomb. Several witnesses have stated that at this point, the man was claiming to be FBI

Special Agent Harrison Mclean. The FBI have made no comment so far.

"Whether there was or not a bomb is as yet unconfirmed, but security guards who were present at the time have told me that they saw the bomb with their own eyes, and that they watched the man claiming to be Agent Mclean disarm it. They also claim, and hold on to your hat, Don, that it was a tactical nuclear device concealed in a wheelchair. Experts from the Bomb Disposal Unit are currently in the General Assembly Hall, apparently examining the alleged bomb, but so far they have not issued a statement..."

Ben was rigid, staring at me. "You have no idea, Lacklan, how angry I am right now."

I gave a single nod. "I am glad to hear it."

He closed his eyes and steadied his breath. "At least," he said, "you performed this much of your part of the bargain." He gestured to Marni.

I shook my head. "No, I didn't. I told her to go to Boston."

He echoed my single nod. "I see. Give me one reason why I should not kill each one of you."

I exploded. "You're out of your fucking mind, Ben! The only reason we, and a hundred thousand other people, are not dead is because I managed to dismantle that goddamn bomb! What fucking planet are you on?"

We had reached the runway and now the jet stopped and the engines began to scream as they prepared for takeoff. Next thing, we were accelerating down the runway and rising up into the sky above New Jersey. I stared at him in silence throughout, then said, "What? You're so mad at me for not letting you kill us, that now you want to kill us?"

"You know, sometimes you are a very stupid man, Lacklan. If you had stayed at the Institute, as you were supposed to, you would not have been at risk. Did it ever occur to you that I might have put you there for your own protection?" I had no answer for that and he went on, "And as for Marni and Professor Gibbons, if they had accepted our invitation in the first place, to join us and work *with* us, they would not have been at risk, either. You were all three at the UN *against* my advice."

Marni turned on him. "*You were planning to murder hundreds of thousands of people!* How can you sit there and *tell us off—like children—*for *spoiling* your monstrous plan? It's *inhuman!* How can you *live* with yourself?"

He gazed at her and shook his head. "I am far too angry to even try to reason with you right now, Marni. I need to spend some time meditating and re-center myself. But you should know that you have both caused us a very serious setback."

I burst out laughing. "You say that as though we should feel sorry." I frowned at him. I had the strange feeling that I was talking to somebody who didn't speak the same language as me, like I needed to articulate everything very carefully in order to make myself understood. "It has always been our intention to screw up your plans, Ben! You must know that! What is the matter with you?"

He took a deep breath. "I guess I thought, after our recent conversations, that I was beginning to get through to you. I thought we were beginning to have some kind of..." He hesitated, like he was searching for an appropriate word. He shook his head again. "Some kind of understanding. Obviously I was wrong."

I nodded. "Yes, Ben, you were wrong. Perhaps the number of Omega operatives I have killed should have been a clue. Now, would you mind explaining to me what the hell we are doing on this plane? The woman at Teterboro told me you were waiting for me..."

He shrugged. "People die. If society could learn to accept this simple fact, the world might be a healthier place. The fact that you killed so many of our operatives told me nothing except that you are exceptionally good at what you do."

Marni looked away. I sighed.

Ben went on. "And I might add, Lacklan, that there is more than just a hint of hypocrisy in your holier-than-thou attitude toward Omega. For you, of all people, to accuse us of murder is a little rich."

He raised his hand and snapped his fingers. The big flight attendant approached. "Bring me another martini, and whatever they want."

I ordered a Bushmills and Marni just shook her head and stared out the window. I asked, "Where are you taking us, Ben? What are you going to do with us?"

"I am taking you to D.C. I want you both to meet somebody."

Marni turned her head and looked from me to Ben. "Both?"

"You and Lacklan. Professor Gibbons... We have different plans for him."

She looked alarmed. "What plans?"

"It's none of your concern, Marni. But in any case, I will fill you in when we are sure of how to move forward. Plans are in a bit of a state of chaos at the moment."

He loaded the words with irony, like he was trying to guilt-trip her. I said, "Who do you want us to meet?"

"Someone who might help you to acquire a slightly more global perspective."

"What does that mean, Ben? You want us to learn how to justify killing a million people?"

He held my gaze for a long moment, then said, "Or two million, or twenty, or a hundred. The number is not important. Let me ask you something, Lacklan, as you like to preach so much about right and wrong. Is it twice as bad to kill two people as one? How do you measure that? Is it worse to kill a mother and her child than it is to kill ten men? What if one of those men is Mahatma Gandhi, and the child will grow up to be Ted Bundy?" He gestured at me with his open hand. "You murder indiscriminately in the name of your crusade, to stop what you see as Omega's evil plans. But what if by doing that, you are driving humanity toward extinction? What if our project is the only way to save humanity? Which one of us, then, is the evil one?"

I had no answer. Or if I had, I had no idea how to articulate it. Marni covered her face with her hands. Her voice came out muffled. "You cannot *justify* the indiscriminate *murder* of hundreds of thousands of people. There *is no justification for an act like that!*" She uncovered her face and looked at him. "How can you not see that?"

He frowned at her. "Who says I don't see it?"

"*What?*"

"I see it more clearly than you do, Marni. For you it is an emotional impulse driven by a primal instinct to protect the tribe. But we are so far beyond the point where we can think in those terms! Look around you. We are hurtling toward eight billion people. About four and a half million people are added to the population—*net!*—every month! Feeding them requires massive industrial production and distribution, a process which is destroying the very environment we need in order to feed these people! *We are parasites, Marni! And we are killing our host!*" He sank back in his seat. "Now I ask you, do you kill that child, knowing he will grow up to be Ted Bundy or Adolf Hitler, or do you let him live, knowing what he will do when he grows to adulthood?"

Marni screwed up her face and turned away from him. "You're sick!"

He shook his head. "No, I am not sick, Marni. What I am asking you to look at and recognize is sick. I am no more sick than the surgeon who removes a cancerous lung."

I sighed at him. "How does killing half of Manhattan help the world to survive overpopulation and climate change?"

He nodded. "That is a good question, but I am going to save the answer for tomorrow. We have some very serious business to transact in the morning, and you have a very important person to meet. For now, there are two things that I need you to do. The first is this. I would like you both to discuss, very seriously, how you would change Omega's policy toward climate change and overpopulation. I am not playing you, this is a genuine request."

I frowned, hard. All my alarm bells were going like crazy. Marni looked stunned, then turned, looked at Gibbons, and back at Ben.

"What about Philip?"

He ignored her and switched the TV back on. We were still at the UN and in the background you could see a gurney being wheeled out of the main doors toward a waiting ambulance. Alia Fadel was talking to the camera and pointing back toward the scene that was unfolding behind her.

"...this latest news has taken everybody by surprise. It is a huge blow to international efforts to get the world to agree on an agenda for sustainable growth, and a terrible shock for the international community. Professor Philip Gibbons was, despite his controversial and often confrontational style, highly respected and well liked. His contribution to this ill-fated conference was, according to his colleagues, going to change the face of international politics and world economy. Exactly why he was murdered by the man posing as Agent Mclean is as yet unclear, as is the whereabouts of his young protégé, Dr Marni Gilbert, whose own contribution to the conference was, apparently, going to have at least as seismic an effect as Professor Gibbons'. He will be sorely missed..."

He switched off the TV.

I shook my head. "You bastard. You're going to kill him and blame it on me..."

He shrugged. "That is very much up to you and Marni. You have a lot of soul-searching to do over the next few hours." He glanced at his watch. "I have arranged accommodation for you both in Chain Bridge Road, between Palisades and Wesley Heights. You'll be very comfortable there. Gibbons will come with us to sleep off his mild intoxication." He glanced at me. "He has very powerful friends, Lacklan, as I have mentioned to you before. They will not be pleased. All of his suspicions about you will have been confirmed." He turned to Marni. "And I am afraid they'll be wondering about you, too." He sighed. "What becomes of him is up to you. What becomes of all three of you, is up to you. Despite what you think, we are not in the business of destroying people for the fun of it. We would much rather have the three of you onside. So please, spend this afternoon and tonight productively, and when we meet tomorrow, be prepared to tell us how you would change Omega if you could. Your lives, and Professor Gibbons' life, depend on it."

We had started to descend toward D.C. He reached in his pocket and pulled out an envelope, which he slid across the table to me.

"The address of your house and two sets of keys. You will be under surveillance, but you will not be controlled or stopped if you attempt to go away. You are not prisoners. All that will happen is that I will be informed. A car will come to collect you tomorrow at two PM, after lunch. If you don't come to the meeting, Professor Gibbons will be executed."

TWENTY

CHAIN BRIDGE ROAD WAS NOT SO MUCH LEAFY AS wooded, and not so much suburban as semi-rural. Our house was set back from the road, among plane trees and pines, with a crescent driveway to the front door. It was a big, stone affair, painted cream, with blue, gabled slate roofs and tall chimneypots that poked up among the trees toward a perfect blue sky.

Marni paid the driver while I unlocked the heavy, blue wooden door. Somewhere a rook, or it may have been a raven, cawed like he thought what I had done might have consequences. Bad ones.

I stepped in. It wasn't super luxury, but it was spacious and comfortable in a pleasant, old world sort of way. There was a big hall with a broad, oak staircase that climbed to the upper floors. A dark, wooden door on the left led to a large living room with an red brick fireplace and the kind of cozy furniture you'd expect from a New England cottage. At the far end, there was a long dining table, and behind it French windows stood open onto a mature garden with stone steps leading down to a well-tended lawn, and a pond. The raven who had laughed at me was now strutting across that lawn, like he owned it.

There was a tray of drinks on a credenza, a couple of large, well stocked bookcases, and a smell of baking coming from somewhere. I turned to look at Marni, who had come in behind me. I smiled. "Welcome home."

She gave a humorless snort. "You think it's bugged?"

I raised an eyebrow. "You think it's not?"

She shrugged. "You think they abducted Rosalia and Kenny too, and they have them baking in the kitchen?"

As if in response to her question, there was a tap at the door and an agreeable woman in her forties looked in and smiled. "Good afternoon, are you Mr. and Mrs. Walker?"

Marni gave a single shout of laughter and pointed at me. "He is Mr. Walker, I am Dr. Gilbert. Who are you?"

The woman looked startled. "Oh, I beg your pardon, Dr. Gilbert. I am Mrs. Henderson. I'm almost finished in the kitchen and I have done upstairs..." She hesitated. "According to the instructions I was sent..."

Marni smiled. "Sure, Mrs. Henderson. I didn't mean to bark. That's great, thank you."

"Pie's in the oven. It needs an hour. Can I get you anything before I go?"

We told her we'd be fine and watched her through the leaded bow window as she cycled away, along the wooded lane. When she'd disappeared from view, Marni turned to me and looked up into my face.

"Lacklan, they are insane. What is this? Tell me you think they're insane as well."

I nodded. "I do. I think they are out of their minds."

"Cozy country house, French windows onto the lawn, Mrs. Henderson cooking us pies, and tactical nuclear bombs at the United Nations..." She shook her head. "*Excuse me?*"

I laughed. It wasn't a happy laugh, it was a bitter one. I dropped into one of the overstuffed armchairs and a wave of profound exhaustion washed over me. "You think they're trying to make a point?"

She watched me from the window. "What point?"

"I don't know. This represents their core values, the bomb represents what they are forced to do in order to achieve those values?"

"You buy that shit?"

I sighed. "No, Marni! I'm the guy who just nearly got vaporized diffusing the bomb, remember?"

She took a deep breath. "I'm sorry, Lacklan, that was stupid." She came and sat in the chair opposite me, then said, "No, I don't think they are making a point. I think they are just insane."

I shrugged. "Is it so different?"

"So different to what?"

"To what so-called legitimate governments do. They send men like me to Afghanistan and Iraq to hunt and kill human beings, they allow multinational corporations to devastate the rainforests, support child slavery, exploit African mines in states where twelve-year-old kids are taught how to behead people and use assault rifles. They allow banks like ITCD to launder the Sinaloa's drug profits. And meanwhile, the men and women who make billions out of all this chaos and cruelty sip champagne in mansions, spend hundreds of thousands of dollars on a single suit or dress, and shoot two hundred thousand dollar sports cars to Mars for fun." I shrugged again. "I don't think Omega is any more insane than our legitimate governments. I think Omega is just the distillation of everything that is our society. It is our society taken to its logical extreme. Are they any more insane than, say, the Third Reich, or North Korea? If anything, they are less extreme."

She was frowning at me. "Are you apologizing for them?"

"Again, no. All I am saying is that, however offensive they may be—and to me they are very offensive—they are not as weird as they may appear. Human beings behave in very strange ways when they become extremely rich and powerful. Jesus! Look at the Bohemian Grove! The Pizza scandal, Wyss..." I spread my hands. "Need I go on?"

She sounded uneasy. "No, but what's your point?"

"I don't know, no real point, just that we shouldn't see them as something freakish or abnormal. I think they represent the status quo."

Now she looked unhappy and changed the subject. "What about this request of Ben's, that we prepare a statement on how we would alter Omega?"

I sighed. "It's pretty cynical."

"They're trying to lure us in, like your dad."

I nodded. After a moment, I said, "His big regret, when he died, was that he allowed them to do that."

Her gaze was lost in the garden behind me. The raven was still cawing. The smaller birds ignored him and chattered, like gossiping mothers in a storybook world where owls read books and bunnies make tea. She puffed out her cheeks and said, "I believe you. My only recommendation for how they could improve would be for them all to make like lemmings and jump."

I gave a small laugh. "I don't think that would be very helpful, somehow."

She raised her eyebrows. "Helpful?"

"Marni, I can't remember the last time I slept. I am more tired than I can describe. Please don't jump down my throat every time I say something that isn't perfectly expressed."

She raised both hands. "My bad. You want to get some sleep."

"I think I have to, but we need to give some very serious thought to what Ben has asked us to do. The implications if we do it, and if we don't, need to be very carefully examined."

She leaned forward, with her elbows on her knees, and rubbed her face. "If we go there tomorrow and offer him a range of proposals aimed at how we think Omega could improve, that will do three things. One, it will be an acknowledgment that we believe Omega can improve to a point where we would consider joining it; two, it will allow them to *appear* to meet our requirements and entice us to join; and three, it will allow them to engage us in a dialogue, effectively a cease-fire. It will give them a beachhead and allow them to try to seduce us, drive a wedge between us... You name it!"

I held her eye while she was talking and gently, discreetly tapped my ear with one finger until I saw realization dawn on her face. She shrugged and spread her hands.

I said, "Of course you are right. But we need to examine both sides of the argument. That is probably their purpose in asking us to come up with these proposals, but what if we don't? What happens if we don't?"

She looked at the cold fireplace. "They'll kill Philip."

"Amongst other things. It will be confirmed that the man who killed him was in fact Captain Lacklan Walker, posing as Special Agent Harrison Mclean, whom he attempted to murder along with his partner, Special Agent Daren Jones. And every tiny piece of advantage that we gained today by exposing the bomb plot will be lost, because we will lose our only allies, the press and the cop on the beat."

"So what do you propose?"

I discreetly tapped my ear again. "I don't know, Marni. Give me a couple of hours to sleep. Then I'd like to see the news, see how the story is developing. Then..." I thought for a moment. "The Potomac is less than a mile to the west of here. There's a nice walk through the woods. Let's take that walk, relax a bit, and try and get a different perspective. What do you say?"

She nodded. She had understood what I was saying. "Sure, that makes sense." She came over and knelt by my side. The kiss she gave me was as natural as though we had been together for the last ten years. She stroked my face and said, "I'll wake you in a couple of hours."

There were five bedrooms on the second floor, but only the master bedroom had been made up. It was ample, furnished in the same old-world style as the rest of the house, and had a large, bow window overlooking the garden. The others had the drapes drawn and the furniture covered in dustsheets. Clearly Ben, or his masters, whoever was pulling the strings in this deep game, wanted us to be a couple for some reason. I was too exhausted to think about it right then. I collapsed onto the huge bed, closed my eyes, and slipped quickly into a deep, dreamless sleep.

When I awoke, the light outside the window had acquired a coppery hue, and the shadows had grown longer and deeper. It was not evening, but the afternoon was thinking about moving that way.

I swung my legs off the bed and realized that my boots had been removed, and so had my jacket and my Sig. I smiled and made my way to the en suite where I stood for ten minutes under the hot jets of water, allowing some of my exhaustion and my confusion to be washed away.

Finally, I dressed and made my way downstairs. I found Marni in the kitchen. It was the only room in the house that had made any concessions to the twenty-first century. It was big and roomy and had a huge fridge and a breakfast bar with stools. That was where Marni was sitting, drinking coffee and watching the news on a TV across the room.

She looked at me as I came in, jerked her head at the screen, and said, "I'm not sure what to make of it."

I went and rested my ass on the table. Jeff Glor was reading the news. He was saying, "...this report live from the UN Headquarters in New York."

They cut to a guy I didn't know, standing outside the gates of the UN building. Behind him, you could see police cars and unmarked vehicles in the plaza, but what was new was the two FBI vans and three Army National Guard trucks that were stationed there, and the soldiers in combat gear standing guard with assault rifles. The reporter was saying, "There is a sense of barely suppressed panic, Jeff. It's as though the administration really does not know what part of this fiasco to deal with first. I am told the president is going to address the nation later this evening, but even that has not been confirmed, as far as I am aware.

"What we know now is that there *was*, indeed, an armed, nuclear device smuggled in through the security gates at the entrance to the building, right under their noses. It *was* concealed in a wheelchair and it *was* taken to the General Assembly Hall. We also know that the timer *was* in fact set to detonate at noon, just as Dr. Marni Gilbert and Professor Gibbons were due to start their talk.

"Critics of the government's policy on the environment are clamoring for an explanation for how this could have happened. Some are even accusing the president of involvement in a plot to assassinate these two speakers who, it is understood, were going to make certain revelations about the role of multinational corporations and western governments in climate change and overpopulation. What those revelations were to be, Jeff, is not known precisely, but some are saying that they would have been damaging to the president and this administration, as well as previous ones.

"However, perhaps the most important question that investigators here are asking is, how did a U.S.-made nuclear device fall into the hands of terrorists?"

Glor's voice interrupted him and the reporter pressed his ear piece into his ear to listen. "Is there any indication yet, Dave, as to exactly who these terrorists were? Has anybody claimed responsibility for the attempt?"

"No, Jeff, some people are pointing to a small demonstration of Islamic fundamentalists who were chanting '*Allahu Akbar*' at the security check a little earlier in the day. But the level of organization needed to set up an attack of this sort is huge, and sources within the FBI are also pointing to the fact that the chair was, apparently, brought into the building by three non-Muslims. Attempts are currently being made to trace those people."

Glor's voice interrupted again, "And, finally, Dave, what more, if anything, do we know about Professor Gibbons' murder?"

"So far, Jeff, there is nothing new. There are unconfirmed reports that the man posing as Special Agent Mclean, the very man who apparently defused the atomic device, also gunned down Professor Gibbons before escaping. This of course raises all sort of questions, including, was Professor Gibbons himself responsible for the bomb? But so far, the FBI are playing their cards very close to their chest and have declined to comment."

"And, before you go, Dave, I see there is now a military presence at the UN."

"We don't know exactly what their purpose is here, Jeff, they arrived about an hour ago and the entire complex seems now to be under military guard. Russian and Chinese delegates have quietly raised questions about jurisdiction, but so far it seems everybody is content to wait and see what the investigation unearths. The president is due to make a statement either tonight or tomorrow morning, so we hope to know more then."

They cut back to the studio and Glor addressed the camera. "Now, the markets have responded badly to..."

I killed it and turned to face Marni. "Let's take a walk and clear our heads. What do you say?"

She sat staring at the black screen for a while, then looked at me like she had only just registered my words. She nodded. "Yeah, good idea. We have at least a couple of hours of daylight. Let's go."

Across from the house, and running the length of Chain Bridge Road for almost a mile, was a stretch of wild wooded parkland. It was unfenced and untended, with a couple of foot paths that wound their way through the trees down to the river. We stepped out of the house, crossed the road, and entered the woodlands. As we went, I turned and looked back to see if anybody was following us, but we were alone, and pretty soon we were deep among the chaotic jumble of trees, fallen branches, creeping ivy, and wild ferns that is nature, when Man leaves her be. Dappled sun broke the shadows on the path ahead of us, above our heads wings battered the leaves sporadically among the canopy, and bursts of song seemed almost to sparkle against the clean blue of the sky.

Marni shoved her hands in her jeans pockets and stared down at her boots as she walked, like she wanted to make sure she placed each step in just the right place. I knew from experience, you can't do that and remain human. She said, "They know that we know the house is bugged."

I shrugged. "Of course. But they also assumed that we would come here to discuss our plans. They're not really interested in what we discuss. They're only interested in our final decision. To be honest, Marni, as far as they are concerned, they have hooked us and they are reeling us in." She flashed a look at me like she was about to get mad. I shook my head. "There is nothing to be gained by kidding ourselves. That is where we are. As soon as they caught you, the game changed."

Her cheeks colored and she looked back at her boots. "Do I need to apologize?"

I smiled. "No, you need to focus."

Voices came to us with that odd, dull amplification that sounds acquire in forests. A woman, a child shouting and laughing, and then a golden retriever streaking through the trees. A red sweatshirt chasing, calling. Three fleeting lives.

I took a deep breath. "They will want your father's research."

She nodded without looking at me. "I know. I have to choose, live with your death and Philip's on my conscience, or hand over the research and give up the fight. It's the choice your father faced, or the next stage of that choice."

We had come to a clearing. The retriever was sniffing furiously, seeking in the tall, wild grass around a large tree stump and a fallen trunk. The child's voice called from the shadows among the undergrowth and the dog bolted after her. Marni approached the felled tree and stepped onto the stump. She smiled down at me. Her face was sad. "I'm the queen of the castle," she said. She waited, looking into my eyes, but I had no answer. "I used to be a little girl, once."

"I remember, I was there. You were quite good at it."

"But you were never a little boy. You were always serious and earnest. Even when you were fighting off dragons to protect me, you did it with a tremendous commitment, for such a skinny little runt."

She burst out laughing. I had to laugh too, until I saw she was wiping tears from her eyes. She smiled and pulled a handkerchief from her pocket. "I'm sorry." She blew her nose and managed to look both awful and beautiful at the same time. "It was what I loved so much about you. Even back then."

I held out my hand to her but she jumped down without taking it. As she moved away, I said, "Marni..."

"I know. We haven't got time for this now. I'm being stupid..."

"Marni!" She turned to me. I moved to her and took her shoulders. She stared up at me. I cupped her small face in my hands, hands that had taken so many lives, hands I had felt ashamed to touch her with when she had come to me, all those years ago in London, when I had turned her away. Now I said what I had been unable to say then. "I love you."

She took my hands in hers and kissed them. Then gave a single, tragic laugh. "Now? Like this?"

I sighed. "In case I don't get another chance." She took my arm in both of hers, rested her head on my shoulder and we walked on through the trees in silence for a while, listening to the crack of twigs under our feet, the shouts of the little girl growing more distant, and the chatter of the birds above in the growing dusk, as they prepared for the night.

Eventually, we stood on the banks of the Potomac, looking down at the great, dark snake moving slow, steady, and irresistible toward the ocean, and she asked me, "So what do we tell them?"

I stared at the great river for a long while. Then I gave a small shrug. "We tell them that we want Omega to gather the world leaders, and start a concerted initiative, a serious program through the UN, to halt climate change and *humanely* reduce the population of the Earth, over the next ten generations, to a number that the planet can sustain. We tell them we want them to invest the same kind of energy and commitment into that enterprise, that they would normally invest in making war."

She smiled up at me and made no effort to hide the irony in her face. "Seriously?"

I nodded. "Seriously."

"They'll laugh in your face."

"Maybe they will, but Ben has a point, Marni, and though I hate everything that he and Omega stand for, when he asked us to come up with a proposal, he *had* a point. We can't only oppose. What are we fighting for?" I turned to face her. "We have been fighting to stop them. But if we stop them, then what? What do we put in their place? Have we got a better option?"

She sat on the grass, on the banks of the river, and I sat next to her. She said, "How do you reduce the population of the world, without infringing people's rights and liberties? How do you make seven and a half billion people agree?"

I remembered Salman Awad's words at Prince Awad's party. I said, "You give them a common enemy, make them aware that they face a common threat."

After a while she shook her head. "That might work with ten people, a hundred, a thousand, maybe even a few million; but seven and a half *billion* people, from different nations, different cultures, with diffcrent faiths and religions..." She shook her head again and threw a small twig toward the river. The breeze caught it and carried it away. "You and I both know that is impossible."

I nodded. "I know. But that's the fight, and we have to fight it."

"So that's what we tell Ben?"

I didn't answer straight away. When I did, I said, "Did I ever tell you it was my mother who chose my name?"

She frowned. "No."

"She was descended from Danish Vikings. She's a tough cookie, hard as nails. The name means 'Norse Raider', a man from the fjords. She loved the philosophy of the Norsemen. She used to tell me, 'You fight, Lacklan, and you keep fighting. You don't give up, ever. One day you will die, and that will be the end of your story in this world. But when that time comes, you must look back over your life and be able to say, I never gave up.'" I smiled. "You give up when you die, not before."

She gave her head a small sideways twist. "Wow..."

I laughed. "Yeah, but there's more."

"More? Really?"

I nodded. "Yeah, after she had given me her talk, she would then lean toward me and fix me with her blue eyes. She would raise one, devastating eyebrow, and say, 'But it's not enough to fight and never give up, Lacklan. You have to win! Win or die!'"

I stared at her sweet, beautiful face and said, "Repeat it with me, Marni, win or die."

"Win... Win or die."

TWENTY-ONE

THE CAR ARRIVED THE NEXT DAY AT FIVE MINUTES before two. It was a black Cadillac and the driver was in uniform. He saluted and held the door for Marni. I climbed in the other side and we took off. We crossed the Chain Bridge and then followed the George Washington Parkway at a sedate pace along the banks of the Potomac, all the way to the Arlington Bridge. From there, we took Washington Boulevard and arrived at the Pentagon at just after two-twenty.

We stopped at North Parking and our driver led us, as I had been led once before, to the Corridor 8 entrance. There we were met by a man in a suit with a wire in his ear, who had 'Secret Service' written all over him. He handed us a couple of badges, then led us through rings E, D, and C to Ring B. The way it works at the Pentagon, the closer you get to the center, the closer you get to absolute, temporal power.

We stopped at Ring B, and there we rode the elevator up two floors to room 32. He knocked on the door before opening it and announcing, "Mr. Walker and Dr. Gilbert, sir."

He stood back, holding the door for us, and we stepped inside. There was the flag against one wall, and a portrait of the president. There were mahogany bookcases, and a nest of black leather chairs and a sofa around a coffee table. A large, oak desk stood by a window that overlooked an internal garden. I knew that having a view of that garden meant you were at the heart of power.

Ben was sitting with his ass on the desk, watching us. There was another man standing at the window, in silhouette. He turned as we came in and the door closed behind us. It was former president Dick Hennessy. There was a moment of awkward silence. Ben broke it.

"Hello, Marni, Lacklan. Come in. I'd like you to meet Beta, though you may be more comfortable calling him Mr. President, or sir."

I took three steps across the room and stood looking at the man. He watched me back, with cold, hard eyes. I said, "I can think of several things to call you, Hennessy, but none of them is sir."

He didn't answer, but Ben said, "Let's not get off to a bad start, Lacklan. Take a seat. Marni...?"

He gestured us toward the nest of chairs and the sofa. Marni sat. I ignored him and crossed the room to where he had his tray of drinks. I poured myself a whiskey and showed Marni the decanter. She shook her head. I turned and looked hard at Ben.

"This is the second time I've seen you in this office, Ben. Whose office is it?"

He was standing by the sofa, waiting for me to sit. He

thought about my question for a moment, then shook his head. "No, Lacklan, you have had enough concessions. I have given you more than your fair share of latitude. Now it's time for you to give me something. Join us, and I will make you privy to that kind of information. Now, will you please sit, so that we can begin?"

I looked at Hennessy. He had his arms crossed and he was watching me with interest. I sipped my whiskey and shrugged. "What's the matter, Beta, you're not going to sit down and join us?"

He didn't answer, but after a moment he walked slowly over and took a chair. Before he sat, he drawled in his strong, Texan accent, "You are one confrontational son of a bitch, aren't you, Lacklan?"

"Yes."

"Well, will you do me the courtesy of sitting with me and discussing a few issues?"

I smiled on the right side of my face. "Sure." I sat. "What issues?"

He and Ben sat too. Hennessy was pensive for a moment. "It kind of irks me, Lacklan, I have to tell you, that I know you are going to take what I'm going to say next, with cynicism, and you will dismiss it. But I'm going to say it nonetheless, because it is the truth." He paused and, oddly, seemed to study Marni's face. "Bob Walker—your father, Lacklan, was my closest friend. I loved him like a brother. More than a brother. He was a comrade."

I didn't hesitate. "Is that why you made him kill his own best friend?"

His answer surprised me. "Yes, Lacklan. That is exactly why. But I am not going to explain that today because there is no way you can understand it. Because it has to do with commitment, loyalty, and love on a level which is beyond the likes of you."

I felt a hot pellet of anger in my belly, but controlled it. "That's a love that kills."

"Like I said, I am not even going to try to explain. You might as well try to describe air to a fish. But I am going to ask you both something. And I want you to understand that we have never before asked this of anybody outside the twenty-seven permanent members. So you can understand that this is a mark of our respect for you, and especially both of your fathers."

Marni frowned. "Both...?"

He nodded. "Your father refused membership. We offered it to him because he was an exceptional man. He refused, even knowing what the consequences would be. So we had to kill him, because he would have destroyed us. But we respected him for his commitment to his own beliefs."

She looked at me, as though she was searching for something in my face. There was a wordless exchange between us, and then Hennessy was talking again.

"I am going to ask you a question which your father was never able to answer, Marni. How can we save humanity from the catastrophic changes that are coming? How can we avoid the millions of deaths, the famine, the flooding, and still preserve all the best that humanity has achieved?"

She stared at him a long time without answering. Finally, he sat forward, with his elbows on his knees, and said, "You condemn us for the way we run Omega. Now I want you to tell me how I ought to be doing my job. And I promise you,

Marni, that I will listen to you with an open mind, and an open heart."

She took a deep breath. "First, Mr. President, the whole world must be informed of what is coming. Every single individual has the right to know the threat that he or she faces. If we are a plague on this planet, as we certainly are, then each of us needs to take responsibility—*personal* responsibility for reducing the population. It only requires each family to have only one baby, and within a generation…"

"We can come to the technicalities later, Marni. Let's stay with the general principles for now."

"Fine. Then the first thing would be to inform the entire world of the *facts* concerning climate change and overpopulation. Second would be a managed reduction of the population, and a steady, phased move away from the global, mass market, so that we can eliminate our reliance on fossil fuels. And third, engage the leading universities of the world in a systematic program to transform the way we get energy—to move away from fossil fuels and toward solar power, wind turbines… The more the population is reduced, the more feasible that becomes."

Hennessy nodded a few times after she had finished, then turned to me. "What about you, Lacklan? Have you anything positive to contribute to this discussion?"

I shrugged. "As you know, we went for a walk last night, where we could get away from your bugs…"

Ben said, "The house is not bugged. If you'd asked me, I would have told you."

I raised an eyebrow at him, then turned back to Hennessy. "We discussed our options; in the end, we agreed that those were the realistic options. I stand with Marni. If we are talking in generalities, those would be the obvious steps."

Hennessy scratched his cheek, then leaned back in his chair. "Obvious, yes, realistic, no, not really. And please let me explain why..." He hesitated. "Then I'll come back to my reasons for asking you, and to my proposal for you both. But first, let me explain why this is not a realistic suggestion. You see, whichever way you cook it, there are always going to be two options. The one you have suggested, and the other one. The other one is to ensure the participation of a small, powerful elite, insulate yourself from the damage as much as you can, and let ninety percent or ninety-nine percent of the population wipe themselves out. Then create a new society that works, with you at the top, running things. After five, ten, fifteen generations, the heirs to that elite will inherit a beautiful, stable, sustainable world."

Marni drew breath to say something, but he held up his hand. "Just hold on, and hear me out. Now that option, the one that you two both detest so much, is open not only to us, but to the Chinese, the Russians, the Muslim kingdoms, and Europe. It's open to anybody who has all the information. Knowledge, if you'll forgive me for using an old cliché, is power. Now, we would have to be plumb stupid to give away the kind of information that we have been able to gather through NASA and other sources, and allow ourselves to be sabotaged so that China, or North Korea, or Saudi Arabia, can seize the advantage and come out on top."

Ben had been nodding throughout this monologue. Now he said, "And that is without getting into the details of how we handle massive climate migration once the droughts start in earnest. The Middle East is already in the midst of the worst drought in recorded history. That can only get worse and spread. Once drought turns to famine on a global scale, as it soon will, and there is not enough—" He stopped, staring hard at Marni, then continued with almost savage emphasis. "*Simply not enough food to feed everybody.* Once that happens—and we are talking a decade or two at the very outside—once that happens, Marni, what do we do? All the information that you want to give these people will only fuel the chaos and the strife that is going to engulf the world. It will not *help* anybody, but it *will* lead to war."

Hennessy studied us both for a moment. Then, he drew breath and started to speak again. "However, having said that…"

Ben cut him short. "It is, Marni, Lacklan, like being in a city with three hundred thousand people all dying of some dreadful disease. And you know that in one, small clinic, there is enough medicine to save only two hundred people. If you spread the word to the city, the consequences will be devastating. And in the end the medicine, if it is not destroyed, will fall into the hands of the most violent and the strongest, the Hell's Angels or the Mafia. Your other option is to select the best, the finest, and offer them a share of the medicine." He turned and smiled at Hennessy. "Dick, forgive me, I interrupted you."

"It is a perfect simile. I was going to say that, in spite of this, because we admire you and because we loved your father, Lacklan, we are prepared to make you a very significant offer."

I raised an eyebrow. "Join or die? I've been made that

offer before, and I've lost count of how many of you people have died since then."

Hennessy sighed. "That is not the offer. We will create a committee for the purpose of studying your suggestions and finding a workable way to implement them. We will go further than that. We will make you both directors of that committee, with executive powers, to give it teeth. You can start as soon as you like, select whoever you want for the committee, and, within certain reasonable bounds, start reaching out to people to find a way forward. If you can make it work, then we will be happy to follow your ideas."

Marni was frowning hard. "*What?*"

Ben laughed. "It's not as incredible as you think, Marni. We are happy to do this for two very simple reasons. First, we don't believe it's possible, and you will discover that as you try to make it work. And second, if you *can* make it work, it will be everybody's preferred way forward."

She stared at him, then stared at me. I sighed loudly and reached into my jacket for a packet of Camels and my Zippo. As I lit up, Hennessy said, "You can't smoke in here."

I leaned into the flame, then snapped the lighter shut, inhaled deep, and blew smoke at the ceiling. "You want to come over here and make me stop, Dick?" I turned to Ben. "I have one, real big problem with your suggestion, Ben."

"I thought you might."

"You planted a nuclear device at the UN. It would have killed somewhere between a quarter and a half of the population of Manhattan, men, women, children, indiscriminately.

"Now, here's the interesting part about that. If you had wanted to cripple the U.S. economy for some reason, you would have picked the financial district. But you didn't, you very deliberately picked the UN. Why would you do that?" I held up a hand. "Don't answer, not yet. Before he escaped, Abbassi told me that Aatifa, Hassan, and Ali were set up, that the canister they thought they were planting was a dummy, that it was never intended to get through security." I laughed and shook my head. "I thought at first that they were intended to get caught at security, while trying to enter. But that wasn't it at all, was it, Ben?"

He shook his head. "No."

"The plan was that I would see Abbassi at the party. That was why you sent me there, and I would go after him and expose the plot to bomb the conference, or at least alert the Feds, just as I did. But I was never meant to escape from the Institute. I was supposed to stay there in a drugged stupor, while you went ahead and bombed the UN. Then Mclean and Jones would have revealed to the president that they'd had a warning that Islamic terrorists were going to bomb the conference with a dirty bomb. Knowing this administration's feelings about Islam, an all-out war was a certainty. What was Prince Awad's reward? Membership of the Alphabet Club?"

He didn't waver in his stare. He just said, "That is not the question, Lacklan. You can do better than that."

"Yeah, you're right. War in the Middle East is nothing new. You don't need to nuke Manhattan for that. But if you can claim that hostile powers in the Middle East, like Iran, have nuclear weapons, then that would justify the president in using nuclear to retaliate in the Gulf. And I can't prove it, but two gets you twenty that Russia would come in on the side of...."

"Don't be naïve, Lacklan. Russia would not come in on the side of Iran. But Europe would impose severe sanctions on the U.S. if we struck at Iran with a nuclear missile. Our military presence in Europe is very significant. We have U.S. Naval Forces Europe, U.S. Army Europe, U.S. Air Force in Europe, U.S. Marine Force Europe *and* U.S. Special Operations Command Europe. In addition to which we have about 250 nuclear warheads deployed in Italy, Turkey, Germany, Netherlands, and Belgium. Now, if those assets were seized by the European Union, driven by general public outrage, how do *you* think this president would respond.?"

A wave of nausea swept over me. I stared at him, and then at Hennessy. I heard my voice, but it was as though somebody else was speaking.

"Dear God... You were trying to trigger a war with *Europe?*"

Ben shrugged. "Why not? The last one was the best thing that ever happened to the U.S. The British Empire was crippled and we became top dog, remember?"

TWENTY-TWO

BEN ROSE AND WALKED TOWARD THE WINDOW that overlooked the internal garden. He stood in stark silhouette and stretched, making his vertebrae clunk. After a moment, he turned back to face us.

"You become pretty tedious sometimes, Lacklan. You're hard work. We need a war. So does Europe. It used to be easy. Countries went to war on a regular basis. Now public opinion has become so damn precious, even when we go to war, people expect our soldiers to get through it without getting hurt." He laughed and turned to Hennessy. "Hell! They even expect the *enemy* not to get hurt! So we needed a new 9/11. More than that, a new Pearl Harbor."

Marni was staring from him to Hennessy and back again. "Why? Why in God's name do you need to go to war with Europe? You must be *insane*."

Hennessy sighed like he was getting bored of having to explain the obvious. "Come on, Marni, get real. Why does anybody go to war? Why has anybody ever gone to war?

Religion? Of course not! Ideology? Of course not! People go to war over resources, land, *arable* land, food, water, minerals."

Her voice was shrill when she answered. *"And we are short of resources in this country?"*

I said, "No, but we will be. Draw a line from Washington, D.C. to Washington state, and in twenty years, everything south of that line will be desert."

She hadn't lost the shrill edge to her voice. She almost screamed, "So what? Now we are going to invade Europe? *Is that it?"*

Hennessy said, "Don't be absurd."

"Don't be absurd? *Really? You* are telling *me* not to be absurd? You want to *start a fucking war with Europe!"*

I said, "Marni." She stared at me like she was ready to hit me. "We should have seen this. This should not be a surprise."

She flopped back in her chair. Ben said, "Are we good?" I nodded. He went on. "Every so often, the world needs a war. As globalization and industrialization progress, necessarily those wars get bigger and their impact is more far-reaching. The wars in the Middle East have been beneficial, but we need something bigger, much bigger. Because when climate change really kicks in, we need to be in a position where we profit from it. Originally, our rival was Britain, then it was Russia, now it's Europe. Does that answer your question, Lacklan?"

"Yeah."

"Good. Now, Dick was going to make a proposal. We establish the committee, as he already outlined. In exchange, we want something from you."

"What?"

Ben looked at Hennessy. "Dick?"

He smiled, like he was granting us some great boon. "We want you to become permanent members of Omega. Lacklan, you will step in to your father's position as Gamma. You will be second to me. Marni, you will come in as Psi. You will both manage the Commission on Education and Reform, and you will marry. You will be man and wife, and you will commit to Omega."

I sat forward. "What? Why the hell...? What fucking business is it of yours...?"

"That's the deal, Lacklan. We know you both have strong feelings for each other. We would like you to marry and have a family." He laughed. "It's not so unusual, guys! All over America, all over D.C., corporate culture is the same: we want you to get married, make a home, have kids! It breeds stability, loyalty, harmony, and integration. It cements the culture of mutual support. Don't you love each other? I think you do."

I drained my glass, stood, and went back for another. I poured a generous measure and turned to face them. They looked complacent, like they already knew the outcome of the meeting. I said, "What about Gibbons?"

Ben said, "He returns to Oxford unharmed."

"What about his supposed murder?"

"A mistake. You are hailed as a hero and ISIS claim responsibility for the attempt, and you and Marni get a period of grace to make your plan work. But there is one thing we have not discussed yet."

Marni said, "My father's research..."

Ben said, "We must have that. That is not negotiable."

She looked at me. We held each other's gaze for a long moment, then she said, "I don't see that we have much option, Lacklan."

I looked at Ben and swore to myself that one day I would kill him. "OK, Ben. You have a deal."

Hennessy smiled. "Excellent. That is very good news, and I am confident that you will not regret the decision you have made today. Marni, where is your father's research?"

She buried her face in her hands and was silent for a long while. When she finally dropped them into her lap, her face was wet with tears. "It's in a box in a bank vault in Oxford. I have to instruct them to send it here." She turned to face Ben. "It must come via the diplomatic bag. The material contained in it is much too sensitive to risk any other means of transport."

He reached in his pocket and pulled out a card. He wrote a name on it and handed it to her. "Have them send it to this man at the U.S. Embassy in London. I'll advise him to expect it and forward it to former President Hennessy at this office, as a top priority, via the diplomatic bag. Will that satisfy you?"

She nodded.

He pointed at the desk. "You can use the phone over there."

"Now...?"

"Yes, Marni, now."

She looked at me, like she was begging me to do something, to stop this from happening. There was nothing I could do. She got up and went to make the call. Ben was studying me carefully. I didn't give him much to read. Finally, he said, "I am quite serious about the marriage,

Lacklan. I want you to see to that straight away. I want you living together and making a real commitment to Omega. Have kids. Be happy. Is that understood?"

I nodded and stood. "It's understood, and now I'd like to get the hell out of here."

Marni finished making her call and came and joined me by the door. She was having trouble controlling her tears. I put my arm around her but she shook her head and pushed away. Hennessy smiled at me, though his eyes were hard and cold. "It'll take a bit to adjust, but give it time. Meanwhile, we'd like you to stay in D.C. just until the package arrives. We'll be keeping an eye on you, just to make sure everything's OK. My advice? Use the time to get acquainted. It's been a long time since you two had a proper conversation." He gave me a friendly punch on the shoulder. "Hell, Lacklan, take your lady out to dinner, show her a good time, talk about the future. Things are going to be good for you guys from now on. You can stop looking over your shoulder."

I held his eye a moment too long, then said, "Yeah, you, too."

I opened the door and we stepped out. We didn't speak in the elevator, or as we crossed the Pentagon rings, moving toward the exit. We didn't talk until we were back outside in the sunshine. Then I took her in my arms and held her for a long while, feeling the cool breeze from the river on my face, listening to the cry of the gulls overhead and the mournful bray of a riverboat in the distance. She looked up into my face and I kissed the tears from her eyelids and her cheeks.

"Come on," I said. "Let's go and get drunk."

———

WE WOUND up in the Free State, a rustic basement on G St SW. It had only just opened. The place was almost empty and we were able to get a small table by the bare-brick wall, with a couple of high stools and a couple of draught beers. We sat in silence for a long while until she said to the table, "Why does he want us to marry?"

I stared at her beer for a moment, at her fingers holding it. "Would that be such an awful thing?"

She looked at me in astonishment and blinked. "If I were ever... If we ever married, Lacklan, I'd like it to be because we chose to, not because some weird-ass organization dreamed up by Chris Carter on a bad acid trip, tells us to."

"I agree."

"Why? What's in it for them?"

I shrugged. "Control. With each of us operating randomly, doing our own thing, we were out of control. We did a lot of damage." She held my eye and it was hard to read her expression. I went on, "You know 'guerilla' in Spanish means 'small war'. If waged in the right way, it can do a lot more damage than a direct military confrontation, not only to the actual infrastructure of your enemy, but to their morale."

"So you're saying they want to convert us from wild guerillas into a small army that they can control?"

I nodded. "It's what empires, ever since the Romans, have done. The Gauls, all of those Nordic and Celtic tribes, they were a pain in Rome's ass, but they were too small and too quick to be effectively confronted by huge, slow moving armies. So they gave them incentives to consolidate, and then they employed them. They became some of the most effective legions in the Roman army. The British did the same in

India and Africa, but they lost America because, here, they failed to do that. Bring the guerillas together into a force you can handle, then either destroy them or employ them."

She sighed. "Literally marry them together."

"Yup."

"So I was right to avoid you for so long."

"No. We need to act together. Marni…" She raised her eyes to meet mine. "I was wrong in London, when I said no. I wanted to protect you from what I had become. But I was wrong."

Her eyes strayed. She nodded. "So what now?"

I stared down into the froth in my beer. It seemed to me to be clinging to the edge of the empty glass for dear life. I knew how it felt. I said, "Will you allow me to digress for a moment?"

She gave a small laugh. "Sure, it can't do any harm."

"I was in Afghanistan. We, the Regiment, we operate in groups of four." I gave a small laugh. "We are recruited for our skill, resilience, commitment… all that stuff. But we are also recruited for being eccentric individualists. Not many people know that. Four eccentric individualists can do an immeasurable amount of damage to a Third Reich, a Soviet Union, ISIS, to any organization that wants to standardize human beings. It's a very English way of looking at things."

She nodded. "I get that."

"It's a long story, but, cutting to the chase, we were in the north of Helmand. We were attacked and we were separated. Sergeant Bradley, Bat Hays, and Nick Barns went one way, toward the extraction point, and I went another. I had to make my way south, back to Camp Bastion, through the desert, where there was no food and no water. So I had to make small raids on villages and farms that were trying to eke an existence out of the sand." I paused and sighed, not sure myself what point I was trying to make. In the end, I said, "I was one man. All I was trying to do was survive. The regime of the Taliban demanded one thing, and one thing only, absolute observance of the Koran, absolute obedience to Allah and his prophet Mohamed. I was a bacterium. I was one, single organism that by its simple presence threatened the integrity of their entire body. Not by anything that I was doing, because all I was doing was stealing a chicken here, a tomato there, a canteen of water from a well. The threat came from the simple fact of my presence. Because I was an eccentric individualist, and my intention was to fight against their culture of absolute obedience."

She studied my face for a long while, then said, "And only give up when you were dead."

I nodded. "They want—they *believe*—that our marriage will make us easier to control. Let them believe that, Marni. But let our marriage be eccentric and individualist, and let our marriage be a virus in itself, that undermines the very fabric of Omega." I hesitated, then went on, "Marni, because you are a mad scientist and I love you, because I am an eccentric individualist, and I love you, will you please marry me?"

She gave a small yelp and covered her mouth with her hands. The barman looked over and smiled. I saw tears spill from her eyes. I laughed, and she laughed and cried and reached for a paper napkin to mop her eyes and blow her nose. After a bit, she leaned across the table and took my hands. "Yes, Lacklan, I will."

We talked then, and made plans. We ate, and talked more, about us, her and me, as unique, eccentric individuals, and what we wanted from our lives. Then we walked through the city streets, down the boulevards and avenues, strolled in the parks and the gardens. Indifferent to whether we were being followed or not, we made our path and we made our plans. And, as the sky turned to copper and the shadows grew long in that city designed by dreamers, libertarians, and Masons, two hundred and thirty years earlier, we fled. We hailed a taxi and fled, holding each other in silence in the back seat of the cab, traveling north and west, toward our temporary home, our refuge in the woods.

When we got there, my car was in the driveway. I felt a brief surge of anger at the thought of one of them driving my Zombie, as though they had somehow violated it. But I suppressed the feeling and told myself I would find the tracking devices later. There would be at least two, one for me to find, another for them to follow. Marni and I looked at each other and shrugged. Then we went inside.

Mrs. Henderson was there in the kitchen, and we told her our news, that we had got engaged. She was delighted and insisted on cooking us a meal that night. She lit the fire, though it wasn't necessary, set the table with a linen cloth, a candle, and crystal goblets, and even retrieved a bottle of twenty year-old Burgundy from a wine cellar we didn't know the house had.

At eight fifteen she placed a roast leg of lamb, a dish of roast potatoes, sautéed vegetables, and the wine on the table, gave us both a huge hug each, and cycled away into the gathering evening, ringing her bell and waving happily.

We stood on the doorstep and, after she'd gone, we kissed, for all the world to see. Then we stepped inside for our engagement dinner.

TWENTY-THREE

As I started to carve, Marni dropped into her chair and buried her face in her hands. I kept carving, but after a moment I asked her, "Are you OK?"

She rubbed her face, then ran her fingers through her hair and heaved a huge sigh.

"Yeah. No. I don't know, Lacklan. This... all this..."

"What about it? We discussed it. The least we can do is try to make it work."

"I know, I know. And in theory, that's fine. But I can't shake the feeling that I am being a hypocrite. That I am somehow betraying my father."

I handed her her plate with three slices of lamb on it. I smiled, though not exactly happily. "Do we have to do this now? We are supposed to be celebrating our engagement."

She looked distracted. "I know. I'm sorry." She helped herself to potatoes and vegetables and I poured the wine. When I sat down, I raised my glass to her.

"Here's to us, and to the future."

She stared at me for a long moment, hesitated, then raised her glass with little enthusiasm.

"To us."

We drank and I set down my glass and leaned back in my chair while she started to eat.

"You know, I was in the Regiment for ten years."

"Yes, I know that."

"In many ways they were very happy years. I made very good, very loyal friends. They were more than friends, more than family. I could have stayed, made major or even colonel."

She was chewing, watching me. She sipped and said, "But...?"

"Two things conspired to make me leave and come back, buy my shack in Wyoming and retire from the world."

"What were they?"

"In no particular order, I grew tired of killing. You develop an emotional callus after a time, but it's strange, your own lack of feeling ends up nauseating you. You *want* to feel. You need to. And when I'd done my ten years, I decided it was time to stop."

I paused, and she said, without looking at me, "And the other?"

"You. Five years earlier you came to London and asked me to go home, so that we could be together. I told you no."

"That's something I am not likely to forget, Lacklan."

"I regretted it the moment I'd said it, and I have regretted it every day since then. When I left the Regiment, I had a hope, maybe it was more of a hopeless dream, that if I came back to the States, maybe, somehow, one day, we might come back together. It is the one thing that has kept me going all this time."

She looked serious and laid down her knife and fork. "This should be a joyful occasion, Lacklan. You know how I feel about you. But we are not alone at this table. Ben is here with us, Dick Hennessy is at this table. The whole damned organization is listening to our conversation, recording every word we say so that they can use it against us if they need to. It's fake. It's not real."

"Marni, we have been through this! We talked about it! We decided it was the only course open to us. We may as well make the most of it. Those were your words."

"Well..." She took another deep breath. "Maybe I was wrong."

I frowned. "What are you saying?"

"I don't know if I can go through with it. I'm sorry."

"*What?*"

"I'm sorry, Lacklan! I am not a hypocrite!"

"So I am?"

"I didn't say that..."

"What about Gibbons? You know what will happen to him if you back out?" She didn't answer, just sat staring at her plate. I pushed. "They'll kill him! And they'll make it look like I did it!"

She turned on me, with bright, angry eyes. "This is *war*, Lacklan! You should know that! In war there is collateral damage!"

"*Collateral damage!* Are you *serious?* He is not collateral, Marni! He is a human being! A good man!"

"A good man that you were prepared to kill less than a week ago!"

"To save *your* life! Not to salve *my* conscience!"

"Well, maybe I am a hypocrite after all!"

"Maybe you are!" I stood and threw my napkin on the table, went to the credenza and poured myself a whiskey. I took a swig and turned to face her. "What will you do? Escape back to England? Shack up with Gibbons in Oxford? Oh, no, he'll be dead! You'll have to find another academic to use! You know what they'll do to me, right? After they have framed me for murder, they'll kill me, too. So that's two men you will have got killed, Gibbons and me, but hey, don't let it worry you. At least your conscience will be intact."

"You are one vicious, sarcastic bastard."

I leaned forward, half-shouting, "You are going back on your promise! You are sentencing two men to death!"

She stood, shouting louder, *"A promise made under duress to an organization that plans to exterminate and enslave the human race!"*

I shouted back, *"No! A promise to me! To stand by my side! To be my wife! And instead of honoring that promise you are sentencing me to death!"*

"Oh for crying out loud, Lacklan! Enough with the melodrama!"

I stared at her. "Melodrama? *Melodrama...?* You are the one talking about exterminating and enslaving the entire race! We don't even know if that's true anymore! We have been offered the chance to change the direction Omega is moving in. You won't even *try*! You won't even give it a chance! You are so concerned with your fucking conscience, you are prepared to sentence two men to death and walk away from the one realistic chance we have of changing this organization!"

She didn't answer. She just stared at me. Her eyes were resentful and her mouth was sour. I drained my glass and put it down. "You know what, Marni? I have had it with you. I have had it with chasing you, with your stupid way of doing things, with your lack of trust, with your screwed-up priorities. You killed my father, now you've killed me. Well, fuck you!"

I grabbed my jacket and my car keys and walked out of the house. I stood a moment in the driveway, looking up at the stars, feeling slightly sick. I lit a cigarette, climbed into my car, and slammed the door. I sat a moment, smoking and thinking, before I fired up the silent engines and pulled out onto the road.

It was a short drive, just fifteen minutes down MacArthur Boulevard and into the city. A left just before Washington Circle and I was on Pennsylvania Avenue. I pulled up outside her block and sat staring at it for a long time. It was a strange, red brick corner building, with arched windows and a jumbled tower at the top. Eventually, I lit up another Camel, pulled her card from my wallet, and dialed her number.

"Hello? This is Dr. Lara Banks. Who is this?"

"Hello, Dr. Banks. It's Lacklan Walker."

"Mr. Walker!"

I allowed an ironic smile into my voice. "I think when you've had a man kicked half to death, you're entitled to use his first name."

"Where are you? What do you want?"

"Don't be afraid. I am not coming after you. Things have changed. Have you spoken to Ben?"

"Yes..."

"I'm in a fix. I need your help."

"*My* help?"

"I know. Life is full of little ironies like that. It's not just me. I think Omega will be grateful. Can we talk?"

She was silent for a moment, like she was thinking. Then, "Yes. Of course. Where are you?"

"Outside your front door. May I come up?"

"Yes." Then, again, "Yes, of course, come on up."

I hung up, flicked my cigarette out the window, and sat thinking for another minute before I climbed out and crossed the road. She buzzed me in to a luxurious brass and mahogany lobby, and I rode the elevator to the top floor. She let me in as soon as I rang the bell.

The apartment was a collection of vast, open spaces rather than rooms. The décor was all in black and white. The floor was black wood with a high polish, and white rugs were strewn here and there, apparently at random. The ceiling was paneled in white wood, and the walls were painted white, except for one, in the area where she had her sofas, chairs, and TV. There, one entire wall was white marble streaked with gray, and set into it was a black marble open fireplace. In the middle of the floor, a black dining table sat on a white rug, with twelve chairs set about it, and a white candle in the middle.

I stood looking around and she closed the door behind me.

"Are you going to kill me?"

"No. I told you. I need your help."

"It was brutal what you did to my nurses." She came and stood in front of me, frowning up into my face. "And to Nurse Rogers. You raped her."

I raised an eyebrow. "I missed the part where she said, 'No.' How much do you know about the deal Dr. Gilbert and I made with Ben?"

She shook her head. "Not very much."

"There is a lot riding on it." I gave my head a quick shake. "It's impossible to overstate how important this deal is."

"I see..." She gestured at the sofas. "Shall we sit? A drink?"

"Yeah, I'll have the same as you, and if you don't mind, I'll watch you pour it."

She poured the drinks, and after she had sipped, I took her glass and gave her mine. Then we sat.

"Dr. Gilbert has got cold feet. We had just got engaged, this afternoon. We'd reached an arrangement with Ben, with Omega, that on the face of it met with all our demands and theirs." I hesitated. "Yours...?"

She nodded. "Yes. I am Omega."

I shrugged. "We were celebrating, and suddenly she started backtracking, getting hysterical, accusing me of betraying everything that we had fought for. I explained to her that she was putting my life and Professor Gibbons' in jeopardy, but it made no difference. In the end, I walked out."

She was frowning, like she was trying to understand what I was saying. When I'd finished, she said, "What I don't understand, Mr... *Lacklan*, is why you have come to me."

I sat back in my chair, crossed my legs, and returned her

frown. "I would have thought it was obvious, Lara. You specialize in manipulating people's minds. That is basically all about persuasion, or am I being naïve? I need you—Omega needs you—to persuade Dr. Gilbert, Marni, to honor the commitments she has made to me and to Omega."

She combined a smile with a frown and made it look like skepticism. "OK, assuming for a moment that I believe you, which is not necessarily the case, why this miraculous turn around? A couple of days ago you were killing us off like flies. And today you are trying to persuade me to recruit Dr. Gilbert onto the team?" She shook her head. "That is not credible."

I snorted. "It's not credible and it's not true. Believe me, Lara, if I had my way, I'd nuke the lot of you. But I am a realist, and the last phase of every war in the last two thousand years has been the phase of negotiation. I know when I am outgunned and out-maneuvered. I also know I can hurt you very badly—but I can't win. So we negotiate. And through negotiation, maybe I can achieve my ends."

She studied me for a few moments. Her expression had changed. She made a face and said, "You sound like a man who could be an asset."

"That's what Ben thinks, and it's what I am beginning to think. But Marni thinks that is hypocrisy. I need you to change her perspective, make her see it differently."

She spread her hands. "Well, do you want to bring her to see me tomorrow?"

"No. We haven't got that long. It has to be now."

"Right now?"

"Right now. If Ben and Hennessy find out about her

change of heart, it could cost me and Gibbons our lives. And that is just the start of it."

She sighed. "What do you expect me to do, Lacklan? I am a psychiatrist, not a magician!"

"I don't know, Lara! But you have to do something. Talk to her! Try to persuade her! She won't listen to Ben, she won't listen to me. She sees us both as having a vested interest. But you, she doesn't know you. She doesn't need to know you are Omega. You are just a friend of mine, somebody impartial. Tell her I used to see you when I got back from England, as a therapist. Just use your techniques to make her see the consequences of what she is going to do!"

She sighed again. "Very well, but I can't promise anything, Lacklan. I honestly think you're clutching at straws."

"If straws is all there is, then that's what I have to clutch at, right?"

She stared at me, then nodded once. "Alright, let's go."

We left our drinks virtually untouched. She grabbed her coat and we left.

As we crossed the road toward the Zombie, in the dull amber of the streetlamps, I asked her, "Have you told Ben I am here?"

She shook her head. "Not yet, but I will have to."

I studied her a moment across the roof of the car. "Just wait till you've talked to her, will you? Let's at least try and make this work. It's not too late yet, but once you tell Ben..."

She nodded. "Let's do it."

We drove in silence, moving through the city toward the river. Soon the city lights were falling behind us and we were in darkness, surrounded by dense trees, a deep wall of blackness against the night sky, and only the amber beams from my headlamps to show the road ahead.

Unexpectedly, as the darkness closed in around us, Banks said, "You scare me, Lacklan."

I answered without thinking. "You only need to fear me if you're my enemy, Lara."

She stared at my face, but didn't reply. Shortly after that, I turned onto Chain Bridge Road and a couple of minutes later, I pulled into the drive. The lights were on and I could hear music. I killed the engine, climbed out, and opened the door. Banks was just behind me. The music was big band jazz from the thirties and the forties. There was a lot of clarinet and it sounded like Benny Goodman or Artie Shaw. It was happy music and made a weird contrast with the stillness of the room. The table was as I had left it, but Marni was sitting in an armchair holding a martini, staring at the fireplace, where the flames were dying down to embers.

Banks closed the door and I went over and switched off the music. Now the only sound was the desultory crack and spit of the burning logs. She still didn't look at me, but I said, "I've brought somebody to talk to you."

She raised her eyes to mine for a moment, then turned to look at Banks, who was still standing by the door. Marni asked, "Are you a friend of Ben's?"

I said, "No, this is Lara. She's a psychiatrist."

Marni threw back her head and laughed out loud. "So because I don't agree with you, I need a shrink? Boy! You really *have* joined Omega!"

I sighed. "Don't be absurd, Marni. Lara helped me a lot when I left the Regiment, to deal with all the issues I had back then. She has nothing to do with Ben or with Omega. I thought, if you could talk to somebody objective—if *we* could talk to an objective mediator, we might be able to resolve this, come to some resolution before it's too late."

Marni looked at her skeptically. "You just happened to be in Washington?"

Banks smiled at her. "No, I didn't just happen to be here. I live and work in Washington. This is my home."

Marni turned to me. "How come you've never mentioned this before?"

There was an edge to my voice. "Maybe because we have never actually spoken, because every time I have tried to get close to you, you have run away." I sighed. "Do you want a drink?" She shrugged. I looked at Banks. "Will you have that drink now? The one you were going to have at your apartment?" She smiled and nodded, and while I poured, she approached Marni and said, "May I sit?"

"Sure."

"Do you mind if we give this a try? I think it's worth it, don't you?"

I handed Banks a martini. She took it and sipped. "Thank you."

I handed Marni hers and for a moment our eyes met. I smiled. "I guess the first thing is that I need to do is apologize. I said things I should not have said, and which I didn't mean. I guess we have both been under a lot of stress."

I raised my glass. "Here's to fresh starts and new beginnings!"

We all three drank to that. But then Marni sighed and shook her head.

"Look, Lacklan, Lara, I appreciate what you are trying to do, and believe me, Lacklan, I do understand why you're mad. But I am sorry, I just can't go through with this. I *cannot* collaborate with the enemy. I can't and I won't."

Banks sipped and then sighed. "Marni, you know, often, when a situation looks simple, black and white, and our options seem limited, a small change of perspective can suddenly throw up a lot of new options. I believe you love Lacklan, don't you?"

She shrugged and stared down at her glass. "Of course I do."

"And you understand, from what he has told me, that if you pull out of this agreement, it will probably cost him and some other people their lives..."

Marni nodded, still staring at her glass.

"Then can we at least agree this much, that it is really very important for us three, tonight, to reach some kind of arrangement that satisfies your conscience, but also ensures Lacklan's safety?"

Marni drained her glass and handed it to me. "Can I have another, please?"

I took the glass and looked at Banks. "You want a refill?"

"Sure."

She drained her glass and I refilled both of them at the sideboard. When I handed them back their drinks, Marni looked me square in the eye and said, "No. You have survived till now, fighting and killing, you can continue doing that. To quote your words just before you left, Lacklan, fuck you."

TWENTY-FOUR

I STARED AT HER, THEN BELLOWED, "*WHAT THE HELL is the matter with you, Marni? Have you gone out of your mind?*"

"Fuck you!"

"*Just talk to me!*"

"*Fuck you!*"

"*For crying out loud, Marni! What's got into you?*"

"*Fuck you!*"

"*You had better stop saying that Marni, or so help me God....!*"

"*What? So help you God, what? What are you going to do? Kill me? Is that your fucking answer to everything? Kill! Kill! Kill! That's all you know how to do, you fucking animal! Well, fuck-you! Fuck you! Fuck you!*"

She got to her feet, walked to the French windows and stood looking out.

My voice was cold and quiet when I said, "It was you who killed my father..."

After a moment she turned to face me. "And he murdered mine. He was a murdering bastard, just like you. You are your father's son, Lacklan. Fuck him and fuck you, too. Fuck you both."

I walked away from her, out into the hall, out into the drive, to my car. I opened the trunk and pulled over my kit bag. I found the Smith & Wesson and loaded it with five 700 grain rounds. I walked back into the house to where she was sitting, with her eyes closed. There was a savageness, a madness to my voice.

"You think you can use me? You think you can tell me you love me in the morning, and then sentence me to death in the evening? You think you can write me off and sentence millions of others to death just to salve your fucking conscience? Well you can't, Marni. Maybe you're right, maybe I am a killer. But when I kill, it's for a reason—a better reason than moral vanity!"

I aimed with both hands and blew her head off at near point blank range. I emptied the five rounds into her, then I went to the garage and collected two of the gallon gasoline cans I had seen earlier. I brought them back to the living room and doused her body and the chair with the contents of one, and the rest of the room with the other. Then I took the candle, went to the door and threw it in.

I climbed in my car, lit a cigarette, and drove away into the night, not following any particular road, just heading north and west, following the Potomac, into the dark, toward the wilderness.

After about an hour, when I had reached the outskirts of Bedford, I pulled over to the side of the road, in the cover of some trees, and took Banks' phone. I sent Ben a message from it.

"One thing I can't forgive, Ben, is betrayal. Marni betrayed me, after I was willing on so many occasions to give my life for her. I have killed her, and I have taken Dr. Banks hostage. If you come after me, I will kill her. Allow me to disappear and I will let her return to you when I am safe. It's over, forget me."

I pressed 'send'. Then, I climbed out of the car and threw the phone into the trees. After that, I spent half an hour finding the bugs in the car and throwing them after the phone. Finally, I climbed back into the Zombie and smiled at the beautiful woman sitting next to me.

"Before you go, I want to show you my house in Wyoming. We'll spend a couple of days there. A honeymoon for the wedding we never had. Then, I'll take you to San Francisco, you can fly from there."

Marni nodded, leaned forward and kissed me.

"I will come back. We will make it happen. I promise."

"I know. We'll never give up."

"Not till we're dead."

———

IT WAS THE NEXT MORNING, while we were having an early breakfast of coffee and scrambled eggs at a service station in Indiana, that we heard it on the news.

"...in a week that has rocked the world, we have barely recovered from the revelation that a United States-made tactical nuclear device was smuggled into the United Nations, armed and set to detonate, with sufficient power to take out most of lower Manhattan and part of Brooklyn, we are barely recovering from this devastating shock, when we now hear that a bomb has exploded in the very heart of the Pentagon, killing three people. But as if that were not enough, we are now hearing that the identity of one of the victims has been confirmed as that of former President Dick Hennessy. A tragic loss to the nation, that has left us utterly, utterly stunned. We can't help but wonder what new horrors are in store for us, and pray, Bill, that this nightmare will soon come to an end..."

We paid, in cash, and as the sun spread its early light over the highway, we climbed into the Zombie and headed north, toward the wilderness.

I knew Banks would be completely unrecognizable—the Smith & Wesson had taken care of any possible identification by dental records, and the fire had taken care of everything else. We had a reprieve, we had some time. Meanwhile, I hoped Mclean would survive, and that he would eventually check his email. Who knew? One day he might become an ally. As for Gibbons, we knew from a phone call to Green College that he was safely back in Oxford. With me out of the frame as his killer, I trusted that Omega would not dare take him out.

And the fiasco at the UN had started to burn out of control. It wasn't enough to bring Omega down, not yet, but it had hurt them badly, and the fight would continue. We would win. We would win, or we would die.

Don't miss A HARVEST OF BLOOD The riveting sequel in the Omega Thriller series.

Scan the QR code below to purchase A HARVEST OF BLOOD.

Or go to: righthouse.com/a-harvest-of-blood

NOTE: flip to the very end to read an exclusive sneek peak...

DON'T MISS ANYTHING!

If you want to stay up to date on all new releases in this series, with this author, or with any of our new deals, you can do so by joining our newsletters below.

In addition, you will immediately gain access to our entire *Right House VIP Library*, which includes many riveting Mystery and Thriller novels for your enjoyment!

righthouse.com/email

(Easy to unsubscribe. No spam. Ever.)

ALSO BY BLAKE BANNER

Up to date books can be found at:
www.righthouse.com/blake-banner

ROGUE THRILLERS
Gates of Hell (Book 1)
Hell's Fury (Book 2)
Ice Burn (Book 3)
Judgement by Fire (Book 4)

ALEX MASON THRILLERS
Odin (Book 1)
Ice Cold Spy (Book 2)
Mason's Law (Book 3)
Assets and Liabilities (Book 4)
Russian Roulette (Book 5)
Executive Order (Book 6)
Dead Man Talking (Book 7)
All The King's Men (Book 8)
Flashpoint (Book 9)
Brotherhood of the Goat (Book 10)
Dead Hot (Book 11)
Blood on Megiddo (Book 12)
Son of Hell (Book 13)
Merchant of Death (Book 14)
Extinction C-14 (Book 15)

HARRY BAUER THRILLER SERIES

Dead of Night (Book 1)
Dying Breath (Book 2)
The Einstaat Brief (Book 3)
Quantum Kill (Book 4)
Immortal Hate (Book 5)
The Silent Blade (Book 6)
LA: Wild Justice (Book 7)
Breath of Hell (Book 8)
Invisible Evil (Book 9)
The Shadow of Ukupacha (Book 10)
Sweet Razor Cut (Book 11)
Blood of the Innocent (Book 12)
Blood on Balthazar (Book 13)
Simple Kill (Book 14)
Riding The Devil (Book 15)
The Unavenged (Book 16)
The Devil's Vengeance (Book 17)
Bloody Retribution (Book 18)
Rogue Kill (Book 19)
Blood for Blood (Book 20)
The Cell (Book 21)
Time to Die (Book 22)
The Reaper of Zion (Book 23)

DEAD COLD MYSTERY SERIES
An Ace and a Pair (Book 1)
Two Bare Arms (Book 2)
Garden of the Damned (Book 3)
Let Us Prey (Book 4)
The Sins of the Father (Book 5)
Strange and Sinister Path (Book 6)

The Heart to Kill (Book 7)
Unnatural Murder (Book 8)
Fire from Heaven (Book 9)
To Kill Upon A Kiss (Book 10)
Murder Most Scottish (Book 11)
The Butcher of Whitechapel (Book 12)
Little Dead Riding Hood (Book 13)
Trick or Treat (Book 14)
Blood Into Wine (Book 15)
Jack In The Box (Book 16)
The Fall Moon (Book 17)
Blood In Babylon (Book 18)
Death In Dexter (Book 19)
Mustang Sally (Book 20)
A Christmas Killing (Book 21)
Mommy's Little Killer (Book 22)
Bleed Out (Book 23)
Dead and Buried (Book 24)
In Hot Blood (Book 25)
Fallen Angels (Book 26)
Knife Edge (Book 27)
Along Came A Spider (Book 28)
Cold Blood (Book 29)
Curtain Call (Book 30)

THE OMEGA SERIES
Dawn of the Hunter (Book 1)
Double Edged Blade (Book 2)
The Storm (Book 3)
The Hand of War (Book 4)
A Harvest of Blood (Book 5)

ABOUT US

Right House is an independent publisher created by authors for readers. We specialize in Action, Thriller, Mystery, and Crime novels.

If you enjoyed this novel, then there is a good chance you will like what else we have to offer! Please stay up to date by using any of the links below.

Join our mailing lists to stay up to date -->
righthouse.com/email
Visit our website --> righthouse.com
Contact us --> contact@righthouse.com

 facebook.com/righthousebooks

X x.com/righthousebooks

instagram.com/righthousebooks

EXCLUSIVE SNEAK PEEK OF...

A HARVEST OF BLOOD

CHAPTER 1

Is revenge any part of justice? It's a question lawyers and philosophers agonize about in the abstract, usually over a fine malt, or a cognac, and a Havana cigar. But ask a mother whose daughter has been taken from her, raped and murdered, and she'll tell you justice is revenge. They are the same thing.

Marni had stayed six months. Omega had left us alone. They had their hands full dealing with the press and the media, and above all, with a very aggressive select committee appointed to look into the UN fracas, and former President Hennessy's death[1]. It was still big news, and I figured it would be for years to come. I never watch TV or read the papers anymore, but even so, it was hard to get away from the debates, the investigations, and the conspiracy theories that had sprung from it. And all of that had Omega keeping a very low profile indeed.

---

1. See *The Hand of War*

So they had been six idyllic months at my house in Wyoming, in the remotest place in the western world. We'd hardly seen anyone from one week to the next, and that suited us fine. We walked in the hills, fished and hunted for our food, and spent the evenings in front of the open fire, reading, listening to music, talking, laughing; healing.

But we both knew our time was limited. Omega had not gone away, and it would not be long before they came looking for us. So, as November drew to a close, I locked up the house, she packed her things, and we headed for San Francisco. There she called Professor Gibbons at Green College in Oxford and gave him a coded message that she was going back. At International Departures, she gave me one last kiss and told me she'd be in touch. The fight against Omega would continue. And as long as it did, we could not be together. It made us too vulnerable.

And next thing she was gone, swallowed by the crowd beyond the security gate, and I was alone. Again.

After that, I had driven east on the I-80, into worsening weather conditions. A weather alert had been issued. An unseasonable freezing front had been reported coming down from the Arctic across Canada and into the northwestern states. There were severe blizzards reported in North Dakota, Montana, and Idaho. It had been cold in San Francisco, but the skies had been blue and I had not expected problems driving back to Wyoming.

East of Reno, I had made a pit stop at a service station. It was three in the afternoon and I noticed that the sky in the north was turning black, and a cold wind had whipped up. I debated staying at the motel across the road, but I was seven hundred miles from home, and I'd figured I'd try and make it that night. In the Zombie 222, my modified Mustang Fastback, weather and cops permitting, I could make it in six hours and maybe beat the worst of the snow.

That was what I'd figured. So I stepped into the warm, noisy diner, found a table with a view of my car, ordered a steak sandwich and a large black coffee, and stared at the TV behind the bar. It was a current affairs talk show and Larry O'Connor was talking to Senator Cyndi McFarlane, who looked as though she was getting mad. She was leaning across the table, stabbing at the air with her finger.

"You know what makes me mad, Larry? I'll tell you. It makes me mad that Professor Gibbons has been publicly humiliated by the press and the media across this country, not because he lied, not because former President Hennessy proved him wrong, not because he was exposed—none of those things happened. He has been ridiculed because a bunch of hecklers made him look comical on stage. But everybody—and that includes you, Larry—everybody is carefully ignoring what he said. And everybody is ignoring the fact that today, in America, we have a select committee asking the question '*How the hell did an American-made nuclear device get into the hands of Islamic terrorists?*'"

Larry played it for the camera, which obligingly closed in on his face. He smirked and said, "I don't think everybody is ignoring it, Senator. It's just that he looked funny up there, getting excited like that. And let's face it, he *does* look like Bilbo Baggins!"

He got a laugh, but not from Cyndi McFarlane. She turned and surveyed the audience, waited for the laughter to die down a bit, and said, "Did any one of you lose somebody on 9/11?" The laughter died and Larry looked embarrassed.

She went on regardless. "Anyone here out of work, or can't afford medical care? Because let me tell you something, somebody put a nuclear device in the United Nations building. And they put it there, partly, to silence Professor Gibbons, the man you like to ridicule so much. And he was there to tell you that *successive* administrations, Democrat and Republican, have spent *seven trillion dollars* waging a war that only cost a few billion. Those seven trillion dollars are *interest*. Interest on money borrowed from financial institutions that belong to the friends, colleagues, and associates of the presidents in office during that war. That is not funny. You think that's funny? I don't. And I think it is very sad that you do."

Larry made a comical, chastened face for the camera, but only got a small, embarrassed laugh from the audience. They were with the Senator. He cleared his throat.

"So, moving on..."

"Who said we were moving on, Larry? I'm not ready to move on." Now she got the laugh, plus some applause. I smiled. I decided I liked her. "I am here to tell you," she said, "and America, something important. And neither you nor your network are going to silence me. There is a web of corruption in this nation of ours. It's a cancer that spreads clean across America, across the border into Mexico and across the sea into China and Russia in the East, and Europe and the U.K. in the west. And this corruption is controlled by a small group of men and women who will stop at nothing, and I mean *nothing*, to further their own corrupt ends. They have attempted to institute an unfettered government within the government and bend our democratic processes to allow them to rule supreme. But neither the legislature, nor the people, of this country, will allow that to happen!"

She got a lot of applause, whistles, and shouts of support, and Larry O'Connor was forced to join in. He was smiling, but you could see he was mad. I wondered if Ben and his cohorts at Omega were watching. I was pretty sure they were. Ben had told me once I could not hurt Omega. So far I had killed two of their senior members and right now I figured they were squirming in their padded leather chairs. But I wasn't kidding myself. They would manipulate the situation, and they would end up using it to their own ends. That was what they did best.

I paid my bill and stepped back into the parking lot. It had grown dark and I was surprised at how far the clouds had spread from the north. The wind had turned from cold to bitter and I shivered as I crossed to my car.

The Zombie 222 is the creation of a couple of crazy geniuses in Texas. The body is an original Mustang '68 Fastback. But under the hood she has twin lithium-fueled electric engines delivering eight hundred bhp, one thousand eight-hundred foot-pounds of torque direct to the back wheels. She'll go from 0 to 60 in one and a half seconds, with a top speed of 200 MPH. And she is totally silent.

I slipped out of the lot and headed west into the gathering dark. As I chased the amber funnels of my headlamps along the endless, straight thread of the blacktop, my mind reached back. The last thing that Marni and I had discussed was where we went from here. My own plan had been to hunt down the twenty-seven members of Omega, one by one, and assassinate them. It was simple and effective, and followed the most fundamental of rules in warfare: Cut off the head and the body will die. But she had dissuaded me and begged me to let her talk to Professor Gibbons, to use his contacts and bring in more allies. I wondered vaguely if Senator Cyndi McFarlane was one of those contacts. Either way, whether she was or not, for now there was nothing for me to do but wait.

Within half an hour, the sky had turned black and it had started to snow. Fifteen minutes after that, I passed the town of Lovelock. There was no traffic on the roads, the snow was beginning to stick and drift, and for the second time I thought maybe I should stop for the night. But fate had other plans for me.

Another fifteen minutes and I found myself in a blizzard, slamming on the brakes because I had realized at the last minute that I was plowing into a intersection that shouldn't have been there, and there was a truck bearing down on me fast from my left. I stopped with my hood three feet over the line and the truck passed within six inches of my headlamps. The blast of air rocked my car and a shower of snow, sucked up by the slipstream, smothered my windshield. The wipers cleared it, but suddenly I had no idea where I was, or how I had got there. Hindsight got busy telling me I should have stopped at a motel in Lovelock, and I was now inclined to agree with it. But hindsight wasn't telling me how I could get back to Lovelock. I knew straight ahead would take me deeper into the storm. The intersection gave me no left turn, so I turned right and hoped for the best.

The road got dark and the snow grew heavier. I began to worry. I would soon need to recharge the lithium batteries, and if I got stranded out here in this snow I would not last long. I told myself that sooner or later I must find a service station, a motel, or even just a house. But hard as I looked, I could see no sign of life. I could see nothing at all except the blackness and the glow of the deepening snow in my headlamps.

From cruising at 120 MPH I was now down to crawling at little more than 20, and if the snow got much deeper I wouldn't even be crawling. I'd be stuck and buried.

Eventually, after maybe half an hour or a little more, I began to see flickering lights on my right. I figured the road would eventually turn that way, but as I crawled on, the lights seemed to stay parallel. That told me there must be a turn off, an intersection, which might be hidden by the snow. But I could not afford to miss it. I needed to get to those lights. It would be ironic, I thought without much of a smile, if having survived ten years in the SAS, the worst that the Sinaloa cartel, FARC, ISIS and the Mujahidin could throw at me in hostile territory all over the world, I were finally to be killed at home, in Nevada, by a snow drift.

Ahead, the glow of my lamps picked out an irregularity on the roadside; a couple of signs, maybe a rest area, a row of mail-boxes, a fallen tree trunk... I slowed, stopped, and climbed out of the car. A million tiny knives of ice tore through my skin. I tramped unsteadily, ankle deep in snow, and saw it was a turn off that led through a blanket of darkness to the small cluster of lights flickering in the distance. There was a wooden sign by the road and I could just make out the name 'Independence' written on it.

I turned back to the car and saw again what I had taken to be a fallen tree trunk. It wasn't a tree. I walked over and hunkered down, wiping the snow from the body. It was a girl, maybe fifteen years old. Her skin was white and her lips were blue. I felt for a pulse. It was hard to tell because my own hands were freezing, but I thought I felt a flutter. I opened the passenger door, picked her up, and placed her with difficulty in the seat. I had a couple of rugs and blankets in the trunk from where Marni and I had gone on picnics. I grabbed them and wrapped her as warmly as I could. Then I closed the door, got behind the wheel, and turned down the track toward Independence.

CHAPTER 2

IT WAS ABOUT TWO AND A HALF MILES OF UNPAVED track. The snow was settling deep and several times I almost got stuck. Eventually, after five or ten minutes, we slowly slithered and ground our way in to a kind of town square, which was actually little more than a broadening of the road. On the right, there was a row of houses, with warm light creeping around heavy drapes to touch the heaped snow on the front lawns. On the left, there was a wooden fence with a gate. Through the gate I could make out a small orchard, a path, and a large wooden building with a sign over the door that read 'Pioneer Guesthouse'. But opposite, as an extension to the terrace of houses, there was a saloon bar that looked something like a large cottage. There were several trucks parked outside.

I left the Zombie by the gate to the guesthouse, opened the passenger door, and lifted the girl out, still swathed in rugs and blankets. She looked dead, but when I put my ear to her nose and mouth I could feel the soft, frail brush of her breath. I carried her across the small square, through the heavy fall of flakes, to the door of the saloon. I opened it with my foot and as I maneuvered myself through I shouted above the hum of voices, "*I have a wounded girl here! I need a doctor! Fast! I think she's dying!*"

Absolute silence fell on the room. Maybe a dozen faces stared at me. A man and a woman behind the bar, three men in their thirties standing at that bar, two tables occupied by middle-aged couples: twelve faces, staring, silent. I roared, "*A doctor! Now!*" An elderly man stood. I ignored him and turned to the nearest occupied table. "*You! Put two tables together!*" They jumped and started moving tables. To the couple behind the bar, I bellowed, "*Pillows! Cushions! Warm water!*"

It was like a chicken coop when Mr. Fox drops in for a visit. There were people all over the place trying to look busy. The two couples I'd shouted at had jumped up and pushed two tables together to form a make-shift bed. One of the men had pulled off his tweed jacket and folded it to make a pillow for her head. I laid her gently down and started rubbing her hands. I noticed the elderly guy who'd stood up was taking off her shoes and rubbing her feet. He shouted suddenly, "*Abi! That water! Hurry! Not too hot! Warm! Tepid even!*"

"You the doc?"

"I am." He glanced around. "Where is Sammy? *Sammy!*" A young man in his mid-twenties stepped up, looking apologetic.

"Yes, Doctor Graham."

"Take over from this man! Keep rubbing her extremities.

Get some warmth into her... You." This last was directed at me. "Get a hot drink inside you!"

But I was looking at Sammy. He had his mouth open and he was staring at the girl's face. I looked at the other people who had by now formed a circle around us. They all had the same expression as he had. I said to him, "Get a grip, Sammy. Start rubbing."

I pushed through the small crowd and went to lean on the bar. I felt suddenly very tired and very cold. I saw Abi bustle out of the kitchen with a pan of warm water and make for the table. There were three men leaning against the bar next to me, watching the proceedings, and as I put my elbows on the counter, they gave me the once over. They weren't hostile, but I got the feeling they reserved the right to turn that way. The guy behind the bar came over.

"What can I get you, mister?"

"Hot coffee, and a double whiskey. You can leave the bottle."

He poured me a generous measure and left the bottle, then went to the kitchen to make coffee. Outside, the wind rattled the windows, whistled, and rose briefly to shriek before settling again to groaning and moaning. I drained the glass and refilled it. The guy standing next to me said, "Passing through?"

I glanced at him. He was six foot, had balding, sandy hair and pale blue eyes. He was bull-necked, had strong arms and a barrel chest. I shook my head. "Nope. I got lost in the storm. I turned right somewhere after Lovelock."

"Where you headed?"

For a moment I thought of asking him why he wanted to know. Instead, I said, "Wyoming."

He gave his head a small twitch to the side. "You're four hundred mile from Wyoming. Reckon you turned south a Mill City." He smiled. It wasn't friendly. "Nobody ever comes to Independence on purpose."

Behind me, I heard the doctor say they needed to get the girl to a warm bed, and to bring some hot water bottles for her. Then there was a bustle of movement and I saw them carry her into the kitchen. I figured there must be stairs there to the upper floors. I watched them go and turned back to the big guy who'd been talking to me. "Where's your sheriff?"

His eyes seemed to half-close for a moment. "Over in Lovelock. He don't never come out this way. We got a whole mountain range between us and Lovelock. What you want the sheriff for?"

I wondered again whether to answer him or not. I took another drink and said, "I found her by the side of the road. I was wondering how she got there. I thought maybe the sheriff would wonder that too."

He didn't answer. He just stared at me with no expression. The young guy came out with my coffee and poured me a cup. I said, "You got any food?"

He looked momentarily astonished. Maybe that was the big thing in this town, being astonished by everything. After a moment of astonishment, he said, "Yuh! Sure! We have beef and red beans?"

I nodded. "Good, and some bread. And give me a beer."

I took my beer and my whiskey to a table and sat. My friend at the bar got the hint and turned his back on me, started talking to his pals. Eventually, the woman called Abi came out of the kitchen with a large bowl of beans and stewing steak, and a basket of bread and butter. She placed them in front of me and sat. I was surprised and told her so with my face.

"Excuse me." She looked distressed. I studied her for a moment. She was very attractive in an un-affected kind of way. She was maybe thirty-six or -seven, wholesome, blonde, blue-eyed; very much a woman. "I just wanted to thank you."

"For what?"

"Peggy. She would surely have died."

"Is that her name? Peggy?"

"Peggy-Sue Martin. Where on Earth did you find her? What happened?"

I was aware that the men at the bar had gone silent and turned to face us. I ignored them.

"I took a wrong turn 'round about Mill City. I was looking for a motel, or somewhere to stay the night. I stopped when I saw the signpost for Independence. Luckily I got out of my car to read the sign. At first I thought it was a tree-stump. Then I saw it was a girl."

She was staring at me like I was talking Klingon, and she didn't speak Klingon. "At the junction? With Bloody Creek?"

I shrugged. "The main road where you have your mail boxes."

"What in the name of the Good Lord was she doing there?"

I shrugged again, this time with my eyebrows, and shoveled a spoonful of meat and beans into my mouth. It was good. I spoke through a full mouth. "I was wondering the same thing."

She turned and stared at the men at the bar. It was hard to read anybody's expression. I said, "Is there somewhere I can stay till the storm passes?"

She turned back to me. "Of course. I have the guesthouse across the way. I'll fix you a room there."

I continued eating. She was about to stand but I asked her, "What about her parents?"

She didn't answer straight away, which made me look up from my food. Then, she said, "They live up the road."

"Is somebody going to tell them?" She didn't answer and I leaned back in my chair. "They didn't alert anybody that she was missing?"

She shook her head.

I drained my beer. "Tell me where they live. I'll go and get them."

My talkative friend at the bar spoke up. "You're a regular good Samaritan, friend. Take it easy. I'm going that way. I'll deliver the news and I'm sure they'll be down to thank you." As he walked past, he put his hand on Abi's shoulder. "Good night, Abi. Be seeing you."

I heard the door open behind me. There was a blast of cold air and the shriek and moan of the freezing wind in the trees. Then the door closed again, shutting out the night behind its fragile wood and glass.

"That's Earl," she said, as though she owed me an explanation, and an apology. "He works at the farm."

I should have let it go, but I could see Peggy's frozen white face, her blue lips and her fragile, childlike body huddled in the snow, and something made me say, "Farm?"

"Aloysius Groves' farm. Al. Most people 'round here

work for the farm. They'll probably be down in the morning."

I frowned.

She said, "Peggy's parents. They'll want to thank you."

"In the morning?"

"They won't want to come out in this..."

It was my turn to look astonished. I said brutally, "Let's hope she's still alive in the morning for them to see her."

She stood and went back to the kitchen. I finished my food and had another glass of whiskey. After that, I asked Abi to show me to my room. She pulled on a heavy coat and hat and I followed her out into the night. It was very dark and our breath billowed like cigar smoke in the freezing air. The flakes were dense and a fitful, gusting wind tossed them this way and that in swirls and flurries. Abi hunched into her shoulders and crunched across the snow, which was now five or six inches deep on the small square. She pushed through the wooden gate to the Pioneer and opened the door to the guesthouse.

It was warm and quiet inside. The walls were paneled in wood. The floors also were wood, and covered in thick, woven rugs. To the right there was a pine reception desk, and to the left a staircase, carpeted in deep green and illuminated by Victorian, glass-shaded lamps. Ahead, double doors stood closed. She opened them, revealing a comfortable living room with an open fire burning large logs. A girl, perhaps eighteen or nineteen, sat before it in a large armchair. Beyond her, a boy of perhaps thirteen lay stretched out on a sofa. They were both reading, but looked up when Abi opened the door.

"Primrose, we have a guest for the night. Will you show him to his room, please? Two B is made up."

Primrose stood and approached. She was more than pretty, but too demure and sweet to be stunning in the Hollywood supermodel sense. She wore jeans and a sweatshirt, but you felt she should be wearing a crinoline. She was the kind of girl a young man might fall seriously in love with, and spend all his time staring at the stars dreaming of rescuing her from evil-doers. She was a maiden, a damsel. She smiled at me and said a simple but pretty, "Hello."

I found a smile somewhere in my weary face and nodded. While Primrose got the key, Abi turned to me, wrapped in her coat and hat. "I must get back to the saloon. If you need anything, just call down to Primrose, she'll make sure you're taken care of..." She hesitated. "And...I don't even know your name..."

"Lacklan, Lacklan Walker."

"Mr. Walker, thank you so much for saving Peggy..."

Primrose turned to stare. I shook my head. "Anyone would have done the same."

She seemed about to say more, but turned and went back into the snowstorm, closing the door behind her.

Primrose led the way up the stairs through the dim light of the lamps. As we climbed, I realized they were oil. It was fortunate. Electricity would never have survived that storm. She opened a door at the far end of a broad corridor and showed me into a large, comfortable room, furnished in the style of the early twentieth century, with an en suite bathroom at the far end, by the window.

"I'll light the fire for you." She hunkered down and struck a match. As she put it to the kindling, she said, "The lamps are oil. We have no electricity or gas here. We're pretty much off grid."

"No phone?"

The flames caught and started to roar in the chimney. She shook her head and the flames danced amber on her face. She stood and turned to me. Her expression was oddly direct. "There's no line, and no coverage for a cell. No TV. No internet. We get some electricity from a generator."

"You're pretty isolated."

She nodded. "Especially in winter, when it snows."

"I guess you get what you need from Lovelock."

She smiled. It was an odd smile, part mischief, part irony. "The farm supplies us with basic necessities. Anything else we might need, we do without. What happened to Peggy?"

"I don't know. I'd like to know. I found her by the road-side, freezing to death."

She frowned and looked down at the floor. It was an expression of distress, but not surprise; not shock. "Was she..." She looked up into my face. "Did they...?"

"Who?"

She hesitated. "I mean, whoever..."

"Do you know what happened to Peggy, Primrose?"

"No! Of course not!" She turned. "I'd better go. Is there anything you need?"

I smiled and showed her the bottle of whiskey. "Just this and sleep."

She smiled, but it wasn't a happy smile. "Goodnight, Mr. Walker."

"Goodnight, Primrose."

She closed the door and I fell into an armchair in front of the warm, dancing fire. I poured myself a generous measure of whiskey and savored it without swallowing, watching the manic dance of the flames as they licked and consumed the dry logs. I told myself that in the morning I would fit the chains to my car, charge the batteries and, whatever the weather, I would head for home. There was a problem here in this town, that much was obvious, but it was not *my* problem, and I must not get involved.

But as I let the fierce amber liquid slip down my throat and warm my belly, I thought of Peggy, barely a child, left to die by the roadside, of cold and neglect. And it was not just the whiskey that warmed my belly, but anger.

CHAPTER 3

I WENT FOR A RUN NEXT MORNING AT SIX. ABI AND her two children were already up and about. Abi was at the reception desk and watched me come down the stairs.

"You're up late, Mr. Walker. Did you decide to have a lie in?"

She didn't exactly smile, but there was a glint of humor in her eyes that could have been mischievous. I considered her for a moment and then smiled. "I've been up for a couple of hours, Abi, but I thought I'd finish translating Genesis from the original proto-Aramaic before breakfast."

She raised an eyebrow. "Really? That is very worthy."

"Now I'm going for a run."

"Goodness. You'll find there is hot water in the shower when you get back, despite the weather."

"That will be a novel experience. Perhaps I'll give it a try. By the way, my name is Lacklan."

As I opened the door, she said, "You really are going for a run..."

I nodded. "I'll have plenty of time to sleep when I'm dead."

It was heavy going down the track. The snow had eased up, but it was a foot deep on the road and six to seven feet in the drifts. It was pitch dark, but above you could just make out a low, leaden ceiling of dense cloud. It was colder than I had expected, I guessed about 5 degrees F. I punched and dodged as I ran, did quick sprints to break up the pace and increase my heart rate and calorie burn.

After about half a mile, I became aware of some lights moving up ahead, and the sound of heavy diesel machinery. As I got closer, I saw there was a snow plow that had cleared a path to a structure about a hundred yards off the road, in the field. A large ten-wheeler truck, with a covered back, was pulling away from it, headed for the intersection. Once it got there, it turned right and moved south.

From what I could make out in the light of the plow and a couple of trucks parked thereby, the structure was some sort of pen, with a barn in the centre. It was big. The pen itself was at least a hundred and fifty yards by the same again square. And the barn was easily seventy feet long and fifty across. I saw Earl standing in the back of one of the trucks. He had a couple of friends with him. They all watched me run past. I ignored them and carried on as far as the road. By that time I had warmed up. I practiced a few kicks and some Tae Kwon Do patterns, and then ran back at a loose, relaxing pace.

In spite of my boast to Abi, I had a hot shower, dressed, and went down for breakfast at seven. She brought me bacon and fried bananas with a pot of coffee.

"There are pancakes and maple syrup if you're still

hungry after. Exercising in the snow will give you an appetite."

I smiled at her. "It did."

"Can I sit down?"

My mouth was full, so I gestured at the chair opposite me. She sat. She didn't say anything, just watched me. I swallowed, drank coffee, and asked her, "Any news on Peggy?"

She shook her head. "We moved her to the doc's house last night, where he can take care of her a bit better. Her temperature's up a bit, but she needs to get to a hospital."

"You want me to take her? I'll need a truck."

"No. There's heavy snow forecast. If you got stuck, she'd die."

She stared at the tabletop, like she was thinking about saying something but didn't know how to. Finally, I said, "What's on your mind, Abi?"

She looked surprised at the question, then said, for no apparent reason, "We're pretty isolated here, even when it doesn't snow. I've never known it to snow like this before. All we've got really is the farm."

"I saw them clearing the snow when I was out."

"At the depot?"

I shrugged. "Big barn off the track, with a fence around it."

"We call that the depot. It's where he stores his produce."

"Aloysius Groves?"

"He provides what work there is around here..."

I raised an eyebrow. "Is he the feudal lord?"

She laughed, but it sounded strained. "Something like that."

"What are you trying to tell me, Abi?"

She made a face like she was going to dismiss my question, then stopped herself and sighed.

I said, "OK, let me ask you something instead. Al Groves has a snow plow. He also has several trucks. Why isn't he either taking Peggy to a hospital or going for help?"

She took a while to answer. "I guess he has other priorities." She sighed again, heavily. "Mr... Lacklan, the weather is going to get worse before it gets better. It looks as though you may be stuck here for a couple of days. You may see or hear things that seem strange to you. It's just the way things are around here. Best if you don't get involved."

I drained my cup and sat back. "Does that include dumping children by the roadside, in the snow, to freeze to death?"

She didn't answer.

"Where is the doc's house, Abi?"

"Two down from the saloon. It has a blue door, and an arch over the gate."

"Thanks for breakfast, and for the advice."

I stood. She spoke in a rush, like she wanted to say it before it was too late, before I left, "It's not as simple as it might seem from the outside."

"I know, Abi. I've seen it before, many times, in Iraq, in Afghanistan, in the jungles in Colombia. You've told me all you need to tell me. I'm going to go and check on Peggy now."

There was a limpid gray light when I stepped outside. The clouds were low, thick and dark, and for the first time, I got a look at where I was. The village of Independence was tiny, and settled in the mouth of a steep canyon that rose to the west. To my right, the east, that canyon opened out into a flat plain that seemed to extend for miles. Right now it was blanketed in dense, luminous snow. Ahead and to my left, the terrain rose steeply into mountains, densely forested and shrouded, like the plain, in heavy snow. I raised my collar and crossed the road.

The doc's house was like something on a chocolate box, or a tin of Danish cookies. It was a cottage on two floors, with two chimneystacks and a black slate, gabled roof. It had a small front lawn enclosed by a stone wall, and a wooden arbor with a creeping rosebush over it, now dead and covered in frozen clumps of white.

I checked my watch as I pushed through the gate, and made my way to the shiny blue front door. It was ten minutes before eight, but I figured in this village people were early risers and I took hold of the brass knocker and rapped a couple of times. He opened the door almost immediately.

"Saw you out running earlier. Was going to call you in for breakfast..." He winked wolfishly, "But I figured you'd rather have coffee and bacon with Abi than me!"

I smiled. "I hope I am not too early."

"Too early? No such thing. Been up since five. Come on in. You'll have some coffee."

It wasn't a question. He led me through a small hallway with a narrow flight of stairs to a comfortable living room with wooden beams, a large open fire, and, arranged around it, leather armchairs and a sofa that looked at least a hundred years old. The walls were lined with books and there was an agreeable smell of pipe tobacco mixed with soot and freshly brewed coffee. A broad bow window overlooked his front lawn and the small square, and afforded a direct view of the guesthouse.

"In the summer," he said, as though he were answering a question, "we get the occasional weekend pioneer, with their luxury RVs and motor homes. But aside from that, I rarely get to talk to somebody from outside. Sit down." He said all this from the open doorway, then leaned back and shouted in a surprisingly big voice, "*Mrs. Entwhistle! Coffee for two!*" Then he closed the door. "She does for me. But I imagine you didn't come here for my sparkling conversation and amusing anecdotes. You came to inquire after Peggy."

I sat in one of his vast, cracked leather chairs by the fire. "How is she?"

He frowned, not at me, at the fire. "Know anything about medicine?"

I gave half a shrug. "First aid. I've seen a few cases of hypothermia, gunshot wounds..."

"You're a soldier."

I nodded. "I was."

He raised an eyebrow like an albino shrimp. "You still are. Believe me, I can tell. Her core temperature has risen. She should be recovering." He sighed. "But she should be in hospital. She has bruising..."

"Mind if I have a look?"

He gave a brief nod. "In a minute."

The door opened and a woman who looked remarkably like the doc, only less bushy, stepped in with a tray of coffee and biscuits. She smiled at me like the doc wasn't there and set the tray on the table by the window.

"Would you like me to pour, or do you think you can manage that?"

I smiled back. "I'm sure we can manage."

"Go away, Mrs. Entwhistle. Go back to the kitchen, where you belong."

She left.

"With a population of less than barely eighty people, you can't afford to sack somebody like Mrs. Entwhistle. Her ironing and cooking are second to none."

"I'm sure. She looks formidable. You were saying about Peggy."

He went and poured the coffee, handed me a cup with two biscuits, and sat in the other chair.

"Either she had a bad fall, or she was beaten. She may, of course, have been struck by a vehicle. Sometimes you get trucks coming this way, to the farm, then they go on down Independence Road, over the Humboldt Mountains." He shrugged and shook his head. "The long way around. I've never understood why."

I studied him a moment. "I found her at the junction, Doc. It's about as flat as it can get without your Mrs. Entwhistle taking an iron to it. How do you fall and get that kind of bruising, at her age, somewhere that flat?" He didn't answer, just stared at the flames in the fire. "There's something else, Doc. The bruising you get from a vehicle is different from the bruising you get from a fist, or a foot. I'm pretty sure you know that. I've seen my fair share of both. I'd like to have a look at Peggy's bruises."

He sighed. "I know. That's why you're here. Fact is, I'd like you to look at them too."

I carried on as though he hadn't spoken. "You see, I am having trouble understanding what a thirteen- or fourteen-year-old girl was doing three miles from her home in the middle of a blizzard, with no coat. So I am thinking that her bruises were not received where I found her. I think she got those bruises somewhere else, and was dumped."

He raised one of his Gandalf eyebrows at me. "You weren't a military policeman, were you?"

I raised a more modest eyebrow back. "Are you telling me you hadn't come to the same conclusion?"

He looked suddenly depressed. "No, I'm not telling you that. Come on, let's go and have a look."

He led me up the stairs I had seen earlier, to a landing with three bedrooms and a restroom. He opened one of the bedroom doors and I followed him in. There were two single beds and a broad window overlooking snowy hills, abundant pine trees and what seemed to be a frozen creek.

Peggy was lying in one of the beds. She had been bathed and her hair washed. I could see now that was blonde; a very pretty child. She had more color in her face and her lips were no longer blue, but she was still unconscious and had a large bruise on her right cheek. I felt a hot twist of anger in my belly and heard my own voice as though it were somebody else's.

"A year ago, she was probably still playing with dolls."

"You're not far wrong. She was just fifteen last month." He pulled back the covers. "She's in a coma, Mr. Walker. She is not aware of what I am doing."

He showed me her arms, and then her neck. There were deep purple marks consistent with having been gripped, possibly strangled. He pulled back her nightgown and on her ribs there was further bruising, consistent with having been punched. He put back her gown and pulled up the bedcovers, then stood staring at her for a moment.

"There could be internal bleeding, I can't tell. As I say, she should be in a hospital." He paused, hesitated a moment, then said, "I keep a rape kit. Nobody in the village knows that I do, but I do."

"Was she raped?"

Now he looked me straight in the eye. "You know that she was."

I frowned. "You saying you think I raped her?"

He smiled, shook his head and sighed. "No, of course not. The logistics alone would be impossible. Where? When? How did you get her there? No, Mr. Walker. I am saying that from the moment you found her by the side of the road, you have been thinking she'd probably been raped. The beating simply confirms it."

I nodded. "It was the only explanation that made sense." I studied his face a moment. "If this village has less than eighty people, plus a handful of men at the farm, and you keep a rape kit..." I shrugged. "That's telling me you have a fair idea who did this."

"Obviously. But I am not going to tell you."

I scowled. "Why not?"

His face became suddenly irritable. "Because it's more than my life is worth! That's why! Hell! I'm taking a risk just talking to you." He sighed again. "But there is something I want you to do."

"Name it."

"When you leave, soon, go back to Lovelock, tell the sheriff what you've seen here. Make them investigate."

I narrowed my eyes at him. "There have been other rapes of young girls..."

"I am not going to tell you another damn thing. You

come in here, throwing your weight around, demanding to see this poor child. You've seen what you've seen, now pack your things and get out of this town. Leave us be... You understand me?" He said it all without a trace of anger or feeling.

I nodded. "I understand, Doc. But there is worse weather on the way. I'm stuck here for at least another twenty-four hours."

"I know. Just keep a low profile, get out of here as soon as you can, and stay out of Joe Vasco's way."

Scan the QR code below to purchase A HARVEST OF BLOOD.
Or go to: righthouse.com/a-harvest-of-blood

Made in United States
Orlando, FL
02 January 2026